A wet, earthy smell and darkness enveloped him like fog.

Before he got to Luanne's door she'd stepped out and closed it. He blinked and let his eyes adjust to the dark. The rim of a cloud began to glow; the moon came out of hiding.

"Listen," she said softly. "Frogs."

He studied her face in the moonlight and wondered how her lips would taste. Was it his imagination, or was she breathing hard?

"The moon is nearly full." He leaned closer and breathed in the potent, floral scent of her hair.

"It'll be full in three nights," she said. "On Thursday. It's called the Hunter's Moon."

"I never would have guessed," he said. With one finger he tilted her chin toward him and lightly kissed her lips. He couldn't have guessed—or cared less—what they called the full moon in late October, but the taste of Luanne Holt's lips was precisely what he thought it would be. Exquisite.

He kissed her softly on the lips and both cheeks, then returned to her mouth for more. This time soft wasn't enough. He pressed and felt a shock all the way to his toes when she opened her mouth and accepted his tongue.

He had only to open his arms and she stepped into his embrace. This must be what "moonstruck" meant; Rand hoped he didn't suddenly aim his chin at the rising moon and start howling. At this point, though, nothing would surprise him.

Reviews...
for the previous book in the Bitter Falls series,
LOVE WITH A WELCOME STRANGER:
This story ranks with the best. The characters were well thought out and easy to fall in love with, average everyday people you might walk by on the street or, if you're lucky, someone you're actually blessed to have in your life in some capacity. This story is about forgiveness of others, of ourselves and our faults. Life is too short to be lived in pain and anger. This story says you may fight, and you may want to walk away, but all good things are worth fighting for, even if the person you have to fight is yourself. I say very well done, Lynnette Baughman, and I look forward to more from you in the future. This book reminds me of why I got hooked on romance at the age of fifteen.

> ~*Breia Brickey, Reviewed in Between the Lines, WRDF Reviews*

I was amazed to find that this was her initial love story because it was so well written and the subject matter was unique. The tension, as well as attraction, with this at-odds couple was powerful. Her secondary characters were remarkable and served to enhance the beautifully developed story of the primary couple. The poignant dialogue and actions between the two was so emotionally charged it was impossible to put the book down. I look forward to more from this author. I highly recommend this book to anyone who likes to escape in a story and appreciates a surprise ending."

> ~*Brenda Talley, The Romance Studio (Rated Five Hearts)*

From the first page...the perfect blend of outstanding characterization and page-turning pacing. I hated to put it down. I can't wait to read more from this wonderful new talent.

> ~*Pamela Britton, bestselling author*

Lovin' Montana

by

Lynnette Baughman

A sequel to
Love with a Welcome Stranger

Lovin' Montana: Bitter Falls Series, Book Two

Cover Art by *Rae Monet*

The Wild Rose Press
PO Box 706
Adams Basin, NY 14410-0706
Visit us at www.thewildrosepress.com

Publishing History
First Champagne Rose Edition, 2009
Print ISBN 1-60154-528-2

Published in the United States of America

Dedication

To Bill. You're still the one.

Chapter One

Rand Monahan hoisted the kayak over his head and climbed the riverbank to his rented Lincoln SUV. Wind rippled through the canyon and shook the aspens, showering him with gold. At the top of the incline he rested the kayak against the car and looked up at the bluest sky he'd ever seen.

The gold leaves showered him with irony, too. Four hours earlier, knowing he'd lose cell phone coverage on the river, he'd pulled his car off the road and checked on the price of gold and palladium on the international markets. As soon as he'd adjusted his personal holdings, he was back on what he called a one-week vacation to Montana.

His cardiologist dubbed it "a visit to the Last Chance Saloon." Seamus Brogen, M.D., whose nose could guide Santa's sleigh, had chuckled at his own joke.

Rand had neither chuckled nor smiled. He'd locked his jaw and stared at the poster of the human circulatory system until the blue veins and red arteries were a purple blur.

He leaned against the SUV and caught his breath after the exertion of carrying the kayak uphill.

"Damn it," he muttered. "I'm thirty-six!"

Yeah, thirty-six, and in great shape—for a man twice my age.

A squirrel with a one-track mind hustled down the tree next to the car and froze in tableau at the sight of the human ten feet away.

Rand laughed, a sound so infrequent that it

1

surprised him even more than it did the squirrel. Even so, the rodent hauled ass up the trunk of a strapping pine tree.

The sound Rand did hear clearly and often, even when it was softer than a leaf landing on the river's surface, was *ka-pump, ka-pump*. How many billion times had that sound echoed through his chest wall? Unheard, unheeded. Underestimated.

He took a soda from the cooler in the back of the car and sat on a log in the shade. *Ka-pump, ka-pump.*

He recalled the day, not quite two weeks ago, when Brogen had given him the prescription: Montana, Relax. *Repeat.*

Sounded more like a sentencing.

He'd felt the stethoscope against his chest and breathed on command. Inhale, hold it, exhale. As he'd waited for the verdict—naively hoping for a green light to return to work full time—he heard the white paper crinkle beneath him and the annoying snap of a failing fluorescent light in the low ceiling.

He'd felt naked, not because he wore only boxer shorts, but because he had no cell phone.

Instead of delivering good news, Brogen had opened the door. Rand's sister entered, followed by Jeff Adler. Dinah took the only chair. Jeff, his best friend and his partner in their international private equity firm, fidgeted with his back against the closed door and one hand in his pocket.

Probably on his cell phone.

Brogen switched from the Last Chance Saloon analogy to football. Rand was "fourth and long, standing in his own end zone."

Dinah and Jeff nodded their enthusiastic agreement. Clearly, Coach Brogen had called in the Special Team.

Instead of a crude drawing of a Hail Mary pass play, Brogen slapped a set of films of Rand's chest cavity up in front of the light and shook his head. Jeff, who wouldn't know an aorta from a toenail, scratched at his heavy five-o'clock shadow and managed to look grave. Dinah nodded, *Oh yes, I see, I see*, as if she'd just popped in from conducting microsurgery herself, instead of from her hair appointment at Bergdorf's.

Rand thought of some choice epithets with which to needle the three of them, but the words had died on his lips. It was their silence as much as their Ghost-of-Christmas-Future faces that alarmed him.

"It's like treating alcoholism," Brogen finally said with a nod to Jeff and Dinah and an armor-piercing stare at Rand, "except I'm not telling you to call a friend and don't touch the bottle. What I'm telling you is this: When you want to pick up a cell phone and move money around, call a friend and have a drink instead."

Rand had laughed until his sides hurt at that absurdity. Brogen was the monarch of metaphors. And yet, under the humor was a serious message. Relax or die. What was the line people threw out all the time without thinking about it?

Are you serious? Yeah, serious as a heart attack.

Jeff had cleared his throat. "Even counting the key-man insurance we carry, you're worth more alive than dead. Of course, I ran the numbers just to be sure. So go to Montana and hurl your BlackBerry into a lake."

Brogen repeated his bromide that Rand's heart had the potential to heal. The stents the surgical team had placed in three arteries could solve his problem, but only if he would lay off the stress. If he couldn't turn the corner on his own, he was facing major surgery.

"And I do mean *major!*" Brogen barked. "I'm not talking about a drive-through."

Rand had argued. He'd followed Brogen's orders,

he said. For the three interminably long months since his mild heart attack—he said it twice—"my *mild* heart attack"—he'd followed his diet and cardiac rehab regimen to the letter of the law.

"And I stayed away from the office," he'd added, palms up to show he had nothing to hide. "We have employees who've never seen me."

Jeff made a sound somewhere between a bark and a laugh.

Okay, Rand admitted, grudgingly, okay. He'd been doing some work from his apartment. By computer and video-conferencing. Only a little. If he didn't, he'd go stir crazy.

"Stark raving mad." He waved his hands in the air. "Boo-gah, boo-gah. Bananas!"

He looked from Brogen's stone face to Jeff, to Dinah. Not so much as a hint of a smile.

Instead, Brogen had looked over his half glasses and down the length of his rosy nose. "You, Rand, are your own worst enemy."

Removing his glasses for emphasis, he gave a grim You-Go-Girl nod to Dinah.

Dinah caught Brogen's lateral and ran toward the end zone with the old standby: "Rand, listen up for once. You can't take it with you."

Good old reliable Dinah. In for the score.

In lieu of gyrating in the end zone, she pulled a T-shirt out of her large purse and tossed it to him. "I had it custom printed."

The word MONTANA arched over what to Rand was heresy: *Make Love, Not Money*. But he'd pulled it on, knowing he was outflanked, outscored...and on his way out of New York.

So, here I am. Resting on a log, relaxing. Meditating. Not moving a mus—

"Smackdown!" He slapped his forearm, his leg, and his cheek. *Damn mosquitoes*. If he sat in the shade any longer, he'd be a quart low.

4

He rose, crushed the empty can, and tossed it in the back of the SUV. As he searched for the insect repellent, he tried to think of the nickname Dinah had given him when he made his first million. *Oh, yeah, Scrooge McDuck.* But he'd been so consumed with making money since he was a kid that he'd had no idea what she was talking about. Watching cartoons hadn't fit into Randall Rockwell Monahan's so-called childhood.

He found the bug spray on the back seat. Closing his eyes, he sprayed DEET on his neck, arms, and legs. With his luck, mosquitoes would consider it the nectar of the gods and work a double shift at the Monahan blood bank.

When he'd watched the DVD Dinah sent him—about ten years and fifty million dollars later—of Donald Duck's greedy, single-minded Uncle Scrooge luxuriating in a vault full of gold, he'd said, *Yeah, okay, and your point is...?*

Dinah's gesture did, however, remind him of the value of Disney stock, and he'd added ten thousand shares to his corporate portfolio and one thousand shares to the portfolios he'd begun for her two kids.

Actually, the fact that he was here in Montana—in a setting so perfect it looked like a computer-enhanced three-D version of the Rocky Mountain West—was for Dinah's kids. When he'd been flat on his back in the emergency room, gasping for his next breath and looking up at the best doctors money could buy, the words that echoed in his mind were Dinah's.

"Don't you want to live to see them grow up?" she'd asked him so many times. "Don't you want to have children of your own?"

He lifted the kayak to the rack on top of the car and fastened the straps that held it tight; then he hiked down to the river to retrieve his paddle, helmet, and life vest. The sound of laughter carried across the river, and he smiled to see a canoe with a man in the back and a boy maybe ten years old in the front.

"Paddle on the left, son. That's the way." The father's voice was encouraging, not critical. Rand felt warmed, and it wasn't entirely from the sun.

Children of your own. Dinah's voice in his head again.

No. For that he'd have to have a wife. *Not happening, Dinah, old girl.* Being an uncle was a good gig though. Erik and Sophie would be enough for him. Oh, he'd had girlfriends over the years, when he'd had time for them, which—all right, tell the truth and shame the devil—wasn't all that much. He'd even gotten serious about one. Serious enough to shop for a five-carat diamond ring.

He returned a wave to the man and boy in the canoe and climbed back up the riverbank.

It had been Erik and Sophie who had unwittingly saved him from a disastrous mistake. Madonna Taylor, a fashion executive he'd dated exclusively for more than six months, had told him she *loved* kids and that *of course* when they were married she wanted to have a baby. "In nine months and a day" was how she put it.

Cooed like a Central Park pigeon over spilled popcorn, she did.

Then he'd kept Erik and Sophie for a weekend, and Madonna stayed at his place to help. Sophie had a painful earache—and Madonna's true colors showed through. A close friend, one who'd warned him that Madonna was after his money, saved a phone message from her. She'd called Rand's five-year-old nephew and three-year-old niece "obnoxious little brats."

"Madonna" wasn't even her real name. She'd taken it, legally, because it sounded so glitzy, and yet warm.

Her real name, he decided after he broke off their wasted liaison, was probably *She-Who-Drowns-Kittens.*

The close call rattled him. He'd come to rely on his instincts in business. The near-catastrophe with Madonna made him realize that women were too unpredictable to be safe. Too many variables in that equation. He was better off as an uncle.

Back at the car, he tossed the gear in the back and changed shoes. He took a deep breath of clean mountain air and told himself this relaxation stuff wasn't half bad.

Not. Half. Bad.

Okay, one day of relaxation wasn't bad. But he didn't see how he could stand it for seven whole days. His calendar had never been so empty.

"Monday: kayak. Tuesday: explore old railroad tunnels by bicycle. Wednesday: take fly-fishing lesson." By Thursday he'd have nothing left to do but trim his toenails and look for funny shapes in the clouds—if there were any clouds.

He resisted the urge to call and see how the markets in Tokyo were expected to open and how the dollar was holding against the Euro in after-hours trading in London. Jeff could handle every detail of their investment fund as well as he could.

He drove back through the woods, admiring the view he caught from time to time. The top of the mountains had a dusting of snow, but it was a hot October day down by the river.

He bounced off the dirt road and onto the two-lane asphalt road that wound through the hills toward the cabin he'd rented for a week. According to the rental agent recommended by his grandfather, Rand would be close enough to the town of Bitter Falls that he could eat at the Roundup Café or the Mineshaft Restaurant, but far enough out that he could "savor the pristine isolation."

Pristine isolation was code, he knew now, for No Internet Access. Cell phone coverage in the whole valley was about five percent of what he was used to. He had nothing against relaxation. Nothing. He simply wanted to conduct business while he did it.

He picked up a brochure from the console. He'd found it on a kiosk at the airport, a colorful tri-fold describing an attractive hotel in Missoula. A hotel with *amenities*. Wasn't the point of being exiled to Montana that he would spend time with less stress? Yeah, that was it. And playing pioneer in Bitter Falls was *increasing* his stress.

Okay. He'd call the realtor and say, "Something came up; the key's on the table." What did she care? He'd prepaid for the week.

His phone rang—*a miracle*—and he recognized the ring tone as his grandfather, Rocky Monahan, calling. He pulled off the road and hoped the cell signal stayed strong.

Instead of saying hello, he thumbed the Talk button and said, "Yes! I'm relaxing! If I were any more relaxed, I'd be a puddle on the floor."

"I'm glad to hear that, Rand. What do you think of Bitter Falls?"

"It's everything you said it would be, and less. Oh, I haven't gone to look at your land yet." He reminded himself to ask someone where Apple Mountain Road was.

"Plenty of time for that. I'm calling about the favor I asked of you, to visit Amelia Holt and arrange to buy her antique photo collection for me."

"I'm looking forward to meeting her, Grandpa." Well, he was sincerely *trying* to look forward to it. That was close enough.

"Ah, then, I have to disappoint you. I've had a call from Mrs. Holt. She has been unexpectedly detained in Arizona and won't return to Bitter Falls for another three or four weeks."

8

"Oh, well," Rand replied, trying to keep relief out of his voice, "you'll be able to come yourself by then."

"I suppose I could, but I want to seal the deal before then. Amelia has given her granddaughter power of attorney. She can meet with you, show you the collection."

Rand frowned but murmured, "That's good. Sure."

"Luanne Holt is a pleasant woman; daughter of Amelia Holt's son. I met her once myself, there in Bitter Falls." Rocky chuckled. "Old fashioned, in a good way. Not bad looking, either. I gather she's something of a spinster, although that term went out with one-room schoolhouses."

"What is she, a librarian?" Rand sighed. His grandfather's description made him think of a gray-haired woman in a long dress on the steps of a white clapboard building, ringing a handbell. But he'd said "granddaughter," so she couldn't be that old. Could she?

He did the math in about two seconds. If Amelia Holt was really old, and her son was born when she was a teenager, and he became a father at age twenty, Miss Luanne Holt could be, at the most, fifty.

He changed the gray hair to mousey brown in his mental picture but kept her hair in a tight, schoolmarm bun.

"Not a librarian, but you're close," Rocky said. "She owns a shop called Memories Mine. She restores old photos, prepares scrapbooks, and teaches customers how to do it. She does a lot of genealogy. Fascinating stuff to an old duffer like me."

Rand groaned. He hoped he could get this favor over quickly. He half-listened to Rocky describe his latest golf triumph.

"...final rounds of a tango contest," he finished.

"What?" Rand realized Amelia Holt's name was in there somewhere close to "tango." What had he missed? "What did you say about a tango contest?"

"I said that's why Amelia Holt is staying in Arizona another three or four weeks. She keeps moving up in the tango competition. I wouldn't be surprised to see her on TV."

Rand had done his math based on Amelia being about ninety. As he often said when weighing alternatives in the markets, his model would have to be adjusted.

"How old is Mrs. Holt?" he asked.

"Age is just a number, my boy." Rocky laughed.

A little warning bell sounded in Rand's mind. *Is Rocky up to something? Am I walking into a trap?*

"And, Grandpa, exactly what does 'not bad looking' mean?"

His picture of a schoolmarm was getting fuzzy, like a pixilated photo of a crime witness.

"Decide for yourself, Rand." Rocky gave him the address of Memories Mine—on Main Street, of course—and said Luanne was expecting him in an hour.

Rand groaned again, said good-bye, and pulled back onto the road. The turnoff to his cabin was six miles ahead. An hour gave him barely enough time to remove the kayak from the car rack, shower, and dress. No time to think of an excuse not to go— which was probably his grandfather's plan.

Dinah's nickname for Grandpa was Wiley, as in Wile E. Coyote. Now *that* cartoon reference he understood.

****

Luanne Holt propped open the door of her shop and looked down the street. Business had been good since eleven o'clock when the three tour buses lumbered down Main Street and parked in back of the county courthouse. It was almost three now, and she hoped to have customers until four o'clock when the buses started loading. For a Monday in October, her sales were gratifying.

The phone rang and she picked up the handset on the counter. "Memories Mine."

"Luanne, can you talk? Or do you have a shop full of people?"

"I can talk now, Grandma, but if some tourists wander in, I'll have to call you back."

Her grandmother had called at one-thirty, but she'd had to postpone their chat. She regretted doing so, as she had a feeling Amelia was up to something, and she wanted to know what it was.

The whiff of mystery had begun two weeks earlier when Amelia, her father's mother, said she was staying on in Arizona longer than she'd planned. Luanne didn't question the extended stay; Amelia had a lot of arrangements to make for her new winter home in Mesa. But then Amelia said that "something might come up" in Bitter Falls while she was away, a business matter. She'd refused to speculate on what that something might be, but said that "just in case," she'd directed her attorney to draw up papers giving Luanne power of attorney.

"I'll talk fast, then, dear. Skipping over the whereas, whereas rigmarole, I'm selling my antique photos to Rocky Monahan. You know I've been considering it. With the big house sold, and me gone so much, it's time to part with the collection."

"Just the ones in the house?"

"No, the Daguerreotypes, too. Rocky has already arranged to donate all of them to the Montana Historical Museum so they'll be properly preserved and catalogued. Here's the thing, though. The deal needs to be signed and sealed this week, tomorrow perhaps, or Wednesday at the latest. So I need you to take care of it."

"Me? Can't you fax documents back and forth?"

"No. It will be better if you do it. You have the power of attorney."

Luanne opened her mouth to object. The start of the Harvest Festival was only four days away, and so much was riding on it. She was searching for a tactful way to say no when Amelia continued.

"Luanne, dear, all of the proceeds will go directly to the Suncatcher Fund. Now you see why it has to be done quickly."

"You'd do that?" she asked, astonished. "I don't know what to say." Rocky Monahan's generosity, donating the valuable collection to a museum, did not surprise her. His philanthropy was famous. But Amelia wasn't rich. Giving all that money away was a sacrifice.

"Because I'll be living in Arizona half the year doesn't mean I love my hometown any less. I know what Suncatcher means to Bitter Falls—and to you."

Tears welled in Luanne's eyes and spilled down her cheeks. "Thanks, Grandma."

"Now, here's what you need to do. Rocky's grandson, Rand Monahan, is in Bitter Falls on a vacation. He's going to meet you at your shop around five o'clock—"

"Today?"

"Of course, today. You take him to see the photographs at the house and the bank, and he'll arrange the wire transfer with Rocky. But Luanne, I must say one thing, even though you don't want to hear it. Don't let your devotion to Suncatcher and all it stands for take the place of having a life of your own."

"Is this where you point out, again, that I'm not getting any younger, and that my chances for a family are sliding down a steep slope—on a waxed sled?"

"I wouldn't have put it exactly that way, but

since you brought it up, yes. When a woman hits the big three-oh, fertility begins to diminish. I wouldn't mention it, dear, if I didn't know how much you love children."

Luanne sighed theatrically. "Okay, you win. I'm writing Get Pregnant on my To Do list, right under Show the Photos to—what's his name again?"

"Rand Monahan."

"All right, I'll show them to Rand. He and his grandfather will do whatever magic rich people do, and the money will appear in the Suncatcher Fund." She thought for a moment. "What's Rocky's grandson doing in Montana? Oh, wait, you said he's on a vacation, didn't you?"

"That's right. It's his first time in Montana; he lives in New York City. You know how Rocky loves Bitter Falls. He even bought more land out by the old Jensen place. When he builds a house, he'll have a big spread with a great view."

"How old is Rand?" Luanne watched two ladies stop outside the store and point at her display.

"Young, I think. But then, I think that everyone under fifty is young."

"Except me," Luanne offered. She used telepathy to urge the women to come inside.

"Oh, I think you're young. But your ovaries aren't."

"I don't believe this conversation. You are seventy-five going on seventeen."

"Age is just a number, my dear. But since you asked, Rand is between thirty and forty. Rocky says he's a techno-dweeb, always has his head in an equation. Numbers, numbers, numbers. He probably wears plaid pants above his waist. And one of those zippy little phones hooked onto his ear like a silver leech. Please be nice to him, for Rocky's sake."

"Sure. Customers coming; gotta go. I love you, Grandma."

At four o'clock the two ladies from Missoula gathered their bags of scrapbook supplies and hurried off to join their bus tour. They were full of enthusiasm for their projects. They'd been especially taken with Luanne's technique of cutting calico frames to tie a scrapbook together in the theme of a family quilt.

She closed the door and gathered the scissors, pinking shears, and material samples. Her feet hurt, and she had a dozen loose ends to tie up about the festival. This business meeting with Rand Monahan would throw her schedule off—but she wasn't complaining. She still couldn't believe her grandmother's generosity.

She perched on her work stool by the counter and rearranged a dozen receipts. The three buses drove down Main Street, heading for the highway outside of town. Business would be slow for the rest of the afternoon.

In the summer she could have customers until nine p.m., seven days a week. Bitter Falls was a boom town from mid-May until mid-September. In October, however, a lot of their business was the Leaf Peepers tours. Thank goodness the leaves were late to fall this year. The tour buses, plus tourists in cars, would be in Bitter Falls in force for the coming weekend. The Harvest Festival was a major cog in the complicated funding for Suncatcher.

Getting the Suncatcher factory re-opened would save the economy of Bitter Falls. Everyone said it would give bright kids a reason to stay or to return after college, and—equally important to her—it would be a fitting memorial to Ted Wilder, the man behind the whole business, and the man she would love forever.

Furthermore, throwing open the front doors of Suncatcher would gently close a door on her past. Life—she knew this was true—was for the living.

She hoped she was ready.

Cory DeSoto, her best friend and a fanatic fan of The Discovery Channel, said she was like an Australian lungfish, an animal that burrows into a riverbank when the river goes dry and stays in a state of suspended animation until the river runs again, even if that takes years.

A lungfish—in a state of suspended animation. And that was her *best friend* speaking. Luanne didn't want to know what other people said. She wished they'd all mind their own business.

She hopped down from her stool and used the small bathroom to scrub some stubborn glue off her finger tips. A glance in the mirror made her laugh out loud. Somehow she'd gotten glitter stuck to the tip of her nose. She washed her face and reapplied a touch of foundation to cover a few of her freckles. With her fair skin, artificial blush would be superfluous.

What the heck, she thought. Lipstick, too. And I might as well brush my hair.

The ultra-dry atmosphere made her thick hair crackle with static electricity.

She couldn't help but wonder what Rand Monahan was like. Amelia had mentioned before, in passing, that Rocky had a married granddaughter and an unmarried, workaholic grandson.

To "workaholic" Amelia had now added plaid pants above his waist, and a metal leech hooked onto his ear.

"Yeah, right," Luanne now said to her image in the mirror. "Methinks, Grand-ma-ma, the lady doth protest too much."

She suspected this power of attorney ploy was a charade, a slick trick to get "poor Luanne" to meet a new man. As soon as her grandmother said Rand was a techno-dweeb, her antennae—and her self-defense shield—went up.

She gave her hair one last brush stroke and smoothed it with her fingers. From a sea shell box, a gift from Ted, she pulled out two ebony combs to hold her unruly curls back from her face, a move that showed the delicate jade earrings that matched her eyes. The earrings, too, connected her to Ted.

Her throat squeezed tight, and she blinked rapidly to keep tears from gumming up her makeup.

Why can't Grandma give up on matchmaking? If I want to find an eligible bachelor, I know how to look around.

I'm not ready.

She said it out loud to shore up her embattled position.

"I'm not ready!" Not ready. In spite of what Amelia and Cory thought.

And in spite of what a certain egotistical newspaper editor thought. She gave about five seconds of thought to Dexter "Can't Take a Hint" Stone. That was four more seconds than she wanted to spare. Grinding her molars, she told herself—once again—that she had to make Dexter understand she wasn't interested in him. Not now, not later.

For a man who spoke and wrote in English, he certainly had trouble comprehending it.

Pondering a showdown with Dexter was like pulling an invoice out of a drawer, determining she had more time until the due date, and stuffing it in a folder marked "L" for Later.

She disliked procrastination, but she disliked confrontation even more.

The bottom line didn't change: She wasn't ready to deal with all the emotional sludge that came with official "dating." She'd learned the hard way that grief wasn't something you blocked onto a calendar with a colored pen. Healing wasn't something you could pencil in, then celebrate with a gold star and the words: Good Job.

No. Not even when the leaves falling from the trees meant more than an entire year had passed. She wasn't ready—whatever the calendar said—and she didn't appreciate Amelia's misguided interference.

Still, a little mascara couldn't hurt; a woman in business should keep her appearance sharp. Her eyelashes were so light that sable mascara was more a necessity than a vanity. She leaned toward the mirror, blinked the mascara dry, and added another dash of lipstick for good measure. Burnt Sienna, the only one she used. Ninety-five percent of pinks and reds looked hideous with her hair.

The day had flown by, but the time until Rand Monahan was due seemed to crawl. There wasn't time to start a new project and have to clean up the work area all over again. She wasn't interested this afternoon in the genealogy search she was doing, and her bookkeeping was all up to date.

She used the time instead to compare catalogs online and fill out orders for new supplies.

"Hello?" a man called from the front of the store.

Luanne looked up, so engrossed in a tedious website that threw her out every time she tried to order acid-free parchment in "Arctic Mint" and "South Sea Sun" that she hadn't even heard the bell over the door.

She slid the keyboard back under the desk and returned to the counter. "May I help you?"

For what seemed like a minute but must have been ten seconds, she stared into eyes the color of Caramel Cappuccino. The man's hair was Sahara Sand with highlights of Honeysuckle Dewdrops. She gave herself a mental shake.

I've been spending way too much time with color samples.

"Are you Luanne Holt?"

She nodded. Her mouth was dry as the cotton

batting she'd just ordered from Quilt Supply Unlimited.

"I'm Rand Monahan." He put out his right hand.

She placed hers in it automatically, but felt a shock and jerked it away.

"Oh—I'm sorry. There must be a lot of static electricity today. Yes, I'm Luanne." She took his hand again, gingerly, shook it, and reluctantly let go. "Welcome to Bitter Falls."

Her voice sounded strange to her, a little—breathy. Odd, because she was having trouble catching her breath.

"Are you all right?"

His question jerked her out of her reverie and her cheeks flamed. Darn. It was pathetic, but nothing made her blush more than blushing. She'd always been that way. It was as if one small embarrassment brought on a cascade of self-consciousness. And with her complexion there was no way to hide it.

"I'm fine. Umm, have you been in Bitter Falls before?"

Her grandmother said Rand Monahan hadn't been there, but right now Amelia Holt's credibility was about ten percent. Techno-dweeb? Plaid pants halfway to his armpits? Ha, ha.

The man in front of her could model for a tall men's clothing designer. She noted the khaki slacks and soft cotton shirt with the sleeves rolled up. Broad shoulders. Jaw like a movie star, but without that skuzzy facial hair some women—not her—thought was sexy. His light brown hair appeared to be damp, and she caught the fragrance of aftershave.

"No," he said. "In fact, this is my first time in Montana. I live in New York."

Okay, score one for Grandma in the Truth column.

Six or seven questions crowded Luanne's mind

like helium balloons in a minivan, but she punctured them with a mental hatpin. Rand Monahan would take care of business and leave Bitter Falls behind. She'd better stay on topic and keep her renegade emotions reined in.

"You want to see my grandmother's photos, is that right?" She tapped her fingers noiselessly on the counter. Part of her wanted to get their business done quickly. She needed money in the Suncatcher Fund. But part of her had been asleep for a long time, and somehow—she couldn't think how this could be—this stranger was waking her up.

I've gone insane. She had to tap her fingers harder to keep from smacking herself in the forehead. This was clearly what psychologists called "magical thinking."

"No need to rush. I see you're busy here." He looked around the display cases, still covered with sample books and picture frames she'd been showing the tourists.

She closed the book nearest to hand and held it against her chest. "Actually, I was about to close for the day. It's the big advantage of being the owner."

Over Rand's shoulder, she saw the UPS truck pull alongside the curb, blocking her view of the whole street. "Excuse me, please."

She laid the album down and moved quickly to open the front door. The young man in a brown shorts uniform carried two boxes in and set them on a table behind the front counter. She signed the delivery receipt, thanked him, and turned back to Rand Monahan. Even taking a deep breath wasn't enough to calm the fluttering in her midsection.

She clutched the UPS receipt as if it were a document of urgent importance—the key evidence in a congressional investigation, perhaps, or the nuclear code that must be signed into a vault. In a voice that once again did not sound like her own, she asked Rand to excuse her.

In the back room she tossed the meaningless sheet of yellow paper in the general direction of her desk and ordered herself to breathe deeply. Calm down.

What was it about Rand Monahan that made her knees knock? He was good looking, no one would argue that point, but his looks weren't the answer. This was, after all, Montana. She could walk into the Aces High Saloon, throw a stick in any direction and hit ten good looking men.

And feel nothing.

Yet into her way-too-busy life strolls a total stranger, someone her *grandmother* picked out for her, for pity's sake! And Luanne Holt, the queen of self-control, time-warps to age sixteen.

Her internal critic was on high alert. *Keep your hands where I can see them and step away from the man.*

Maybe she was exhausted; maybe she had a fever. Maybe she should move to Arizona and learn to tango.

Whatever the genesis of this wake-up call, Luanne could feel the effect humming inside her like a tuning fork. Two words for her reaction: Wildly Inappropriate.

She looked at herself in the mirror over her sink. She looked the same. Well, except for the residual redness in her cheeks and neck. She ran cold water on a washcloth and dabbed it to her temples and cheeks.

She had to relax; she had to appear cool and professional. In other words, she had to keep Rand Monahan from reading her mind.

Chapter Two

Rand ran his finger down the textured cover of a scrapbook. Soft classical guitar music came from a CD player at the wall end of the counter. A fragrance he couldn't identify scented the air.

Opening the thick book at roughly the middle, he smiled at the photo that appeared. Two babies leaned out of a metal washtub. Yellow headbands with bows decorated their little bald heads. The page was bordered and trimmed in yellow and white checked cotton.

He'd wanted to get this chore, buying Amelia Holt's old photos, over with, but something about Luanne Holt made him want to slow down.

After all, isn't that what Brogen told him to do when Rand stopped by his clinic for a fare-thee-well? Brogen's exact words had been: "Smell the flowers, watch the leaves fall, kiss a pretty girl."

When the cardiologist said it, in the white-walled room that would smell forever like rubbing alcohol, the words were banal. Cliché. But in Montana, today, especially in a store called Memories Mine, it made sense.

Rand grinned. He'd like to take two or three kisses from pretty Luanne Holt's lips and call Brogen in the morning. This small town in Montana, even in a cabin with no internet access, was suddenly a lot more appealing.

Call his doctor in the morning? *Uh-oh*. That reminded him of the two phone calls he'd made right before he walked in the door of Luanne's shop. One to Mountain Realty to say he'd be leaving in the morning instead of staying seven days. And a call to Mike's Bikes to tell Mike to leave the new bicycle in the shipping carton so he could take it with him.

In a stroke of good luck, he'd gotten answering machines at both businesses and left his number, no messages. Quickly, he called them again. To the machine at the realtor's office, he said to disregard his previous call. To a man who answered at Mike's Bikes, he confirmed that he'd be picking up the assembled bike at eight a.m.

That would make Mike and his mechanics happy. He imagined them examining the Trek Madrone with the reverence of archaeologists at King Tut's sarcophagus. Mike Hogg told him when he'd called from New York that he'd seen a Madrone at a trade show, but never had one in his shop.

He took a quick look around the front of Memories Mine. Two lady-sized chairs with girly ruffles bracketed a table maybe thirty inches in diameter. Beneath the glass top, a bright blue tablecloth—more ruffles—exactly reached the floor. On the wall adjacent to the broad front window was a poster announcing that the Harvest Festival would start in four days.

The jumbled stack of pumpkins on the poster made the connection in his mind with the fragrance in the shop. Pumpkin pie. It must be in the candle that burned on a mirrored display above the cash register.

On the partial wall, which separated the shop's back room from the customer area, hung a large framed watercolor of a lush green valley at the base of jagged mountains.

He glanced over and smiled as Luanne returned from the back room. There was something tremendously attractive about the color of her eyes. They were as green as...

Oh, hell. They're the color of money.

The jolt of self-recognition rocked him back on his heels. Dinah was right; his grandfather was right. And so was the psychiatrist he'd visited three times because Brogen insisted he do so.

Now he admitted, with the greatest reluctance, that his self-worth was tangled up with eight-digit numbers. Any man who could look at Luanne Holt's eyes and think of money was Looney Tunes for sure.

Those eyes, set in a pale, heart-shaped face and haloed by wild, curly red hair, met his gaze and quickly looked away. He'd been so wrapped up in himself he'd failed to notice, but now he did. Luanne was shy. All the women he knew—and he did mean all—were powerful, confident.

Comparisons danced through his mind, and he searched for one that didn't involve stocks, bonds, oil or precious metals. At last he had it. The women he knew, Madonna Taylor one prime example, were like bulldozers. Brand new bulldozers with gleaming paint and sharp blades.

Luanne Holt, on the other hand, was...a surrey with the fringe on top.

He angled the album toward her and pointed at the photo of the bald babies in the washtub. "Cute babies. Are they twins?"

"Yes. Rebecca and Rachel. They're six now. I went to high school with their mom and dad." She looked up and he could swear he heard a little catch in her breath when their gazes met and held tight. "Uh, we can go to my grandmother's house now if you're ready."

The old Rand Monahan would hustle through the obligation, probably frowning all the while, eager to break away and see if the Federal Reserve Bank was raising the prime discount rate. But something was shifting inside him, and he liked how it felt.

"I think I'm too hungry to appreciate antique photos. Would you join me for an early supper at the

Mineshaft?"

She hesitated, and he recalled his grandfather saying Miss Holt was "something of a spinster." Rocky must have laughed his butt off when he got off the phone. A woman as pretty as Luanne Holt probably had men lined up, and Rand was a dimwit to act like she had no dinner plans.

Oh well, if he'd put his foot in a cow pie, his Italian leather boots wouldn't smell any worse with the other foot in it, too. And if that wasn't an old cowboy saying, it should be.

"I don't know anyone in town," he persisted with what he hoped was a disarming smile, "and I could use some advice on what to see while I'm here."

The front door opened, and Luanne stepped slightly to the side to see who was coming in. Something about the way her sunny eyes darkened made Rand turn as well.

"Evenin', Luanne." A man roughly Rand's height and age, but about forty pounds heavier through his chest and arms, gave Rand a four-second examination from toe to forehead. Clearly unimpressed, he focused his gaze on Luanne. Rand felt more static crackling in the air than when Luanne shook his hand and drew a spark.

"Hello, Dexter. I wasn't expecting you," she said.

The words were polite, no inflection, but Rand was pretty sure the temperature dropped ten degrees when this Dexter guy made his entrance.

"I finished up early at the mayor's meeting. I thought I'd stop by and see you." Dexter tipped the bill of his John Deere cap back a quarter inch.

"I was about to close up the store. Oh, Dexter Stone, this is Rand Monahan. Dexter is the editor of the Bitter Valley News."

Dexter smiled with his mouth, not his dark, calculating eyes, and held out his hand. Rand guessed that he was in danger of getting his hand crushed. He stiffened his hand and squeezed Dexter's hand before he became the "squeez-ee." Dexter's smile evaporated.

Rand had been in pissing contests like this many times, but always over money. In international finance, there were two parts to the Golden Rule: "The one that has the gold makes the rules," and, "Do unto others before they do unto you." This time the issue wasn't money. It was territory. And Dexter Stone was clearly territorial about Luanne Holt.

Rand guessed—or was that feeling hope?—that Luanne wasn't all that into Dexter. *Well, as we say at the blackjack table, it's time to double down.*

"Glad to meet you, Dexter. Luanne, shall I wait for you, or come back in a while?" It was a risky move, but if he was any judge of eyes, Luanne wanted to leave with him.

"I'm ready now. Dexter, would you excuse us, please?" She came around the counter and turned the sign on the door so the word CLOSED faced the sidewalk. Then she held the door open.

The chilly smile returned to Dexter's face, and he ambled out the door. Before she closed it, he turned. "Oh, by the way, if you have anything else about the festival for Wednesday's paper, I can take it until eight o'clock tomorrow night. Gill said you've got some new booths."

"Yes. I'm still working on the details, though. I'll talk to you tomorrow."

"There's something else..." He hesitated, smiled.

Rand expected a long, reptilian tongue to slide out of Dexter's mouth. But, no.

"Something else?" she asked.

Dexter tipped his hat. "I'll call you later."

She gave a nod and closed the door behind him.

Miss Holt might have a serious boyfriend, Rand thought, but Dexter isn't it.

She took a deep breath and let it out slowly. "I'll go shut down the computer. Then we can go to dinner." She turned and disappeared into the room behind the back wall of the store.

Rand glanced back at the open scrapbook and slowly turned the pages. He had taken pictures of Erik and Sophie, but they were all on his hard drive, as neatly digitized as his puts, calls, options, orders to sell short and orders to convert Euros to yen. Had he ever printed a single photo?

His mind flashed to an evening he'd misplaced his BlackBerry. When he found it, between the couch cushions at Dinah's Connecticut home, he'd held it aloft like the Holy Grail and said, "My whole life is in here."

His sister had crossed her arms and cocked her head, her standard stance to deliver a zinger. "That's the saddest true statement I've ever heard."

He did have one current picture of his nephew and niece in his wallet, but only because Dinah put it there. He wished now that he could turn a page and see them as they used to be. Tiny infants with lungs like bellows, wailing their outrage at slow service from an uncle inept with a bottle warmer. Toddlers who did intricate math in their heads, calculating how to hurl their bodies safely across the cosmos of space—all the way from the coffee table to Rand's leg.

He'd tried to talk Dinah into having another baby or—better yet—two, but she'd laughed until she had to lean against the wall to stay upright.

"Get your own," she'd finally managed to say. "Or to put it in terms you might understand, pull your head out of the futures market and shove it into a future of your own."

"I'm ready." Luanne looked as if she'd changed clothes, but Rand saw that she'd removed her pale green apron and added a black straw hat that matched her dress. It even had a small flower by the crown that looked like the dinner-plate size flowers on her black dress.

The flowers weren't roses; that he knew. Roses were the only flowers he could identify with better than seventy percent accuracy. But, since women always liked getting roses, and he kept the phone number of a reliable Manhattan florist on his speed dial, he figured he knew enough. Why clutter his mind with trivia?

He knew enough about women's shapes, a subject that was most definitely not trivia, to be sure Luanne Holt was perfectly proportioned. Five feet six, give or take an inch.

"Nice hat," he commented.

"Thank you. I have a big hat collection. I have to avoid too much sun or I burn."

He liked that she simply said, "Thank you." It always frosted him when he complimented a woman, and she said something like, "What? *This* old thing?" as if he had the fashion sense of a musk ox.

"Is the Mineshaft all right with you?" he asked.

"It's my favorite place." She turned off the lights and stepped out the front door. "Of course, in Bitter Falls that's faint praise. I think there are seven places to eat, and that's counting the ice cream parlor and the big glass refrigerator inside Wesley Jett's gas station on the west end of town."

He watched her lock the door and turn toward him with a smile as open as the great outdoors.

"New York City has hundreds of restaurants," he said, "but I probably eat at the same seven all the time anyway."

Make that six. His days of eating thick, juicy steaks and gourmet burgers at Smith and Wollensky in Midtown were over. Brogen's voice of doom reverberated in his head. Eat right, exercise in moderation—instead of the maniacal triathlon training he'd done for four years—and slow down his quest to see his name on the list of the 100 Richest Men in America.

"Unless," Brogen had said with a smirk, "you don't care if your name goes on the list posthumously."

In other words, smell the flowers, watch the leaves fall—and kiss a pretty girl.

Rand opened the door of the Lincoln SUV, and she stepped up and in, folding her full skirt against her like a girl going to a prom. Not that he'd ever taken a girl to a prom. During his junior and senior years at prep school, he'd made a fortune on tuxedo rentals and subcontracting limousine rentals. *Kaching.*

Rand wondered, as he had many times since coming out of anesthesia at the New York hospital: *What have I missed?* It had been six months since he'd broken off his almost-engagement to fashion exec Madonna Taylor, but that, at least, was a conscious choice. How many relationships before that had simply died of neglect?

As he strapped on his seatbelt and pulled away from the curb, he wondered what it would be like to open up and have a real relationship. Was the risk greater than the potential profit?

"Oh, Rand, could you stop for a minute?" Luanne's face lit up as she waved at two little girls three blocks down from her shop. They rushed to the curb and windmilled their arms to get her attention.

Sure, he mused, there was a risk in relationships, but maybe this was the right time to take it. Getting more of Luanne Holt's high-voltage smiles was better than gold at nine hundred eighty dollars an ounce. He pulled the car in toward the curb and stopped.

She pressed the button to lower her window. "What's up, girls?"

"Mom said we can tell you first," the girl on the left said. They both bounced on the front of their feet and their dark brown hair went up and down. Rand had seen twins before, but he'd never seen two girls more identical than these. A very pregnant woman with light brown hair smiled over their heads at Luanne.

"Mom's going to have two boys," squealed the girl on the right.

Their mom laughed and stepped close enough to the SUV that Luanne could reach out and hug her.

"Cory, that's wonderful." Luanne leaned out for the hug, then sat back in the seat and looked over at Rand. "Cory DeSoto, this is Rand Monahan. He's here from New York. First time in Montana."

Cory reached her right hand in the window, and Rand leaned over enough to shake it.

"Nice to meet you, Rand. These are my daughters, Rebecca and Rachel."

"I'm Rebecca," the girl on the right said.

Rand said hello to her and to Rachel. Looking hard for differences between them, he noticed that Rachel had a bandage on her knee and Rebecca wore a red barrette. Not much to go on.

Luanne gave Cory another hug and thanked the girls for sharing their news with her. "You make me feel very special, girls. Remember, you need to be extra helpful so your mom gets plenty of rest."

"We will," they shouted in tandem, still jumping.

"As soon as we stop at the grocery store, we're going home," Cory said. "I'm on bed rest from here on out."

"I'll go to the store for you! Go on home and get off your feet."

"Well, if you're sure you don't mind. Kent will be home tomorrow afternoon."

"I'll call you in a while and find out what you need."

"You're the best. It was nice to meet you, Rand."

Luanne waved again and powered up her window. Rand drove on to the Mineshaft.

"They're a great family," Luanne said. "How big is your family?"

"My sister, her husband, and their two kids. They live in Greenwich, Connecticut. Plus my grandfather, Rocky." He pulled the Lincoln in at the end of a row of pickup trucks. "I thought we were early."

"For dinner, yes," she said. "But it's happy hour. The bar will be full."

He walked around the car and opened her door, took her elbow to help her down. As she slid off the high seat, her skirt caught on the gear lever. Before she could tug it free, her skirt went up like an umbrella to her panty line, showing her shapely legs to good advantage. She brushed the skirt down and again he saw pink blossom on her pale cheeks.

Rand wracked his brain for the last time he'd seen a woman blush, but nothing came to mind. A lot of the women he knew in New York used language that would make a sailor blush.

The restaurant and bar shared a common entrance, a wooden passage that looked like a miner's shack. The pickaxes and lanterns along the walls might be the real thing.

"Luanne, good to see you," said a tall woman with short gray hair and a nametag that identified her as Zelda. "Two for dinner?"

"Yes, thank you." Rand felt Zelda's fierce, appraising look, probably meant to warn the city slicker not to mess with her friend.

He had to stifle a snicker. In Montana Zelda might be considered scary, but Rand was used to New York women. They'd eat Zelda for a light lunch and use her bones for toothpicks.

Couples at three tables looked up and called out

greetings to Luanne. Again Rand felt the air crackle with distrust. He wondered if they acted that way toward all outsiders, or only outsiders who dared to place a hand on the elbow of Luanne Holt.

"I guess you know everyone in town," he said when Zelda had handed them each a menu and left. "For better or for worse."

Luanne took a drink of her water and opened her menu as if she were starving. Well, she supposed it was true. Starving, but not for food. The words on the menu floated in and out of focus.

For better, for worse, yes. For richer, for poorer.

She heard the distant echo of the magical words. Ted's face and voice were harder to conjure now. Sometimes—only at night—she allowed herself to drift deep enough in memory to remember him clearly. It seemed like no one ever said his name when she was nearby. She knew it was out of kindness to her, but sometimes she wanted to stand in the middle of Main Street at high noon and shout her grief and anger that Ted Wilder was gone. She would never be Luanne Wilder. She would never be the mother of Ted's children.

Now this total stranger had innocently said words that pulled her backward through time. For better or worse? Oh, definitely worse. Fourteen long months of worse.

She cleared her throat. "I grew up here. Except for going to college in Bozeman, I've never lived anywhere else." She closed the menu and took another drink of water. She hoped he hadn't detected the catch in her voice.

What is wrong with me tonight?

She set down the glass and held her hand, in a fist, against her belly. Her flat, empty belly. Her grandmother had no idea how much her teasing about dwindling fertility hurt. She'd even looked into getting pregnant through a sperm bank, but she

31

didn't have the money. She shoved it out of her mind.

"Would you like some wine?" Rand asked.

"That sounds good. I'm not a gourmet. Whatever you choose will be fine."

"What are you having for dinner? The rib eye steak looks good. So does the pan-fried trout, and the salmon." He looked up from the menu and laughed. "Sorry. I'm sure you can read the menu. In fact, you probably know it by heart."

She smiled. Rand Monahan was an odd mix of sophistication and boyish charm. "I'd like the trout and a salad. They have a terrific house dressing."

He picked up the wine list. When their waitress approached with more water, he ordered a Washington varietal, Dungeness Riesling. The waitress returned with a bottle of wine with an Olympic Cellars label and poured him a little to try.

"That's fine." As the waitress poured a glass for Luanne and then filled his, he told her they would order dinner in a while.

"I thought you were ravenously hungry," Luanne chided when the waitress left. "Too hungry to see antique photos, I think you said."

"I'm trying to slow down. This is part of my new regimen. I'm getting off the information super highway, so to speak. Pulling into a rest area for a while."

"You turned at the right exit. Bitter Falls moves in slow motion." She sipped her wine. "This is good."

"And how do you feel about this slow town? You're still here."

"Truthfully? I'm ninety percent contented." She drank more wine. "Lately, I've wondered if I stay because I belong here, or if I'm afraid of the world outside." She noticed his eyebrows raise a little and felt her old enemy, a blush, rise to her hot cheeks.

His eyes twinkled. Or maybe that was the

candle.

"A ninety percent contentment rate is pretty spectacular." He poured a little more wine in both glasses. "I don't know anyone, except my grandfather, who enjoys his milieu more. And, come to think of it, he has three houses and two luxury condos, so 'No place like home' is a hollow endorsement coming from him."

"I met him once," she said. "He's like a force of nature."

Rand nodded. "He's passionate about what he does. If he could clone himself and carry a stack of books to every classroom in the country, he would. The next best thing is his foundation."

"Cory's husband, Kent DeSoto, is a teacher. Thanks to your grandfather, he went to a seminar three years ago on getting more science and math into the curriculum. He came back hot as a prairie fire. Three kids who had no thought of going to college before that became National Merit Scholars."

"So they're going on to college?"

"Yes, thanks to the Monahan Scholarship Fund. Rocky Monahan is a hero around here. Probably in five hundred other towns, too."

"Luanne, how pretty you look, all dressed up." A woman's voice, right by her shoulder.

There was no mistaking who it was, nor her motive.

"Gerri Woolsey, I'd like you to meet Rand Monahan." Luanne watched him stand and looked up at the two of them shaking hands. Gerri, in high heels, was nearly as tall as Rand. As Gerri Melman, she'd graduated from Bitter Falls High in the same class as Luanne and Cory, but they'd never been buddies. Gerri had been what Luanne's very proper mother had called "fast."

She'd returned to town after two divorces, no children. When she got home and took over the bed and breakfast that her father had left her, she discovered that she disliked the hospitality business. She sold the inn and the sprawling property around it to a developer for an assisted living center.

When she'd returned to Bitter Falls, Gerri's figure could be described—charitably—as voluptuous, but now she'd gotten closer to fighting weight. It was no secret that the former Gerri Melman was looking for more excitement than small town Montana had to offer.

"You must be from out of town," Gerri said.

"New York," he said. "Here on vacation."

"Well, I hope you enjoy our quiet little town." She stepped back and cooed at Luanne like they were the best of friends, "I saw Dexter in the bar. I wondered why he kept looking in here."

Luanne got the message. Dexter was watching her, and at least a dozen people were watching him. She caught the eye of the waitress, not hard to do since the waitress was one of the people following Dexter's steely stare.

Sometimes Bitter Falls seemed like a gigantic room with four mirrored walls. They didn't need surveillance cameras.

"Are you ready to order?" The waitress set a basket of hot rolls on the table. Gerri took the hint and said again that she hoped Rand would enjoy his vacation.

He sat down and ordered salads, pan-fried rainbow trout, polenta, and grilled peppers. They handed the waitress their menus.

"I think we were talking about my small family," he said. "How about you? Do you have much family?"

"Even less than you do. My parents died in a cruise ship accident, in Canada, the year after I finished college. I'm the only child of an only child, so—it's just me and my grandmother. And you've probably heard by now that Amelia Holt is the tango

34

queen of Arizona. I think she got tired of me not leaving the nest, so she sold the nest and flew south."

The waitress brought a bottle of olive oil and a plate of butter squares. Rand thanked her and said the sourdough rolls were delicious.

"Do you bake them here?" he asked.

Luanne gave scant attention to the waitress and Rand discussing baked goods.

Amelia had been painfully clear about what she thought Luanne should do. Whether she should stay in Bitter Falls or move away wasn't the issue. She needed to get over Ted.

Get. Over. Ted. Move on.

The truth was, Luanne knew that Amelia, and Cory, and all the people who cared about her were right. When she'd come out of the period of grief when her heart seemed to be beating at half speed, as if her blood were thick and cold and hard to move, she'd seen the path back to life and health. And it led right through the front door of the closed Suncatcher Solar Cell factory. Once she'd made Ted's dream come true—and gotten even with Allied Advent Technology—she'd be free to move on.

"You lived with your grandmother?" Rand asked when the waitress finished telling him who baked their rolls and pies. "I understand her place is a Victorian mansion."

"It is. Albion House, a three-story monstrosity that begs to be updated. But it was never my home. I live in a ranch house off East Valley Drive, my parents' house." She buttered a roll and poured dressing on the salad set in front of her by the waitress.

"More wine?" he asked.

"Yes, thanks." She watched the golden liquid reflect the light and took a sip.

"To say Amelia's tossing me out of the nest is an

exaggeration. I've been on my own for a long time."

She described the overwhelming amount of remodeling the new owners would be doing on the mansion, pausing to enjoy the crisp greens with balsamic vinaigrette.

"The new owners, Ann-Marie and Tess Riker, are distant cousins of mine. I never knew they existed until a year ago."

"Now that sounds like a story," he said.

"Too long to tell. A genealogical and private detective agency saga. No hugging involved, but I hope we'll get to be friends."

"How old are they?"

"Ann-Marie is twenty-eight; Tess is twenty-seven. Their mother, who died of cancer four years ago, was the only daughter of the only grandson of Goldie Jones. That's who built Albion House."

"And Goldie was your—"

"My great-great-great aunt. Her sister, Violet, was my great-great grandmother. I hope you're taking notes."

He tapped his temple with a finger. "Up here. But I'd like to see the organizational chart, I mean, family tree, on paper."

"Ann-Marie and Tess and their father are moving here from Seattle. They do something there in the hotel business, so I guess they have some good ideas of how to restore Albion House and reclaim its elegant history."

She thought, but didn't say, the reclamation would be a case of resurrection from the grave. Everyone connected with Albion House, even heirs who'd never heard of it, was dead. All but Amelia and Luanne, and now Ann-Marie and Tess. It was time for a change.

In most instances, Luanne didn't like change. She particularly didn't like having Amelia move away, even though she said she'd buy a small condo in Bitter Falls and spend most of each summer there.

And what could she say to her grandmother except, *I'm happy for you?* Amelia liked to golf, bicycle and dance. If she found life more fun in Arizona, then she should be there. *Use it or lose it* was Amelia's favorite saying, and apparently she was using it to good advantage on the dance floor.

Life is for the living.

That was another of Amelia's favorite sayings, and there was no question to whom she directed that arrow of wisdom.

As they ate their entrees, Rand told her about his kayak trip on the river.

"Today I was limited to the stretch of river out by Horseshoe Bend, where I could leave the kayak on the shore, take the car to a pickup point downriver, and hike back two miles to the start. I'd like to do it again with a guide dropping me off six miles upriver. Then I'd haul out at the same spot."

She said no to dessert but urged Rand to try the pumpkin pie. Yes, she told the waitress, she'd like decaf coffee.

"Excuse me," she said to Rand as she pulled her cell phone out of her purse. "I have to check in with Cory and see what she needs at the store."

She made a quick call to Cory and wrote down the items she needed.

"This pie is terrific," Rand said when she put the phone back in her purse. "Are you sure you don't want some?"

"Really, no. Just coffee."

Rand finished his pie and coffee and paid their check with a credit card. While they waited for the waiter to bring the receipt, he pulled out a picture of two cute towheads. The boy wore a totally preppie outfit including a tie. The little girl looked like a princess in a blue and white confection and matching ribbons in her twin ponytails.

"They don't dress like this all the time," he said. "My sister, Dinah, had the photographer come to the house and catch them during the five minutes they looked perfect. Erik—he'll be six next month—is happiest on a muddy soccer field. He has great coordination; he could walk at ten months. You should see him on a pogo stick, and on ice skates. I'm going to take him to his first Rangers game in December."

She liked the way his eyes shone as he held out the photo.

"Sophie is three. She has an ear for music and she'll start violin lessons next May when she's four."

"You're very close to them," she said with a grin. "And extravagantly proud."

He laughed and nodded. "I know you want to ask but are too polite. Yes, my brother-in-law and I *both* handed out cigars when they were born. I was pacing the floor outside the delivery room both times, and the nurses had to pull the curtains closed on the nursery to get me to leave."

The waiter returned with Rand's credit card, and he signed the receipt.

"Would you excuse me for a minute?" she asked. He stood and pulled her chair back.

In the ladies' room she applied fresh lipstick, surprised to realize she didn't want to rush home. On the occasions she'd accepted a dinner date with Dexter Stone or one of the other local men who invited her out, she'd tried hard to enjoy herself. But it was impossible. She'd been in love once, and she knew what that was like. She'd rather stay home with her dogs, Laddie and Max, than go out with the men she knew.

She'd asked herself many times why she went out at all. Probably because Dexter was so persistent that she ran out of excuses. Then, to keep him from acting like he owned her, she went out with others. The whole situation grated on her nerves.

Maybe she should move somewhere else and start over. Somewhere that the ghost of Ted Wilder wouldn't trail in her wake like the filmy train of her wedding gown.

For the first three or four months after Ted died, she'd been so numb that nobody even bothered to advise her. Then she'd taken up the cause of reopening the Suncatcher factory, and her goal gave her strength.

But as the anniversary of his death—the anniversary of their wedding day—approached, people seemed to clear a path around her wherever she went. Conversations stopped, then started up with a tinny note of humor.

That day passed, as all days must. She'd sat alone on the banks of the Bitter River and recalled how her wedding flowers had wilted in the August heat. Someone had taken her wedding cake back to the bakery. She'd wondered idly if it had been recycled, separated into its component parts and rebuilt for some other occasion.

Now, with Rand Monahan showing her pictures of his niece and nephew and waxing poetic about how smart and funny they were, she felt a window open inside herself. Only a crack, but it let in a lot of light and warmth.

Some of that warmth was kindling a fire in her midsection and her breasts, stirring memories that transcended photos and word descriptions. She'd waited a long time to make love with Ted, and it had been better than her most vivid daydreams. But then—suddenly, tragically—it was over. He was gone, and her body missed his caresses as if it had a memory of its own.

She took off her hat and puffed her hair up with her fingers. And thought...maybe a short romance with a man who'd be gone soon would do her some good. They were both adults, unmarried. No strings attached.

"Ridiculous!" she said aloud to the red-headed romantic in the mirror. Rand had invited her to dinner. That didn't imply he wanted anything more. Proper *or* improper. He'd probably be shocked that she was paying such close attention to his lips, and not only for the words.

She returned to the table as the waiter stopped by with the coffee pot. Yes, she nodded. She'd like more.

When they came out of the Mineshaft, she was surprised to see it was dark. How long had they lingered over coffee?

"I thought we'd have time to go to my grandmother's house," she said, "but I forgot how early it gets dark in October. And we're still on daylight time. In two weeks it will be dark by five."

"Winter nights are long here, I guess." He helped her up into his car. "May I see you tomorrow? You can show me your grandmother's collection when the light is better."

"That's a good idea. Her house is rather spooky at night. Only the bravest kids trick or treat there."

He said nothing, but stood beside the car with her door open. She sensed that he wanted to kiss her. Or was that more of her wishful thinking?

"I have to go to the grocery store, for Cory," she said. "My car is behind my shop."

"Why don't I take you? I need some coffee and fruit. You'll be doing me a favor, showing me the store before they roll up the sidewalks."

She looked doubtful. "Cory and Kent live west of town, beyond the store. I was going to Safeway on the way to their house."

"I'd be glad to take you over to Cory's." He left the invitation open.

She thought it over. Why not? The thought of having a fling with this stranger—the idea that sounded like such a good idea twenty minutes ago—scared her, but what harm could come from a trip to the dairy case at Safeway?

"Okay, thanks. If you're sure it's not too much trouble."

"No trouble at all." As he closed her door and walked around to the driver's side, she looked at the almost full moon peek over the mountains across the valley.

Trouble was a word with more than one definition.

Chapter Three

Rand stood in the aisle at Safeway and smiled. He was a fish out of water. And yet, more at ease than he could remember.

There was something strangely intimate about shopping for coffee with Luanne Holt. She held out an open bag of beans she'd downloaded from a plastic bin and held it out for him to smell.

"Think of it as aromatherapy."

He inhaled. "It's terrific." He thought, but didn't add, *And sensual as hell.*

"It's called Chocolate Velvet," she said. "Nice to wake up to."

Their eyes met; she smiled—and wet her lips. And he wondered—hoped—they were thinking the same thought: early morning, the two of them with steaming mugs of coffee. Nice image.

But his imagination went a lot further. A *lot* further. Tangled sheets, her skin flushing with embarrassment as the sheet falls from her breasts. Her nipples dark against her creamy skin.

Oh. My. God.

Rand dropped to one knee in front of the vast display of coffee, and grabbed the first package of beans he saw. Starbucks, whole beans from Sumatra. How much Starbucks stock did he own? He should get some more. He studied the label while his steamy thoughts cooled enough to handle...and while his physical reaction to such thoughts could, uh, shrink.

At last he was ready. He rose and followed Luanne down the aisles, getting a box of cereal she said was healthy, and a variety of apples, and nonfat milk. Following her had a distinct advantage; he could watch the sway of her hips in her full skirt and the shape of her breasts in the fitted, clinging top of the dress as she stretched for a can on a top shelf. He stepped in close behind her and reached beyond her fingertips to get the can of cranberry sauce.

"Thanks." She consulted her list and moved to the next aisle to get the other items Cory had asked for, plus two small dog treats.

"Laddie and Max are waiting impatiently for supper," she said as they headed for the checkout stand. "This is my blatant attempt to regain their affection in the face of starvation."

He started to say, conversationally, that he didn't have a dog but that his sister had an English spaniel. But the words stuck in his mouth like ash. Why did he settle like that, settle for a dog-by-proxy?

What was next for him? Getting a robot dog like the faux pets so popular in Japan?

Luanne went ahead of him at the checkout stand. The checker was full of questions about the Harvest Festival.

He glanced at the rack of women's magazines. The common themes were how to lose weight, how to have more orgasms, and "How to overcome a man's fear of intimacy." He was surprised they didn't have his picture by those words.

Dog-by-proxy, kids-by-proxy. Apartment cleaned by an efficient crew he'd never laid eyes on. Meals prepared—and delivered in cartons, as often as not—by nameless strangers.

Hell, all his financial deals, for his personal holdings and for Morning Select Investments, were indirect, "one off" at the least. Each Buy or Sell order was paper, not something real. Even calling it "commercial paper" was one off. It was a series of zeros and ones in a mainframe computer, not

43

something tangible. Not like the crisp locally-grown apples and organic cereal he'd placed on the rolling mat.

He and Jeff had gotten rich by some incredibly lucky business moves, especially their development and sale of an internet-based matchmaking company back when the conventional wisdom was, "The internet is a fad and nobody will ever make money with it."

Then they'd gotten *really-really rich* by trading in the world financial markets, trading not straight stocks and bonds, but their delightfully profitable stepchildren: derivatives. Options and futures. Market inefficiencies. Risk management.

Adding straight stocks and bonds to their portfolios had come more recently, like adding more fiber to their diets.

He set the quart of milk on the counter, pulled out a ten dollar bill and studied the portrait of Alexander Hamilton. Even that bill wasn't "real." It was a rectangle of paper, a fungible and agreed-upon way to trade. Better than handing over a live chicken or a pound of iron filings in exchange for milk.

Come to think of it, milk is real, but isn't milk in a carton a "derivative?"

If I'm so tired of life-by-proxy, maybe I should get my own damn cow.

Okay. Back up; that's extreme. Maybe I should start with a dog of my own.

On their way out of the store, an older man with a grizzly two-tone beard stopped Luanne to ask when her cousins would move to Bitter Falls.

"Soon. Maybe before Thanksgiving," she said. "They'll be renting a house until Albion House is ready to live in." She introduced Willie to Rand, who juggled the paper sacks in his arms to free his right hand.

"I'm going to have my crew plus four temporary guys start the new roof on Albion tomorrow. We can't waste this weather."

Willie spoke to Luanne, but he was studying Rand and projecting the same silent *Watch yourself, stranger* message Rand had been getting ever since he met Luanne. At least—unlike Dexter Stone—Willie wasn't actively in pursuit of the lady.

"You're right, Willie," she replied, "and it's supposed to stay gorgeous for the Harvest Festival."

Willie nodded. "I know how much that means to you. I mean, how much it means to the whole town. You all have a nice evening, now."

As they strolled across the parking lot to the SUV, Rand asked about Albion House. "Sounds like a big project. I'm looking forward to seeing it."

"I shudder to think what it's going to cost to rewire the place and to remodel the kitchen. The bathrooms all need work, too. My grandmother, Amelia, closed off all the bedrooms except hers, the largest one on the second floor, to save on utilities."

"Your cousins—Ann-Marie and Tess?—must have resources to take it on," he observed.

"Resources came with the deed. Goldie died in 1960, at the age of ninety-seven, without finding her only direct heir, her grandson's daughter. That would be Ann-Marie and Tess's mother, Martha. Goldie left a trust fund for her direct heirs that has doubled and re-doubled and so on, so Ann-Marie and Tess have deep pockets. And Amelia says they have a love affair with history."

She laughed, a sound he was drawn to more and more. "Except for the pockets, I guess that describes me, too. My happiest hours are spent in the past."

"Not in the present?" He put the sacks in the back seat, closed the door, and looked down at her. The present was working extremely well for him, but it would be working better if he could taste her lips.

45

He stepped closer and rested one hand above her on the frame of the car.

Her perfume was something floral. Something tantalizing. She shivered, and he used that as an excuse to pull her close to his chest.

"I should have brought a jacket," she said.

"Ah, I have the solution to your problem." He walked to the back of the car and opened the hatch. The windbreaker he'd worn on the river and the extra jacket he hadn't needed were still there.

He closed the back of the car and wrapped the fleece jacket around her. "You were saying?" he prompted. He wrapped his arms around her to warm her up. Any excuse would do.

"I was?" she asked.

"You were saying your happiest hours are spent in the past." He looked down into her face. If she wet her lips, he was going to claim them. Propriety be damned.

"I was speaking figuratively. I like connecting to the distant past through pictures, journals, even business ledgers. I know pioneers had painful, exhausting lives, but I think I would have fit right in."

He looked down into her eyes and said nothing.

"What are you thinking?" she asked softly.

"The truth?" he asked.

"Yes, of course."

He grinned. "I was thinking that if I were transported back to the Wild West I'd last about twenty minutes. The agility to drive a Porsche on an eight-lane parkway and the know-how to trade stocks on the London Exchange do not translate to survival skills in Montana Territory."

"So if somebody yelled *Stampede*, you might have a heart attack?"

A what?

He stepped back and put both hands in his

pockets. "Yeah, I guess you could say that." He opened her door and held her elbow as she climbed in. He got in the other side and started the engine. She gave him the simple directions to Cory and Kent DeSoto's house.

"So, about Amelia's photo collection, I could meet you at Albion House at noon. You go six blocks west from my shop and turn right. Prescott Street is four blocks up. Believe me, you can't miss the house. There's nothing else like it."

"I'll be there. Would you like to go out to lunch after I see the pictures? That won't take long, by the way. I don't know an antique photo from cheap wallpaper. As soon as I laid eyes on you, I knew my grandfather had set me up. Rigged me like a three-masted schooner. What did your grandmother tell you about me?"

Luanne laughed. "She was vague, in a sly way. Let's just say I'm surprised to see that your shoes match."

Rand joined her in laughing. He was pretty sure Rocky Monahan and Amelia Holt were chortling up their respective sleeves, too.

He ran his hand through his hair. "I wish I had a pair of horn-rimmed glasses with masking tape around the nosepiece."

"Not that being a techno-dweeb is a bad thing," she said.

He winced. "Techno-dweeb? That's harsh." He turned where she directed, onto a dirt road beside the irrigation canal.

She pointed to a light on a pole about a half mile down the road. "That's Cory and Kent's house."

"Techno-dweeb," he muttered again. "I think my manhood is being called into question." Abruptly, he pulled off to the berm of the canal, beside a large tree. He cut the engine and headlights and stepped outside.

47

A wet, earthy smell and darkness enveloped him like fog. Before he got to Luanne's door she'd stepped out and closed it. He blinked and let his eyes adjust to the dark. The rim of a cloud began to glow; the moon came out of hiding.

"Listen," she said softly. "Frogs."

He studied her face in the moonlight and wondered how her lips would taste. Was it his imagination, or was she breathing hard?

"The moon is nearly full." He leaned closer and breathed in the potent, floral scent of her hair.

"It'll be full in three nights," she said. "On Thursday. It's called the Hunter's Moon."

"I never would have guessed," he said. With one finger he tilted her chin toward him and lightly kissed her lips. He couldn't have guessed—or cared less—what they called the full moon in late October, but the taste of Luanne Holt's lips was precisely what he thought it would be. Exquisite.

He kissed her softly on the lips and both cheeks, then returned to her mouth for more. This time soft wasn't enough. He pressed and felt a shock all the way to his toes when she opened her mouth and accepted his tongue.

He had only to open his arms and she stepped into his embrace. This must be what "moonstruck" meant; Rand hoped he didn't suddenly aim his chin at the rising moon and start howling. At this point, though, nothing would surprise him.

He cupped her shapely rear, and she stretched her arms up and around his neck. He pulled her hips against him and moved his, hardening in four seconds flat. Every cell in his body was on red alert. A rush of testosterone sent every organ to its battle station.

Dive, dive, dive. Prepare torpedoes!

"Rand?" She broke off the kiss and murmured his name. He loved the purring, husky sound of her voice. "Rand?"

"Yes?" He kissed her cheek and nibbled at her earlobe, but his attention was centered below his belt buckle, along with eighty percent of his blood volume. He kept one hand on her rear, pressing her even closer, and moved the other one to the side of her breast and inched forward along the soft swell.

"Oh, Rand," she whispered. Her breath came in short puffs.

He covered her lips with his and took her breast in his hand. Her heart raced as if to catch up with his.

Target acquired. Torpedoes at the ready. Stand by.

Good Lord, he marveled, *how long has it been?*

Wrong question. Why has it never been this good before?

"Rand—" Again she broke their kiss but this time she nipped at his lower lip. "I think, umm, I think we should, uh..." She lowered her arms and put some space between them. "Your manhood is no longer in question. I'll testify on your behalf."

"What a relief. You've saved me in the nick of time. Now, what can I do for you?" He tried to pull her close again, but she put both hands against his chest.

"We're making a delivery, remember? A mission of mercy."

"Oh, you're so right. Mercy, mercy." He felt her press harder. "Okay, I'm on the job. Let's go see Cory and the girls."

He took a deep breath and exhaled slowly.

Shut the torpedo tubes. Repeat, shut the torpedo tubes. This was only a test.

****

It was nine-forty-five when Luanne pulled into her long driveway. Laddie and Max, two-year-old Golden Retrievers from the same litter, ran to the fence to meet her, barking furiously. They'd been Ted's dogs, and she'd taken them when he died. There had been days when getting up to feed and exercise the dogs had been her only reason to get vertical.

"I know, I know. You're weak with starvation. I'll get your food as fast as I can." She unlocked the door to the house and closed the garage door. Before she could open the can of dog food her phone rang. As she picked it up, she saw that she had seven messages.

"Hello?" She propped it against her cheek with her shoulder and pressed the can into the automatic can opener.

"I want details!" Cory blurted. "He's gorgeous, and I want to know everything."

During the hour or so she and Rand had spent at Cory's house, Cory had smoothly wheedled more information about his work and family out of Rand than Luanne had asked about.

"He's good looking, he's nice, and he's only here for seven days," she replied.

"A lot can happen in seven days."

A lot had already happened—in less than five hours—but she wasn't going to tell anyone, even Cory, that news. She hadn't had time to process it herself. Had she actually stood in the filtered moonlight and pressed herself against a man she'd barely met?

A delicious shiver ran down her back and her nipples hardened. Rand Monahan's manhood was intact, all right. It was her rigid shell that showed signs of impending fracture.

"I've got to feed the dogs and check my messages. I'll call you back before I go to bed."

"I guess that will have to do. Hurry."

She mollified the dogs, taking the extra time to make them sit and wait until their bowls were down on the concrete patio before they ate. Ted had trained them that way, saying she'd be glad when they got big enough to knock her over that they obeyed the "wait" signal.

Five of the messages were about the Harvest Festival; all announced good news about details coming together and problems getting solved. Three callers asked her to return the call, but said tomorrow would be fine.

The sixth message was from Dexter Stone. His excuse for calling was to say he was giving front page coverage on the Wednesday paper to the Harvest Festival and the city council's declaration of Saturday as Suncatcher Day to honor Ted Wilder.

His real reason for calling at nine-thirty-two, she was certain, was to see if she was home yet.

The seventh message couldn't wait. She made a cup of mint tea and took the oversized mug to the bedroom she used as an office. With her paperwork at hand, she steeled herself for the sound of Ted's brother's voice. Ted and Finn Wilder had been as different as a Lear Jet and a crop duster, but there was something about their voices—the tone, timbre, something—that always gave her a jolt of déjà vu. If she placed the call, she had the advantage of mental preparation, the way she did if a nurse rubbed her arm hard and said, "This is going to sting."

It was a few minutes past ten o'clock mountain time; a little after midnight on the east coast. Finn would be up at least another hour. She booted up her computer and went online so she'd be ready to look up anything he told her about.

Finn was representing his brother's company, Suncatcher, without pay, but the legal costs to his firm for research and document preparation and court costs still mounted. Plus, they were paying unbelievably high fees to Yost and Collyer, a firm specializing in intellectual property law. Who would guess ten minutes could cost so much?

She'd used what remained of Ted's life insurance money, after funeral costs, to pursue the heartless bastards of Allied Advent Technology, AATech, but she was Daniel in the lions' den.

The money she expected the Harvest Festival to raise, including part of the auction income, was already owed to the patent attorneys. She'd had to beg them to keep going; she was sure they were close to winning.

The money Amelia was donating from the sale of her antique photos, plus more than half of the auction income, should go to starting production. However, if that cash was the only way to prevail, Luanne would give it to Finn with one word: Win.

She rested her cheek in her hand. Their "win" would be a Pyrrhic victory if they won back the rights to Ted's invention, but couldn't open the factory.

"Please be good news," she said as she dialed his number, "please, good news." One ring; click.

"Finn Wilder. How are you, Luanne?"

"I can't answer that until I know how things are going with you."

Finn cleared his throat. "It's not good news."

She let out the breath she'd been holding. Whatever happened to the good old American way? The headline she'd written in her head so long ago that she'd come to believe it was inevitable: *Underdog wins! Factory opens tomorrow!*

A bell rings—and another fairy gets its wings.

But Finn said it *wasn't* good news. She stifled a groan.

Not only was she Daniel in the lions' den—she was slathered with A-1 Sauce and tender to the bone.

"Go ahead, Finn. I'm listening."

"I took the train from D.C. to New York this

afternoon. Allied has filed an injunction to stop Suncatcher's suit cold. I've already answered it and one federal district court judge will hear arguments tomorrow. Actually, today. I'm polishing the brief right now."

She sighed. "Oh, Finn, can't I just shoot somebody?"

"As refreshing as that might feel in the short run, I have to advise against it. There is a glimmer of good news, though. I mean beside the extremely good news that I, Finn the Great, am the cold-blooded bastard in the white hat representing Suncatcher. The law firm for Percival is filing a brief on our behalf."

"Whoopee," she said with a groan. "If those jerks hadn't sold out to Allied, we wouldn't be in this mess." She tried to remember what character in Greek mythology got his liver pecked by a giant bird. Had he been more or less deserving of that fate than the CEO of Percival Partnerships, Limited?

"I know," Finn said. "The whole thing stinks like road kill. But I'm not giving up. It's personal." He paused. "I'm worried about you."

"I'm okay. Honest." She sighed again. "Call me as soon as you know anything. I've got to get something in the paper about this. So many people are working so hard, and have so much riding on it. I have to tell them what's going on."

"You want me to send something directly to the paper? I've got Dexter's email and his fax number."

"That's a good idea. I'm afraid I'd bungle the terms. Or add some words like blood-sucking vermin, or ulcerous intestinal parasites, or carrion-licking necrophiliacs."

"Good, that's colorful, I'm getting all this down. Necro—good. I might be able to work that into my brief."

"Glad to help." She urged him to get some sleep

but knew he only needed about four hours of sleep to be ready to fight the forces of evil.

He said he'd be in court much of the day for Suncatcher and two other cases, but would call her around three o'clock mountain time.

A few seconds after she hung up, the phone rang again.

"You said you'd call me back," Cory said. "Before bedtime—and I need to get to sleep. Or what passes for sleep with four feet doing the Texas Two-Step on my bladder."

"Rand is a very attractive man, and yes, he kissed me."

"Please tell me you kissed him back. Please."

"I kissed him back." Remembering how hot her response had been made her close her eyes and shake her head in dismay. What must he think of her? She was torn between embarrassment—a little bit—and relief—a lot—that all her systems were certifiably sound. As were his.

"Well, thank goodness for that. My voodoo doll worked."

"You mean it worked at last. I know you hoped for results before this."

"With whom? Dexter Stone? Give me some credit. I only wish Dexter were harmless," Cory said with a sigh. "Somehow he got the idea you'd turn to him as soon as you got over Ted."

"I'm not over Ted. I will never be over Ted." The words tumbled out as they had many times, but this time she felt a pinch of guilt. If she was so "not over Ted," what had she been doing with Rand Monahan by the light of the waxing moon?

"Fine. I'm going to bed."

"Don't be mad. You're right; Dexter's delusion of romantic attraction to me is a problem. Ted is gone; I'm thirty years old. And yes, yes, yes. I enjoyed kissing Rand."

"Are you going to see him tomorrow?"

"Affirmative. I have to show him Amelia's photo collection. We're meeting at Albion at noon." She'd told Cory while she was dropping off the groceries about Amelia's donation to the Suncatcher Fund.

Cory whistled softly. "Amelia is playing hardball."

Luanne didn't have to ask what Cory meant; she hadn't set foot inside Albion House since the day that was *supposed* to be her wedding day. Amelia knew she had to face it, and she'd found a way to force the issue.

The thought of going inside the old mansion made Luanne's stomach lurch.

"I'll be fine," she said brightly to Cory. "We'll look around the house and go to the bank to see the Daguerreotypes Amelia keeps in the vault, and then we'll toddle off to lunch. Nothing to it."

"Sure, sure. Umm, Lu, I need a favor. Could you drive the girls to school tomorrow? Rachel has a big social studies project that will be wrecked if they go on the bus. And, as you know, I am on my back."

"Sure. I'll come by at seven-thirty and get all of you some breakfast."

"I like Rand Monahan," Cory said emphatically.

Luanne laughed. "I'm glad to hear that. Does the fact that your daughters adore him have anything to do with your endorsement?"

"Kids are smart. Almost as smart as dogs—and my dog would give him a kidney. You saw how the girls were reading to Rand and the way he encouraged them. I don't think he was acting."

Of course Luanne had seen that. When she and Rand had gone into Cory's house, she'd put the groceries away and cleaned up the kitchen. But she'd managed to look around the corner now and again to watch Rand and the girls.

Rebecca and Rachel had been barnacles with

books, each vying to show how well she could sound out words, and how much Rebecca knew about crocodiles, and how Rachel was doing a "very major project" on Alaska, complete with a map the size of a Twister mat.

Luanne said goodnight to Cory and went back to her own kitchen. The light set the dogs running in circles and whining to come in. If she left them outside, she'd be safe from raccoons, porcupines, and skunks. With them inside, she'd be safe from intruders—and not face the possibility of dealing with muzzles full of quills, or with dogs that needed a bath in tomato juice.

She opened the door and knelt to accept their slobbering devotion.

One glass of wine and a quick shower later, she crawled into bed and listened to Laddie and Max snuffle around and get comfortable on their beds.

Sleep didn't come quickly, though. The occasional pinpricks of guilt she'd felt all evening, guilt that she might be disloyal to Ted, returned in force. She couldn't lie here and recall making love with Ted, not after she'd been kissing Rand. And she couldn't lie here and think about kissing Rand. Not when she'd loved Ted for so long and so deeply.

So this is what a turning point feels like.

She turned on her bedside light and read a chapter of a time-travel novel. Maybe she'd fall asleep thinking of a dashing Scottish laird, and herself a lusty lass in tartan plaid with the wind in her thick, curly red hair.

She yawned. It might work. She had the hair for it. *And the lust.*

At last she fell asleep—and laughed aloud in the dark when she dreamed she saw Rand Monahan in a kilt. And made another noise, more like a cat's purr, when she discovered what he *didn't* wear beneath his kilt.

Chapter Four

"I didn't call to discuss business," Jeff Adler snapped, "so you can take your price-of-gold questions and drop them in a brass spittoon."

"Hold on." Rand released the chin strap on his biking helmet, leaned his gleaming new bike against an enormous willow tree, and surveyed downtown Bitter Falls. The Silver County Courthouse loomed in front of him, balanced across the grassy square by a similar granite structure. He could see the words "Carnegie Library" carved in stone over the front door.

Removing his helmet, he sat on a bench beneath the tree. With a sigh, he put the phone back to his ear.

"Okay, Jeff, not business. Then why did you call? Oh, wait, I know. You need advice on romance."

Jeff snorted. "From you? Ha! You couldn't identify Romance in a line up with War, Pestilence and Famine. But, yes, the R word is on my mind." He groaned and lowered his voice. "Serena won't sign the pre-nup."

Rand visualized their office in Manhattan. They'd opted for an open floor space with their analysts and traders; no showroom private offices. It was good for *esprit de corps* and saved a gigabuck on rent, but came up short on privacy.

"She packed up and left my place," Jeff muttered. "She won't even answer her phone. I think it was romance that got me here."

"So, I don't need to order a new tux for a December wedding?" He shaded his eyes from the mid-morning sun.

"Not yet. Damn it, Rand! Serena used to understand my reluctance to get married again. Lord knows I have good reason."

Jeff had lost a literal fortune when his first wife, the French model Taychell, hired the meanest barracuda in Manhattan for a divorce. After two years of marriage that began when Jeff was not quite thirty, Taychell had to settle for less than she hoped to net, but the two legal firms got everything they wanted.

Jeff had been an ogre for about six months, until Serena soothed and, ultimately, tamed him. When she moved into Jeff's apartment, Rand sent her flowers—roses, of course—on behalf of the grateful analysts and traders at Morning Select Investments.

"Refresh my memory, Jeff. And—dare I say?—your own. Why did you ask Serena to marry you?"

"Hold on." There was a sound of other voices, then of Jeff speaking to someone else and swearing. "Up six percent intra-day? Get out!" Then back to Rand, "I'll call you back. Irrational exuberance is calling my name."

"What's going on?" Rand barked. "What's up six percent?"

His question went to a dial tone. He folded the phone with a snap of annoyance. A jolt of adrenaline had speeded up his heart and he braced himself. Nothing, nothing. Good.

He concentrated on relaxing; he carried nitro tablets in case of angina, but he'd only needed to take four since the stents went in, and that had been the second and third weeks out.

Relax, take it easy. Remember what the ceiling of the operating room looked like right before the masked gnome said, "Count backward for me, Rand. One hundred, ninety-nine."

Along with *Relax*, his instructions from Brogen's

post-surgical assistant had been to Exercise. His initial reaction was, *Exercise? Sweet, bring it on.* He loved exercise. His standard weekday routine to keep up his muscle tone had been to run on a treadmill. He had one at home and one—to share—at his office.

He logged miles every day while watching CNBC, reading the *Wall Street Journal* and *Business Week* online, and taking calls.

And then, there were weekends. For years, his idea of a perfect weekend had been a fifty mile bicycle race or running a half-marathon.

None of those activities were on his post-surgical assignment sheet. He was supposed to...walk.

"Walk?" He'd squawked the word like a parrot choking on a walnut.

Walking had only one virtue as far as Rand could see. He could text message better walking than running.

Kayaking and biking could be too fluid an interpretation of the phrase "moderate exercise," even this long after his heart attack, but he really was taking it easy. The kayaking had been on a deep stretch of the river, wide enough to be almost placid. He'd simply steered as the current did the work. And this biking? Easy stuff. User-friendly trail, well maintained. No elevation to speak of. An embarrassing waste of a Trek Madrone, in fact. He might at any moment be passed by a kid on a pink bike with a white basket on the front.

"Learn to listen to your body," said the brochure they'd given him at the cardiac gym. He'd hated that the picture on the cover was of an old man showing a boy how to hold his bat.

"An old man," he'd said to the pretty young physical therapist as he slapped the brochure with his other hand. "I'm not an old man."

The therapist shrugged, but a white-haired

gentleman walking by with a towel around his neck brought Rand up short.

"The point of all this is to get to be old!" To punctuate his point, he's actually called Rand "Sonny."

Gradually, Rand's attitude improved. The feel-good, woo-woo posters hanging all over the gym annoyed him less and actually lifted his mood.

The scene in front of him would make a good poster, in fact. *Watch the leaves scud across the grass. Enjoy the moment.*

It worked. He bent forward to get sand out of one biking shoe.

He tried calling Serena; no luck. "Rats!"

Jeff and Serena had been at the foot of his hospital bed one of the times he'd roused himself from subterranean dreams. Sometimes he'd surface in a beautiful lagoon. More often he'd be looking for sky but couldn't find his way out of an underwater cave. In the worst dreams he had fistfuls of money and couldn't buy air.

Serena had come forward and kissed his cheek. "The doctors say you're going to be fine. We brought you flowers. Roses, your favorite."

That had struck him as hilariously funny, but laughing was out of the question. "Coals to Newcastle," he'd said. From the look on her face she didn't get it. "Never mind."

Jeff and Serena stuck to the official party line, about what a good idea it would be for Rand to go to Montana once he'd graduated from cardiac rehab. When he was well enough to travel, but not well enough to work.

Rand had already dismissed his grandfather's Montana campaign out of hand, but he said nothing.

"I hear it's beautiful," Serena said, resting her hand on his shoulder. "Pretty enough for a honeymoon."

Seeing Jeff's eyes widen comically, Rand muttered, "Good luck with that, Serena." Jeff had already told him the wedding would be in Manhattan on the first Friday night in December—after the closing bell on the stock exchange—and the honeymoon would be an expensive but time-efficient weekend in the Hamptons.

Jeff gave his signature snort, and Serena shot him a look. He held up his palms and shrugged. The Guy Defense. Tight-lipped, she looked from Jeff to Rand and back, a look that would wither lesser men.

"I don't know which of you is more in need of brain surgery," she said. "Listen to me, Rand. I think there's a chance *you'll* listen. Three words: Money isn't everything."

Jeff had laughed explosively—not a wise choice given Serena's aggravation—and Rand had closed his eyes and drifted back to sleep.

Money isn't everything. Serena's voice, and his sister Dinah's voice, and his grandfather's voice. Even now, in Montana, in his pristine isolation, Rand heard them.

How many times had he laughed like Jeff did at those three words? Or raised a glass in toast and said, "Yeah, it's not everything. But the rush of making money is better than whatever comes in second place."

Two teenaged boys in shorts and helmets clattered by on skate boards, pursued by a dog trying to bite their ankles. He watched them fly on the long concrete diagonal toward the library, then angle toward the courthouse. A younger boy raced after them on foot, laughing and calling the dog.

Rand pulled up Jeff's office number on his speed dial. Hesitated. Closed the phone.

Jeff had been his best friend since summer camp when they were fourteen years old. While all the other boys at Camp Mohasset were short-sheeting the counselors and sneaking across the sand dunes to fire off potato guns, Rand and Jeff found a way to hack into the camp computer and check technology stocks on the NASDAQ.

At sixteen, while other boys at their Connecticut prep school traded magazines full of naked women, Rand and Jeff started an online film investment company. As long as no one saw them—and found out they only had to shave twice a week with a Lady Bic—they could move freely in the speculative world of very small independent films.

They'd parlayed one success into another all the way through M.I.T. When other graduates applied for ordinary, predictable jobs, Rand and Jeff saw the fantastic opportunities coming with the spread of the new "world wide web." They formed the first huge online matchmaking company and made money hand over keyboard.

Timing was critical with such untested business models. At the best possible time, they sold their sixty percent stock position for a thirty-six million dollar profit. As a celebration gift—and an inside joke—Jeff gave him a pen holder with three letters on the plaque: B.T.S.

Better Than Sex.

But now? Kissing Luanne Holt last night made him revisit that mantra. As he sat in the autumn sunshine, looking across the Bitter River Valley toward a jagged ridge of mountains, he was giving second and third thoughts to a lot of things he used to take for granted.

Rising and shaking out the kinks in his leg muscles, he removed a water bottle from the holder on the bike frame and drank half of it.

Jeff had joked about Rand's wealth of ignorance about romance, but the knife cut close to the truth.

Everything Rand and Jeff did in investments was, at its core, math. So, putting it in mathematical terms, women were "outliers," properties that lie an abnormal distance from other values and therefore distort ratios.

He adjusted the straps of his helmet, secured it on his head, and moved the attached tiny mirror a couple millimeters until he could see it better. There. Twenty-twenty hindsight.

Woulda, coulda, shoulda.

Matchmaking, in the abstract, was their forte. But when it came to real women, Rand and Jeff were way behind the curve. They had the social skills of men raised by wolves—or by chess masters on a bleak island. The girls they knew were either as nerdy as they were and therefore great pals, or unapologetically sexy and available. With the first they enjoyed beer and pizza after marathon work sessions; with the latter they enjoyed Anatomy 101. "Dating," as the word is usually defined, came later.

He grinned at the memory. Efficient algorithms for data mining had worked extremely well in matchmaking, but nothing about math helped the two rich coneheads understand women.

They had to hire a trainer to get them polished enough to get into the swing of New York dating and business entertaining. They had to learn how to dress, how to order wines and dine like Agent 007, and how to buy and furnish co-op apartments on the Upper West Side. "Décor," they discovered, was a French word meaning, "Destroy those NASCAR sheets and pillow shams. Ditto for the Mardi Gras beads on the goose-neck floor lamp."

Their trainer, a society snob named Calista Karan, said with a sniff that Rand and Jeff would be the most challenging makeover since Professor Higgins met Eliza Doolittle. It had taken copious flattery by Dinah to persuade Calista to take on the boys-to-men project.

The two of them caught on quickly and were

often on the society pages in the company of beautiful women.

But knowing how to seduce—and be seduced—was no substitute for understanding women. Neither of them knew the first thing about lasting relationships. Rand could see that Jeff's disastrous marriage was statistically predictable, as was his own near-miss with Madonna "I-want-to-have-your-baby" Taylor.

He punched in the phone number for Memories Mine, and then paused. Luanne's voice, even on a machine, would get the taste of Madonna out of his mouth. He pressed Talk.

****

"Does everyone in this town know I had dinner with Rand Monahan last night?" Luanne crossed Cory's living room and handed her a glass of orange juice and a small prescription bottle with the lid removed.

She'd dropped the twins at school and filled a prescription Cory needed. The girls' teacher, then the pharmacist, and then the checker at the counter had all asked her about the good-looking stranger.

"Of course they do." Cory made a noise somewhere between a laugh and a cough. She drank some juice to wash down one pill and pressed the lid back on the container.

Luanne plumped the bed pillow she'd brought out to the couch and Cory lay back.

"You've got to know that your date with Rand is hot news. It's the most entertaining event in Bitter Falls since Bess Clark found her dream man at the recycling center. Her fourth husband; his third wife. Textbook-perfect case of recycling."

When Luanne returned to the house and took a good look at Cory, she said she wouldn't go to her shop until Cory reached her doctor. She'd been off her feet, as ordered, but her ankles were swollen and she'd had a miserable night with back pain.

Luanne looked at her watch. "Are you sure you were clear with the doctor's answering service? It's been twenty minutes."

"He'll call soon. You'd better go open the shop."

"No rush. The phone forwards to my cell. And I might ask Nancy to work today; she's planning to help for the weekend as it is."

The stay-at-home mom worked for Luanne three days a week during the summer, and weekends during the school year. She would be glad to put in some more time with the festival coming.

"Well then, at least sit down and drink your coffee before it gets cold," Cory insisted. "You make me nervous."

Luanne sat down and pried the lid off the coffee she'd bought when she was out. "I like it cold."

"Liar!" Cory laughed. "You might like it hot, too, if you get my drift." She batted her eyelashes and wet her lips.

"If I did 'like it hot,' everyone in Bitter Falls would know about it before my back hit a mattress."

Her cell phone rang and she flipped it open, glad of the interruption. "Hello."

"Luanne, this is Rand Monahan."

Deep breath, deep breath. "Oh, hello, Rand." She avoided Cory's eyes, knowing she'd be making faces like they both did in high school when a B-O-Y called.

"I'm looking forward to seeing you today."

She smiled and twirled a strand of her hair around her finger. "What a nice thing to say. I'm looking forward to seeing you, too." Out of the corner of her eye she saw Cory pantomime playing a violin.

"I know I have you tied up for the middle of the day to show me your grandmother's house and pictures, plus lunch, but I wonder if I could lure you away from work long enough to find my grandfather's land."

"Oh, this afternoon? I don't know. I'm at Cory's right now. How about I call you after I check my schedule?"

"You're free!" Cory hissed. "Say yes."

Luanne glared at Cory and made a claw with one hand. "And I can't make any plans until I see how Cory is doing. She's got a call in to her doctor. Swollen ankles, plus back pain. And—this is the most troubling symptom—she's very, very bossy."

Cory's phone rang.

"That's probably the doctor now," Luanne said. "I'll call you in a little while."

The doctor wanted Luanne to drive Cory to his office for tests on her blood and urine. She called her part-time employee, Nancy, to be sure she could handle the shop all day, then called Rand back to suggest they meet at Albion House at two o'clock, after Cory's husband got back to town, adding that she'd show him Rocky's land after that.

"If we can't do lunch, may I take you to dinner?"

"Dinner?" She saw Cory nod vigorously and turned her back to keep from laughing. "I'd like that."

"What are you going to wear?" Cory asked as soon as she'd hung up. "Give me a boost." She put out her hand and Luanne pulled her off the couch to her feet.

"I'm going to dinner in Bitter Falls, Cory. I'm not walking down the red carpet at the Oscars. I'll wear what I have on."

"That old thing?" Cory curled her lip at the A-line skirt and sweater set Luanne wore. "You're so used to dressing like an old maid so you won't attract attention from men like Dexter Stone—" she made a sour pickle face, "—that you've forgotten how to play up your considerable assets."

Luanne huffed. "Don't you need to be getting

some clothes on yourself?" She followed Cory into her bedroom and opened her closet. "What do you want to wear?"

"I'm so big I have only two outfits to choose from. The ugly brown or the ugly black. Hand me that brown thing, please. I'll go as Friar Tuck."

Luanne took her bathrobe and helped her into a brown knit maternity dress. "It won't be long until you're wearing pretty clothes."

"Nice try, girlfriend. But pretty soon I'll be wearing a nursing bra and a bathrobe. Rebecca and Rachel weighed a total of thirteen pounds, and I only lost eleven pounds in the hospital, so I'm realistic in my expectations, clothes-wise. It was two months before people stopped asking when my baby was due." She stretched her mouth in a wide smile. "I'm in my fourth trimester. Thanks for asking."

She pressed a hand to her side and winced. "And my clothes are not the issue, here. We were talking about what you should wear to dinner."

"That's not important."

"Yes, it is." Cory sat on the bed and put her feet in loafers. "Men like Rand Monahan don't land in Bitter Falls every day. Or even every year. Propinquity knocks, girlfriend."

It was a buzz word they'd picked up from some teen magazine when they were about fifteen. In order to attract the boy you liked, you had to make propinquity work for you. Put yourself in his vicinity as often as possible and you had a better chance to work your way into his mind. When sophomore Cory found out that junior Kent DeSoto would be lab assistant to the biology teacher, she developed an overwhelming need to know more about the inside of frogs.

"Propinquity, huh?" Luanne said as she gave Cory another boost and followed her to the kitchen. "That notion is at the root of this whole charade."

67

"Say, what?"

"Oh, I should have spotted this scheme a mile away. Amelia and Rocky Monahan put their heads together and came up with getting me to show Rand the antique photos. I hope he doesn't think I had anything to do with it."

"I don't see Rand Monahan running for the state line."

"Well, not yet. But as I keep telling you, he's only here for seven days."

"Seven days can change the course of a river, Lu. Seven days is all you need."

"What the flip are you talking about? All I need? Need to—what? Snare some poor hapless bachelor? I have half a mind to call him back and cancel."

"Now, now, don't be hasty," Cory said. "I simply mean seven days is all you need to change your attitude toward life in general and romance in particular."

Luanne tried to look annoyed, but a goofy grin gave her away. "All right, I'll keep an open mind. I'll even change outfits. Remember the green dress I bought in Missoula?"

Cory gave her a playful punch in the arm. "This couldn't happen to a nicer guy."

****

Rand tucked his elbows close to his body and his head down toward the handlebars for the last mile of what had been a fantastic ride. The trail along the river was an abandoned railroad bed, so he had no problem with elevation. He wore a heart rate monitor that gave a readout on his watch and beeped a warning if he overdid the exertion. He'd kept it nice and even, the way Brogen said to.

Except that Brogen was referring to keeping it nice and even while walking a little faster than last week's pace.

The bike was a perfect blend of technology and

design; the best bicycle money could buy. Three hours ago, when Rand picked it up at Mike's Bikes, he'd watched the shop owner and technicians circle the Trek Madrone as if it were a holy relic that might cure disease.

Part of him was ebullient that he'd ordered the bike a week before he left New York and had it shipped to Mike's for assembly. But the men's slack-jawed adoration of it, and the talk he knew would circulate about its cost, made him uneasy.

Rich men acting like even *richer* men was the norm in his world. The guy with the best toys was the one on top of the pileup; nobody he knew would play down his wealth. Hell, that would be like a model saying she weighed twenty pounds *more* than she did. *Duh!* Wall Street, the home of "Greed is good," was simply a variant playground. Or, another kind of jungle.

Get a load of my tail feathers, sugar beak. How'd you like to have a piece of this?

But it didn't take him long to realize the gauge was different in Montana. Funny thing was, yesterday he didn't care about fitting in. So what if he stood out like his red Porsche Carrera at a truck stop?

Today, his perspective had shifted.

He slowed as the county road sloped down into town, and came into Mike's Bikes by an alleyway. Naturally, the alley reminded him of kissing Luanne good night behind her shop when he'd driven her back to get her car. He wouldn't have minded a slow-motion replay of their delicious clench from earlier in the evening, but she was in a hurry.

Why was that? Something he'd said? Something he hadn't said, but should have?

His record of reading women's minds was as good as flipping a coin one hundred times and betting every other time on heads—a statistical inanity—but he still thought she'd been nervous, maybe even afraid of something.

Something that had nothing to do with him.

Maybe the lady had been treated badly by a man. No, that was too implausible to contemplate. He wished he knew someone who could tell him something about Luanne Holt. Correction, someone who *would* tell him something. To all her friends, he was an alien from a galaxy far, far away.

At least Cory DeSoto liked him. She'd made that clear the night before, and he heard her on the phone this morning telling Luanne to say yes to spending the afternoon with him.

The garage door of Mike's was up and two young men were working on bikes. Rand saw a look pass between them and wished, again, that he'd ordered an ordinary bike. Who did he think he was, Lance Armstrong?

Oh, well. What's done is done. He called out a greeting and walked the bike into the bay of the garage.

"You did a great job of putting this together, Roddy. It runs like a dream."

"You do any road racing?" the other man, younger than Roddy asked.

"A little. There's a big one all the way out Long Island that I try to do every year. I finish in the pack, nothing to brag about."

"You do any fat tire racing?" Roddy asked.

"No way. I'm as likely to ride a bike up a mountain as I am to hire on as a logger. How 'bout you?"

"I do some. Walt here broke the record in the Apple Mountain race this year."

The younger man with the black ponytail held out his hand; Rand guessed he was about twenty-five. "I'm Walt Hogg. Mike's son."

"Glad to know you," Rand said. He asked about

the race, quickly at ease in the talk of sports. In addition to fat tire bike racing, Walt had collected a roomful of trophies from motocross. The big trophy Rand had seen in the store must be one of his. Roddy bragged on Walt's behalf about his showing in ESPN's X Games in Los Angeles.

"I finished out of the money. No big deal."

"I ought to kick your butt," Roddy said with a laugh.

Walt strolled over to a small flatbed trailer at the side of the garage and pulled a big gray tarp off two motorcycles. He put his hands lovingly on the handlebar of one. "This here is my two-fifty, and my four-fifty is getting an overhaul in Bozeman."

Rand admired the motorcycles and thanked them again for getting his bike ready. "I need to drive out to my cabin now. I'll ride again tomorrow. I need to get in as much trail time as I can, since I'll only be here a week."

"Maybe you'll like it so much you'll come back," Walt said. "You can't see much in a week."

"Your grandfather likes it here," Roddy added. "He's a real nice man."

The door to the front of the building, the company's display area and business office, opened and two men came out. One of them Rand was glad to see.

"Well, Mr. Monahan," Dexter Stone said, "fancy seeing you here. Look out you don't get any good old Montana grease on your New York duds."

"How you doing, Rand?" Mike Hogg asked. "You got a problem with the bike?"

"No problem. I just stopped in to thank Roddy."

"Whoo-ee," Dexter said, "look at that bicycle. I'll bet that cost more than your truck, Roddy." He adjusted his John Deere cap and crossed his meaty arms. With his jeans and western shirt, he wore a corduroy jacket with leather arm patches.

"You must be getting ready to ride through the streets of Paris, France," Dexter said. "Wear that yellow jersey, like on TV, huh?"

Dexter wasn't flicking a fly on the surface of the river, trying to get a bite from Rand. He was throwing handfuls of bloody chum into the ocean, hoping to attract a shark.

"Thanks again, Roddy. Glad to meet you, Walt." Rand gave a half wave to Mike that regrettably had to include Dexter and wheeled the bike out to the alley and around the building to his SUV. He put down the back seat and slid the light bike in through the back.

"Say, Mr. Monahan." Roddy stepped out of the space between the buildings and strode toward him. "Here's a tool to put in your pack."

"Thanks."

Roddy handed him a small metal implement and lowered his voice. "I'd watch my back if I were you. Dexter Stone can act uglier than he looks." He laughed. "I know that's a stretch."

"Thanks."

"I probably shouldn't say anything, but the reason he'd like to see you leave town is Luanne."

"I barely know her," Rand ventured, "but I don't think his picture is on her dresser." He closed the back door of the SUV.

"No, sir," Roddy said, "that place is reserved for Ted Wilder."

"Who is—?" His head and Roddy's head jerked around at the sound of the front door of the bike shop banging open.

"Have a good one." Roddy slipped back between the buildings.

Ted Wilder, huh? Rand wanted to ask who he was, but it would have to wait. He got in and drove away. The thought of seeing Luanne again in two or three hours gave him a pleasant buzz. He put his window down and proceeded out the road that led to his cabin.

He laughed, thinking he felt like a teenager. But he'd never *been* a teenager, so how would he know? Well, sure, he was alive from twelve to twenty, but—he'd missed a lot. While other guys fifteen, sixteen years old were cruising the mall, eyeballing the chicks and playing video games, he was home finessing financing for independent film projects in Canada. One of which, a documentary about a rock band, was a veritable jackpot.

Jeff's backdoor career path was similar but involved more banking and commodities trading experience thanks to his dad and his two uncles.

No wonder they'd needed a personal trainer to carry out The Great Nerd Rescue.

Luanne had admitted—with a laugh he wanted to record and play back on demand—that she was surprised his shoes matched.

He mused aloud as he wound his way up the switchback road to his cabin. "If you only knew."

Chapter Five

Luanne arrived at the hulking, ornate mansion thirty minutes before Rand was to meet her. They'd talked at ten, while she waited with Cory for test results, and again around eleven after she'd driven her home and helped her get comfortable.

The results of Cory's tests were good. She just needed to stay off her feet. Kent got home from his trip in plenty of time to pick up the girls after school.

Memories Mine was open for business, thanks to Nancy, which left time for Luanne to work from home on the Harvest Festival, and time to change clothes.

She climbed the mossy stone steps to the imposing front yard of the mansion, but paused at the bottom of the wooden porch stairs. The place needed a lot of work. More than anything, it needed an infusion of life and laughter. To her right, branching in all directions and probably sending roots into the plumbing, stood an oak tree planted when her father was a little boy. Dangling from a thick arm of it she could see the shredded remains of a rope swing she'd loved when she was maybe six years old.

She looked toward the river, hidden by trees that must have been saplings when she was a kid. Memories were all around her, but worry about Suncatcher's future forced them out of sight.

The festival auction was sure to be a tremendous success. At first she'd been reluctant to let go of the reins, but now she was relieved to have a professional in charge. Cog Cochran, famous for his horse and livestock auctions, especially in Scottsdale and Fort Worth, took on the Suncatcher Fund Auction as a labor of love—at no charge—to benefit the town he grew up in. With a national publicity campaign on the internet and coverage by newspapers in California and the mountain west, Cog arranged a satellite feed that could bring in big money.

Every valuable item donated seemed to pull in three or four more. An Arabian colt with excellent bloodlines; a photo safari to Africa; airfare to Tahiti. She was stunned at the generosity of people.

The dance wouldn't make much money, but it would get nearly everyone in the county involved. Ditto for the booths with their modest fees. Not much income for the festival, but the vendors were delighted to have one more chance to sell their goods to tourists before winter came.

Plus, there was always the hope of being "discovered." Everyone knew how local knitter Ming Lee's cloche hats caught the eye of a vacationing Hollywood designer, who subsequently used them in a popular vampire movie. A poster of the movie's star wearing a Ming Lee hat filled the window of Lee's small shop.

And if Luanne got her miracle, some of those Friday night dancers and weekend vendors would have good jobs before Christmas at the Suncatcher Solar Cell factory. Right here in Bitter Falls; exactly as Ted always wanted it.

She'd talked to Dexter twice about the front page coverage in Wednesday's paper. He said at one o'clock that he hadn't received anything from Finn Wilder, but he'd be on the lookout. He said again, preening like a cock, that he would hold the deadline Saturday night to cover the auction for Sunday's paper.

There was something about Dexter's "concern"

that made her uneasy. There'd been no love lost between Dexter Stone and Ted Wilder. Dexter had once expressed the inflated idea that Luanne would have been his girlfriend if Ted hadn't messed up everything. In spite of his smarmy dedication to "honoring" Ted by helping to open the factory, she had a nagging fear that Dexter would enjoy the project's failure.

If Ted had married her six or seven years ago, Dexter probably would have forgotten he'd ever been interested in her. But Ted was too busy, too absorbed in his work.

There it was.

The sad, insidious, underground cache of truth. A truth that leached into the soil like mine tailings.

As much as she'd loved Ted—still loved him—she'd always come second to him. She believed in every corner of her convoluted mind that she would have changed that—with time. But time ran out.

When Dexter found out how much trouble Suncatcher was in, what would he do? The answer was painful to contemplate, but too obvious to ignore. He'd drive the 'dozer over Ted Wilder's memory.

Thinking about Finn and the threat of an injunction, she looked at her watch. When would he call?

She climbed the stairs and paced back and forth on the wide porch, putting off the moment she had to go inside. If Rand was beside her, it would be easier. She'd concentrate on him, on the antique photos, on what she'd heard of Ann-Marie and Tess's remodeling plan.

She'd forget the ghosts, or—failing that—she'd whistle past the front parlor. If she didn't look in the elegant room with its massive fireplace and marble mantel, she'd be all right.

At ten minutes after two, she unlocked the front

door, pushed it open, and stood back. A musty fragrance, something like potpourri and sachet, floated out toward the sunshine.

She'd laughed last night with Rand as they unmasked the sly machinations of Rocky Monahan and Amelia Holt. But there was a lot more to her grandmother's puppetry than getting Rand into Memories Mine.

There was this. *Getting me inside Albion House.*

A car door out at the street made her turn. Rand was here. Relief flooded through her, making her knees weak. If he hadn't come, she would have locked the door and left. She waved and watched him climb the limestone stairs cut into the hillside.

Directly in front of her, to the south, the sun hung near the top of its autumn arc. In two months it wouldn't be that high, and the valley that stretched out before her like a green and gold patterned quilt would be uniformly white.

She nodded and smiled as Rand apologized for being late, but her thoughts were tied up in layers like scraps of paper, feathers, and straw in a bird's nest. It was all she could do to act as if she felt at ease.

The dress she'd decided to wear, one she'd bought in Missoula two years ago, was a good color for her. But the hunter green jersey clung to her breasts like a second skin and the sleek skirt felt short when she stood still. What would it look like when she sat down?

She had to admit, however, that the look on Rand's face as he'd climbed the stairs made her tingle with pleasure.

"You must have been crazy about this place when you were a kid," he said. He walked to the end of the porch and looked at the garden on the east side. "I'll bet this is pretty in the summer."

"It is, but in a wild, out of control way. It's like a

forest of lilac; it needs serious work to get it back to what it should be. I'll show you pictures of it fifty years ago."

He'd dressed up more for their business meeting and dinner than he had the night before. Charcoal gray slacks, a dark blue shirt open at the neck, and a herringbone sport coat with blue threads that matched the shirt. His face was ruggedly handsome, but he didn't seem to know it.

There was a lot to like about Rand Monahan. High on that list was the way he truly seemed to listen when she talked. And his natural warmth toward kids. When he'd shown her the pictures of his niece and nephew, his eyes sparkled.

If she had to name the moment her shell began to crack, that was it. Erik on a pogo stick and Sophie with a tiny violin.

She pondered why a man who liked kids so much wasn't a dad himself. When Cory said, as they'd waited to see the doctor, that Rand Monahan would improve the gene pool in Bitter Falls by four hundred percent, she'd laughed. Now, as she looked at him from the back, leaning out over the railing, she thought Cory was on to something.

She stifled a groan. Her emotions were running away with her good sense. She'd been alone too long.

He's leaving in five and a half days. We have nothing in common.

Then why do I ache at the thought of saying goodbye?

He walked back down the curved porch stairs and looked up at the house itself. She tried to imagine what it looked like through fresh eyes. Probably like a conglomeration designed by putting all the popular styles of the late nineteenth and early twentieth centuries in a paper sack, shaking it, and pulling out a scrap of this, a suggestion of that.

Some of the worst ideas, a flirtation with gothic

revival, had disappeared in a fire in the 1920s that damaged the west end of the house. The Queen Anne style that battled for dominance over the gothic and the Italianate won out in a major remodel in the late '20s. The chimney where the fire started, in what was then a kitchen with servant quarters above it, was demolished. In reconstruction, the second floor was left off that end in favor of a grand solarium with windows in an arc of almost one hundred eighty degrees.

At the same time, the kitchen was relocated to an addition on the back of the house, and the servants had rooms above that. All that had changed after 1950, as had the bathrooms.

The solarium was Albion House's best feature. It would be perfect for the B&B's breakfast room, and also an evening wine and cheese room. The rest of the house, with its two turrets and narrow, gabled rooms on the abbreviated third floor, was dour, with photos and painted portraits of people who must have worn sandpaper underwear.

Rand returned to the porch and smiled. She thought again how his eyes were the color of cappuccino. "Are there any ghosts?" he asked with a chuckle.

She caught her breath at the unexpected question. "I suppose there are. In fact, later I'll tell you more about Goldie Smith, who built the place. She and my great-great grandmother Violet were the daughters of a sod-buster in Minnesota."

"Goldie," he repeated.

"Her real name was Hazel, and all accounts say she was born for adventure. She got the name Goldie when she struck it rich in the Klondike in 1896."

With a start, she realized she'd crossed the threshold and strolled into the house. She hadn't hyperventilated; so far, so good.

She followed Rand's gaze upward from the entry

hallway to the right-angle series of stairs with landings that led to the second and third floors. The hallways of both floors flanked this central space.

"Do you see the parquet pattern in the ceiling way up there?" she asked. "It's the same as the pattern in the floor at our feet. And the way the banisters slope makes it look like the space between the staircases is smaller on the third floor than the second, but that's an optical illusion."

He walked to the great onion-shaped tops of the banisters and stroked the wood. "It's beautiful work."

"Honduras mahogany."

She wiped away dust from the foot-high metal statue of a goddess on the right hand newel post. The goddess held a glass torch above her head.

"It was a sign of wealth and modern technology in Goldie's day to have an electric light on the newel post. Sadly, this one is another wiring nightmare."

"How old is the house?" He studied the intricate wood pattern at his feet.

"Construction began in 1907. Bitter Falls used to have a spur railway, and the town fathers had delusions of becoming a metropolis. But the railroad barons found a mountain pass they preferred. The town gradually found other reasons to exist, and Goldie settled in."

She pointed to a small framed photo on the wall near the stairs and he moved closer to see it.

"That was Goldie in Seattle in 1897. She'd just returned from the Klondike on the first steamship. News of the fortunes in gold on board started the gold rush."

"And who is this?" he asked.

"That's a copy of a picture of 'Pa and Ma.' The original is in the vault at the bank, with the Daguerreotypes. 'Pa and Ma' is what we call Goldie and Violet's parents. You know, 'Little House on the

Prairie.'"

"How long did Goldie live here?"

"From 1907 until she died in 1970. She was ninety-seven. There's a picture upstairs I'll show you of Goldie at the train station. The railway was used for about thirty years for lumber and cattle, but eventually it died and the rails were torn up. A lot of the right-of-way is a bike trail now."

"As I discovered this morning. It's great. Yesterday I didn't think I'd find enough to do for seven days; now I see I've barely scratched the surface."

"Maybe you'll want to go for eight," she mused aloud, "or nine. You know, happy trails and all that."

"I'm liking Montana more every hour." He caught her hand and gently tugged her closer.

She felt a rush of attraction, a pleasant shiver of anticipation of kissing those lips, of feeling her breasts press against his muscular chest. She looked up, hungry for that sweet feeling of being wanted. But before their lips touched, her brain took in where they were standing—at the archway to the front parlor.

She recoiled from his arms as if burned, and stood, breathing fast. Too fast, too shallow. Hyperventilating; exactly what she feared.

"Luanne, what's wrong? You look like you saw a—"

"No! Don't say it. There's no such thing as ghosts. There are only people who—" She moved quickly toward the bright solarium.

"People who what?" he asked.

She walked to a window and took deep breaths. At last she turned toward him.

"There are only people who won't let go. People who can't move on." She turned to the cherry wood cabinet and took out a crystal decanter. Without a word, she poured two small glasses of sherry.

Her hand shook as she reached to give one to him; she turned away and held on to the wood as she raised the other glass to her lips.

Rand tasted the pale yellow drink, glad it was a dry rather than sweet sherry. Luanne moved away from the cabinet. He watched her gracefully climb two stairs to a platform for a white baby grand piano and stand by a low window directly between him and the sun. The bright light filtered through her skirt, leaving little for his vivid imagination to create. He took a large swallow of sherry.

Much as he enjoyed the sight of her shapely thighs and panty line, she'd be embarrassed if she realized what she was displaying. He cleared his throat. "Why don't we sit down?"

She crossed the platform and walked down the second set of steps to the main room. He followed her to a conversation grouping of a loveseat and two armchairs. She looked undecided where to place herself; finally took one chair. He sat on the loveseat, as close as he could get.

"I'm sorry," she said.

"For what?"

"For—" She waved her hand in the direction of the entry hall, exhaled, sucked air into her lungs. "—for acting so strange."

He nodded. No use saying she hadn't acted strangely. But he still wanted to take her in his arms.

"Luanne, there's something I'm wondering about."

He waited until her green eyes were on his face.

"What?"

"Who is Ted Wilder?"

She jerked reflexively and had to hold her glass with both hands to steady it. She took another sip, and another. Liquid courage in a ladylike form. She smiled; she frowned. She cleared her throat; shook her head.

Reading Luanne Holt's body language was a graduate level course, and Rand never took Women 101. If he could ask for outside help, like a "lifeline," he'd call Dinah.

"Ted was the inventor of the solar cells that the Suncatcher factory should be fabricating right now. Getting it open is the *raison d'être* for the Harvest Festival."

"And?" he asked. "Who was he to you?"

She closed her eyes. "Ted and I were going to be married. But—" She opened her eyes and fixed them on his. "But he died. It was completely unexpected. And my friends say I need to move on. Forward."

"I see," he said. "And how long ago did this happen?"

"Fourteen months. August of last year." She stood abruptly and set her glass on the coffee table. "Let's go up to Amelia's suite of rooms and I'll show you her photo collection. About half is here and half is in the vault at First National Bank."

Had her fiancé died in an accident? he wondered. *Completely unexpected* didn't explain anything except her shock.

He set his glass down beside hers and rose to his feet. The afternoon sun caught gold highlights in her red hair, or maybe the color was what people called auburn. Whatever the label, he wanted to thread his fingers through the silky curls and see if sparks would fly.

The scent of her perfume, too, pulled him like a magnet. But there was something so fragile about her that he didn't act on his attraction.

"We could do this tomorrow, if that would be better for you," he said.

"No," she said softly. "Today is better. I'm already inside. In fact, I'm feeling better."

He followed her out of the light-filled room,

through the entry hall and onto the stairs. He noticed she looked anywhere but into the stiff, formal room they probably called a parlor.

Part of him wanted to back away from Luanne Holt. She was beautiful and warm and alive, and sexy as hell, but there was something gnawing at her. He tried to understand his ambivalence, his...okay, his cowardice in the face of strong female emotion.

Or was it cowardice at his own strong emotion?

And was that strange, strong emotion...love?

Was he teetering on a tight rope over a river, afraid of falling in and going over the falls? Rand Monahan, the man's man, Wall Street whiz, the guy with nerves of steel who never missed a money-making deal? The guy who never waded past his knees in soupy, scary, hot emotion?

No, not me, he told himself. I'm not an "old black magic" believer. And I'm getting out of Montana in five and a half days. Getting further involved with a woman stuck in grief is not what the doctor ordered.

Still, it would be worth a lot to taste her lips again.

With one more look into the parlor, he followed Luanne up the stairs. He didn't *see* any ghosts. Of course, isn't that pretty much the definition of *ghost*?

****

Luanne struggled to get the balky deadbolt lock to click into place. Rand offered to try and succeeded.

She was struggling with a lot more than a mechanical problem. What had Grandma been thinking when she planned this misadventure? Amelia knew how hard it would be for her to go inside Albion House. So why did she have to push it?

Amelia's plan to put Rand Monahan and her granddaughter together had backfired. Instead of bewitched, he'd been bothered. He'd seen for himself what a basket case she was.

And, damn it, as much as she'd told Cory in person, and Amelia by phone—and herself in the mirror—that she wasn't interested in Rand...he'd unlocked something inside her, and if he turned his back on her, it was going to hurt something fierce.

If he turned his back? Make that when.

"I can leave my car here," she said, "but I'd rather leave it behind the shop."

"I'll follow you," he said, then paused. "On second thought, would you like to leave it at your house? That strikes me as safer."

She opened her mouth to argue that alleys in Bitter Falls were not like alleys in New York City, but decided he was right. And even if his concern for her safety was unnecessary, good manners dictated a simple, "Thanks."

From her car on the street, she looked back up toward the front of Albion House. Ted had wanted to use it as a showcase for heating and cooling with his solar cells along with a state of the art heat pump system. Would Ann-Marie and Tess be willing to give it a try?

Would there even be such a thing as Suncatcher Solar Cells? She looked at her watch and willed her phone to ring. Of course, that didn't work. She plugged it in to the charger in the dashboard to be sure she had plenty of power.

A short beep to her left. Willie the roofer waved as he drove to the hidden driveway that wound up the back side of Albion Hill. She'd spoken to a member of his crew while she showed Rand the house; Willie had gone for more scaffolding.

As she pulled away from the curb, she looked up again at the history-drenched house. So much sadness. Goldie's history with the pain of losing contact with her only child, her son Stanley, thanks to her own anger and obstinacy. Never seeing Stanley's son, Lucas, her grandson, who'd been as wild and adventurous as Goldie. Never seeing Luke's daughter.

And then there was Amelia's history, losing her only child in a cruise ship accident.

And—her own history of loss. First her parents, and then Ted.

It would have been a beautiful wedding.

She was powerless to stop the geyser of memories set off by going inside the old mansion.

She dabbed at her eyes with a paper napkin she found on the console. Glanced in the mirror; the Lincoln SUV was right behind her. Took in a ragged breath and wiped her eyes again.

It would have been a beautiful wedding.

The poet who said it was better to have loved and lost than never to have loved at all was full of hooey. When Ted dropped dead—and that's what happened, none of this "passed away" crap—she'd felt as if all the blood had been drained out of her body. Cory and Amelia were the only people she had let come near her.

"You're white as a sheet," they both said.

White as your wedding dress was what they were thinking.

She wouldn't take it off. As long as she wore it, she told herself, Ted might be revived. She'd heard of people waking up in morgues, or under sheets at the scene of an accident. Declared dead, and then— alive. If time were absolutely linear, that is, if one hour in her time were really one hour, then her superstitious wait for good news could make no sense at all. But her time was bent, wrinkled. As long as she wore the dress, she could suspend time. Twenty hours, thirty hours. Day, night.

Magical thinking.

No meal time, no sleep time. No time at all. She'd hurled her watch out the window, unplugged the electric clock, and stopped Amelia's anniversary clock with her hands.

Finally Cory got through to her and she began to cry.

She'd reached such a state of exhaustion by then that much of that third day was a blur. Going into Amelia's room today brought a lot of it back. Unwelcome memories.

"Enough already with the Miss Havisham reenactment," Cory had snapped at her.

"What on earth are you talking about?" She vaguely remembered sitting in Amelia's rocking chair, her lovely dress draped around her in clouds of tulle.

"Charles Dickens, eighth grade English class," Cory said. "*Great Expectations*. Miss Havisham. It's time to get the dress off, Luanne. I brought a suit for you to wear to the funeral."

She'd given in then and done what was required. She stood and felt the zipper slide easily down her back; she watched the dress fall away into a cloud at her feet. And she showered, and dressed in the black suit.

A combination of numbness and the good manners drilled into her since childhood kicked in like an autopilot. She made it through the funeral and the reception at the home of Ted's favorite teacher. Ted's brother, Finn, was there from Virginia to be best man at the wedding. Instead, he'd made all the funeral arrangements.

Finn, like everyone else, said to her, "Is there anything I can do? Anything at all?"

No. Nothing. Thank you.

It was a month later, maybe more, when she'd opened *Great Expectations*, trying to understand what Cory had been ranting about the day of the funeral. When she found it, she laughed for the first time since Ted died.

Pip goes into a mansion and finds Miss

Havisham in the cobwebs. The shriveled, bitter old woman has been wearing her wedding gown for something like half a century, ever since the day she was abandoned by her fiancé. Her bitterness extends beyond the macabre dressing room and dining room where nothing changes except to rot further. She's made it her purpose to raise Estella, whom she's adopted, to be cruel and to break men's hearts.

By then Luanne was back to work in Memories Mine, and probably acting sane about half the time. What had wrenched her out of her mental fuzz was what happened to Suncatcher—what those bastards at Allied Advent Tech were trying to do.

Gradually, the idea of saving Ted's invention and opening the factory he'd planned grew and grew. She'd made it maybe ninety percent of the way, had put everything she had on the line, but it wasn't there yet.

In fact, it could all fall apart.

That might be happening at this very moment.

She drove down to Main Street and turned right, drove on autopilot to her house, two miles outside of town. In the driveway she clicked the garage door opener. Laddie and Max stood at the fence, barking and leapfrogging over one another, jockeying for position. Pet me first, Pet me first.

She dropped her phone in the pocket of her dress and got out to introduce Rand to "the boys." He went to the fence and reached over to pat the roiling masses of golden fur.

"Don't believe anything they tell you," she said. "They're notorious liars. And they're acting like wild Dingos to make me look bad—but they actually have certificates from obedience school. I'll prove it." She opened the gate and they piled out, a two-headed, eight-legged creature. Before they could leap onto Rand, she gave them a voice and hand command.

"Laddie, down. Max, down." Immediately—to

her relief—they lay on their bellies and fastened their eyes on her. She turned her back and walked ten yards away. "Max, come."

He raced to her feet and sat down. Then she called Laddie and he did the same.

"They were Ted's dogs. They need more attention than I give them, though, and more dedicated training." She told them to go back in the yard and closed the gate.

She was about to say, "Let's go look at Rocky's land," when her cell phone rang. Finn Wilder. "Would you excuse me, Rand?"

She walked to a white rocking chair on her porch and pressed Talk. "Hello, Finn. What's your news?"

"I'm standing outside the courtroom now, and I only have a minute before I have to turn my phone off. The whole docket was delayed, and I'm trying to get the judge to hear it now instead of postponing it."

"I can't believe this. I thought we'd already won." She hugged her arms close to her stomach.

"How are you holding up?"

"I have the creature from *Alien* inside me. Other than that, I'm fine."

"I talked to Dexter Stone twice today. He's got his shorts in a twist." He laughed.

"Why?" Her mind was on the case, racing from best outcome to worst outcome and back again.

"Apparently he has some competition for your attention. Anything to that rumor?"

"I went to dinner with a very nice man who is here from New York and who is handling some business with my grandmother on behalf of his grandfather. And, by the way, the proceeds of that business deal are being donated to the Suncatcher Fund."

"Hey, I was just curious."

"And where does Dexter Stone get off thinking

Rand—or anyone—is competition for him? I have no interest in him."

"Okay, okay. Hey, they're waving me to come in," he said. "I'll call you later."

She tried to shake off her aggravation at Dexter—Lord knows she had enough other things to worry about now—but it was hard to shake off. His jovial one-of-the-boys persona and his tender concern for "poor Luanne" might fool some people, but not her. She'd been a victim of Dexter's smothering attention before, and she wasn't about to let it happen again.

The fact that she was, number one, ashamed to have allowed him to bully her in high school, and number two, too "nice" to go around bad-mouthing him now, gave him tacit permission to try again to control her.

Well, here's a news bulletin for your front page, Dex: That's not happening. Now or ever. And it's not because Rand Monahan fell into Bitter Falls like a meteorite.

It's because I am wise to your tactics. As they say in New York, *fuhgeddaboutit.*

She stood and took a deep breath as she dropped her phone back in her pocket. It was easy to tell herself she was wise to Dexter's games. It was a lot harder to make it stick in a town full of people he'd somehow lined up on his team.

She wondered, as she had many times before, why he'd come back to town. Managing editor of a small five-days-a-week newspaper was a big comedown from the successful Los Angeles career he bragged about. His official line was that he'd "come home" to take care of his failing mother. Luanne didn't believe that for a Bitter Falls minute.

Jean Stone lived in River View Care Center. Her mind was fine but her body was a wreck thanks to severe osteoporosis. Luanne had heard from more than one of Jean's friends that Dexter visited his mother so seldom that he probably couldn't find her room without stopping for directions.

But Dexter and his agenda couldn't distract her now. She had to show Rand the photos, complete the deal, and replenish the Suncatcher Fund. Even if it seemed like two steps forward and two steps back, she had to keep trying.

Too late today for the bank. They could do that first thing in the morning. *Or am I putting it off, looking for a reason to see him tomorrow?*

She walked toward Rand, who was in the back yard, clapping his hands, laughing, and tirelessly throwing a tennis ball to two dogs who would follow him to the ends of the earth.

She chuckled and shook her head ruefully. A woman could do worse than take advice on men from dogs and children. A voice in her head said, *Go ahead, jump.*

She had a bizarre flashback to her childhood. Gemstone Lake. A day so hot little kids broke eggs open on the concrete boat ramp to see if they'd cook.

She'd been on a wooden raft tethered to the bottom of the lake; she was about ten years old, a good swimmer. All around her people were leaping into the water, giddy with laughter and the exhilaration of the cold water. Each time someone climbed aboard the raft, he—or she—leaped again. Luanne alone was afraid of the deep black water.

Uh—and I'm reliving that embarrassment, why?

"Heads up!" Rand called and she snapped to attention in time to catch the ball.

"Oh, yuck. This thing has dog slobber." She laughed and threw it to Laddie, who leaped a good four feet off the ground and caught it in midair.

I want to jump in to this—this whatever-you-call-it thing with Rand—I do.

I want to yell, "Geronimo!" and leap into the air.

I want to crash through the glassy, reflective surface of her life and risk the shock of cold, heart-stopping water.

Can I do it?

Chapter Six

Rand glanced over at Luanne as he followed her three-word blips of directions to Rocky Monahan's land.

"Turn left here." Then, a mile or so later, "Turn right here." She was definitely avoiding eye contact, and she kept worrying at her lower lip with her teeth.

The voice on his Porsche's GPS had more inflection. It even had more warmth since he'd selected the sultry British voice he called Duchess.

"In one-quah-tah of a mile, entah the motah-way."

Something was definitely aggravating his red-headed passenger. He'd sensed her tension ever since he stepped onto the porch of the moody-looking mansion. But *Uh-oh* had been his second impression of Luanne Holt today. His first was *Wow*.

In fact, as he'd climbed the mossy stone steps, he'd scarcely registered the architecture of Albion House. He was too enthralled with the splash of color on the front porch: Luanne in a dress the color of emeralds. A dress, he'd noticed when he got closer, that brought out the color of her eyes.

The dress fit her like a wet T-shirt with the bonus of showing her shapely legs in high heels. The modest neckline didn't display cleavage, but the swell of her breasts under the clinging fabric was actually sexier than skin.

"Turn right here," she said. "At the moose."

"At the what?" He did a double take, then slowed and turned at a plywood cutout of a moose.

On its side he read the phone number of a backcountry outfitter and the words: Trail horses and pack animals provided. He wondered if that was the actual size of a moose.

The road quickly morphed into a steep combination of rocks and holes. The Navigator shifted automatically into four wheel drive.

He caught Luanne's eye and smiled broadly, but earned a very small return on his investment. Even more than smiling, he'd like to get her talking, find out what was eating at her. But how? Talking about emotion was as appealing as running a maze in the dark, through the worst neighborhoods of New York.

When Calista Karan's lessons in social skills had focused on conversation, Rand recalled that she offered one silver bullet.

"All you need to know in order to appear charming," she'd said, with a sneer of disbelief that anything could work that miracle for Rand Monahan and Jeff Adler, "are the following four words: *Tell me about yourself.*"

Rand had penned four words on the back of his business card and slid it over to Jeff: *So, what's your sign?*

Below that he'd written the amount they were paying Calista, the oracle and self-proclaimed gatekeeper of societal standards, for her pithy advice.

He discovered later, on his own, that the four words most of the women he dated were looking for were: *I am a millionaire.*

And as for "Madonna" Taylor, her sign was not Aquarius, or Taurus, or Virgo. It was the symbol above the "4" on a keyboard.

The dollar sign.

"This is it," Luanne said when they emerged from deep shade to a flat section in bright sunshine.

He parked the car and drank the last water in

his bottle. Before he could get around to her side, she'd opened her door and slid to the ground. She set off like a race walker across the flat ground covered with pine needles and started up a grassy knoll toward what appeared to be an expanse of flat meadow.

He lengthened his stride to catch up.

"There was a cabin here a long time ago," she said, "but the roof collapsed under the snow. You can see where the rock chimney was. Oh!" Her headlong progress came to a sudden stop when her high heels sank into the sod. She flailed her arms to keep her balance.

From behind, he lunged and clamped his hands around her waist to steady her. She lurched forward, coming out of both shoes.

They stared at the shoes, mired in muck, and she burst out laughing.

He extricated them from the soil; the heel of one shoe hung loose. To his surprise, she laughed even harder. If this had happened to any of the New York women he knew, the air would be blue with their expletives.

"Something tells me these are not Jimmy Choos," he said.

"Jimmy who? Oh, yeah, the designer. No, these cost seventeen dollars. Would have been twenty-six, but I got two pairs for thirty-four." She worked the broken heel up and down like a puppet's mouth. "You got any bubble gum?"

Rand looked at her eyes, her freckles, and her mouth; the music of her laughter washed over him like cooling mist at a sidewalk cafe. And he thought of...red hearts, pink roses. And a pudgy cupid with one arrow taut in his bow.

Zing, through the clean mountain air. *Zap.* Into his heart.

Wham. Like nothing he'd ever felt before.

Cupid's arrow? *Like hell!* There wasn't a cloud in the sky, but Rand knew he'd been struck by lightning, electrified to his smallest capillaries by undeniable, unbelievable, un-buy-able force.

Love? He thought...*Yes, maybe, if...*

No. Enough already with thinking. He reached out instead and pulled Luanne into his arms.

"Resistance would be futile," he murmured.

"I'm not resisting."

"I was talking to myself." He looked down at her lips, took a deep breath, and claimed them. She leaned forward, filling his arms and his senses like a down comforter and molding herself to his sharp angles. He felt as if he'd tumbled out of a tree and landed in a cloud of lush clover. Not ordinary clover. The four-leaf variety.

A sound like music interrupted his reverie. It took a few seconds for the notes of "Pretty Woman" to travel from his ears to his brain and a few more to register that his phone was actually ringing. *How did I get a signal here?*

And why now, when he least wanted it?

He didn't need to look at the screen to see who was calling. "Excuse me." He thumbed Talk and said, "Hello, Serena."

He lowered the end of the phone a few inches, away from his mouth, and said to Luanne, "My partner's fiancée."

"Oh, no, I'm not!" Serena shouted in a raspy voice. "It's all over. I don't ever want to see him again."

"Serena, are you crying?"

"No," she croaked. Pause, sniff. "Maybe a little."

"Where are you? In New York?"

"No. I'm thousands of miles from there, but not far enough, yet. I hate New York."

"Where are you? Do you need anything? Jeff is worried about you. I'm worried about you."

"You needn't worry. I have money of my own; I don't need his damn money." Now she started sobbing and hiccupping. He held the phone out so Luanne could hear.

"Serena, where are you? Please tell me."

She said something but he couldn't make it out. Then the phone lost its signal. He swore and tried to call her back. No Service Available appeared in a white message box.

"Man, talk about conflicted," he said as he shoved the phone in his pants pocket. "I want to stay up here and kiss you as long you'll kiss me back, maybe 'til the moon rises, but I also want to drive to town and reach Serena."

"I should get back, too."

"Soon enough, we will." He hugged her against him and found her lips, parted and eager. "Make that too soon we will. Way too soon."

His tongue pressed into her warm mouth. He felt her shiver—or was that him? Hard to say, and who cared? He was so far from reality he might defy gravity and float above the earth.

Abruptly, she pulled away. "This is crazy." Her breath came in fits and starts. "I don't do this. I mean, this is not like me."

He grinned. "It's not like me, either. It's a big improvement."

"You're leaving town." She held up her hands, clearly exasperated. "What am I, some way to pass the time?"

He wondered if she was angry with him or with herself, but he knew better than to ask. The result was the same. The twelve inches between them grew, doubled, widened into a yawning chasm.

She picked up the soil-caked shoes she'd dropped in favor of the embrace and walked in mincing steps to a point twenty or so yards up a rise. "From up here you can see why your grandfather bought this land."

He climbed the hill in a more gradual arc and stood beyond her. The exertion at this altitude made him stop to catch his breath and rest his heart. *Ka-pump, ka-pump, ka-pump.*

That swishing, rhythmic unappreciated sound must have been in his ears all his life. But now the complex pump in his chest commanded respect. It was a tyrant that gave no quarter; arbitration was out of the question. Chin to floor obeisance was required, and more.

A team of surgeons had interceded for him, made a treaty with the tyrant, bought him time with a tube threaded through his femoral artery and a few dollars' worth of fine wire mesh, for which he'd paid umpteen thousand dollars.

Then they'd ritualistically washed their hands of him.

He, Rand Monahan, had to keep the peace; he had to live up to the treaty's terms. He lived alone on the island with the man-eater.

The man-eater. No wonder the *ka-pump, ka-pump* so often reminded him of jungle drums coming closer.

He strolled toward the site of the ruined cabin. There he rested again, pressed two fingers of his right hand on the inside of his left wrist, and watched the sweep second hand of his watch.

Good. No pain. Not even a twinge. Enjoy the moment.

The sound of the wind high in the pines floated around him, prettier than a Julliard string quartet. The flat acre where he stood was perfect for a house. Huge windows should face the south to catch as much winter sun as they could. The view would be framed by enormous pines. A lake centered in the distance and mountains beyond the lake looked too perfect to be real. How could Rocky wait to build his house? The view alone was worth three million dollars.

He sighed. The only thing that would make the "location, location, location" more appealing was a cell phone tower on the ridge behind him.

"It's beautiful," he called. "What's that lake?"

"Gemstone; it's a reservoir." She climbed toward him, studying the ground before each step. The feet of her pantyhose were shredding.

"Ouch, ouch, son of a gun," she exclaimed as she hopped on one foot and held the other up like a can-can dancer.

In no time flat he was by her side, holding her up. "Lean on me; let me see your foot."

"Whoo-ee, it hurts, but I don't think it's cut."

"Umm, I see some blood." He brushed the dirt off her foot. "Let's go down the hill, easy does it. Hold onto my arm, no, put it around my waist. That's a girl."

"Cory and I were champions at the three-legged race." She pressed herself close to him and he wrapped his left arm around her shoulders.

"The what?"

"You know, teams of two get their inside legs tied together and race other teams."

"Get their legs tied? Why would anyone do that?"

"You're kidding, right? I thought everyone did three-legged races. It teaches cooperation. Balance, too. Cory and I had it aced."

She lurched to her left and he pulled her upright.

"We need more practice," he said. When they finally got close to the car, she leaned on the back side panel. With a quick movement of her hands under her skirt, she shed the ragged pantyhose and stuffed the balled up nylon in her pocket.

"This wasn't a good test," she said. "I would have

to be able to use my right foot in conjunction with your left. And besides, you're too tall. I mean, too tall for me. I mean—"

He grinned and squeezed her close to him, lowered his head and stopped her chatter with his lips. One long, satisfying kiss plus butterfly kisses up her jaw and into her hair.

"Too tall for you?"

She hooked her arms around his neck and murmured, "It's a problem, but I'm willing to work around it."

He'd just found her lips and moved his hands to the curve of her rump when—again—they were interrupted by a phone. Hers this time.

"Sorry, Rand. I have to answer."

She flipped open the phone she carried in a side pocket of the green dress. Her face, dreamy and brimming with laughter a moment before, changed. A replay, he noted, of her attitude adjustment when she got the call in front of her house.

"Hello, Finn. What do you know? Did the court rule?"

Rand opened the back of the SUV and made room for her to sit. While she listened to her caller, he poured bottled water on her cut foot and patted it dry with the new hand towel he'd bought at Mike's Bikes.

"I don't understand, Finn. Where are they getting their legal opinions? From a Magic 8 Ball?"

He kissed her forehead, took a granola bar from the fanny pack beside her, and walked away from the car. At the rim of the pull-out where they'd parked, the ground fell away sharply into acres of briars. Maybe blackberries as he'd seen near the river? No, they might not grow at this altitude.

Insistent chatter drew his attention to a stand of pines close by. The source of the scolding, he saw, was a squirrel. The bundle of gray fluff on the trunk of a tree leaped to a lower branch, then another one, then bounced from the trunk to the ground. Slowly, Rand tore open the wrapper, broke off a quarter of the bar, and lobbed it gently toward the squirrel.

With beady eyes fixed on this forest invader, the squirrel raced out ten yards, snatched the prize, and flew across the ground to his home base.

This little guy was as focused on acquisition as the squirrel he'd seen by the river. *Single-minded, like me.*

For a squirrel, it made sense. *And for me?*

The white head of a large brown bird caught his eye. "Hot damn!" he sputtered. "A bald eagle."

He wouldn't admit it without a swift kick, but it was the first eagle he'd ever seen. At least, that he remembered seeing.

And then he saw—*another one.* That made a one hundred percent increase in eagle sightings in less than a minute.

He watched them soar, weave back and forth, then settle in pine trees. Behind them, jagged as the Dow on a volatile day, were the mountains. Not just pretenders like the Adirondacks and the Berkshires. These Montana mountains were by-God genuine *purple mountain majesties.*

One of the eagles took flight, directly over his head and out of sight into the forest. Rand felt—okay, he knew it was crazy and he wouldn't say it out loud to anyone—but he felt *blessed.*

Oh, boy. Here it is, your moment of Zen.

No. He squared his shoulders against the sniping of his inner cynic.

That eagle flying over his head was better than July Fourth fireworks over the Brooklyn Bridge. Better, even, than the Statue of Liberty. No wonder these magnificent creatures were our national bird.

His cynic, persistent as the rising price of oil, sniped again. *Of course you love eagles, Monahan!*

They're engraved on U.S. currency.

He shook his head. Self-knowledge was, more often than not, a bitter pill.

Everything around him since he'd arrived in Montana was fresh. Was this heightened perception a side effect of his near-death experience?

"Rand," Luanne called. She was standing beside the car. "I lost my cell signal. I have to get back to town."

He backed up toward her, unwilling to take his eyes off the eagle still in the tree to his left. He needed to buy some binoculars.

"Look, an eagle!" He pointed toward the tree. "Another one flew right over us."

He looked over his shoulder at her. "Oh, duh," he said, feeling sheepish. "I guess you see eagles all the time. Me, not so much."

"Sure. But I always stop to watch them. There's something mystical about eagles."

He helped her hop around to her door and boosted her into the seat. She placed the hand towel under her bare foot.

"Do you have a first aid kit at your house?" he asked. "Or should we stop at the store?"

"I've got it all. Let's go straight to my place. We can both try to get in touch with people."

He moved to close her door, paused. "One for the road." He leaned in to kiss her again. If luck was on his side, he'd be doing more of that soon.

Luanne snapped her seat belt on and waited while Rand walked around the big car.

She'd had to clamp her lips tight to keep from laughing at his excitement over the eagles. It was stretching the truth to say she always stopped to watch them. Maybe she watched them one time in five. There were quite a few eagles around here.

But she enjoyed seeing them with his fresh perspective. It reminded her she lived in paradise. A good thing to remember, especially when her world was caving in on all sides.

The SUV bumped down the ruts, dodging and weaving like a skier on a bad slalom course.

"My grandfather is going to have a hell of a time paving this driveway," Rand muttered.

"And this is as good as it gets," she said of the axle-banging five mile stretch. "In the winter it's beneath ten feet of snow, and in the spring it's all mud."

Instead of asking her about her call, he told her about Jeff and Serena, starting with how long he'd known Jeff and how Jeff's first wife, Taychell, had hired the law firm of Shock and Awe to represent her side in their divorce.

"Who did Jeff hire?" she asked.

"That would be Burn and Destroy. A venerable old firm. But that's all history. Or should I say her-story? The good news is, Jeff was left with both of his kidneys. What's distressing now is that he hired the same firm to draw up a pre-nuptial agreement with Serena. Not a good idea, it now appears. Serena is a bona fide angel compared to Taychell, who proved that the devil does, in fact, wear Prada."

"I take it, from what I could hear on your phone, that Jeff and Serena have broken up?"

He slowed to turn back onto the asphalt road. "You've got that right. Jeff called me this morning and said Serena won't sign the pre-nup. He didn't know she'd left New York, though. I wonder where the hell she is."

"Does she have family outside of New York?"

"I don't know." He wrinkled his brow. "Before Harvard and Lehman, I don't know anything."

"How did they meet?"

"Business. She was preparing an IPO, an initial public offering, and she came to see us at MSI. Jeff took her to dinner."

"Your company is MSI? What does it stand for?"

"Morning Select Investments. We picked Morning in honor of our initials, A and M. Adler and Monahan."

"Oh."

"Hey, we were young."

"You were saying Jeff took Serena to dinner." She pointed ahead. "Turn left here and I'll show you a short cut to my place. Bumpy, but scenic."

He described how irascible Jeff had been after his divorce and how Serena had changed him. By the time he pulled into her driveway, Luanne was laughing so much she'd almost forgotten about Finn, the federal court, and the avalanche coming down the chute.

"Some people said the change in Jeff was due to, well," he crooked two fingers to add parentheses to the phrase, "the power of love."

"Some people, but not you?" she asked. "You don't believe in such mystical power?"

"It's not—" He turned off the ignition and made no move to open his door. She wondered what he would say.

The silence in the car continued. Laddie and Max stood by the fence, their front paws on the top rail, their tails wagging hard enough to generate electricity if someone could figure out how to harness the energy.

She put her hand on her door handle. "I'd better—"

"Wait. I—I didn't used to believe in the power of love," he said. "But three people have made me reassess my cold calculation. First Erik, then Sophie, and now..."

He placed his hand on top of hers and she felt tears well in her eyes. "Don't, Rand. Don't say something you can't take back. I have too much on my plate now, too many people relying on me to solve problems—" She choked back the tears and wiped her cheeks with her right hand; she took a deep breath.

"I don't have time to be unselfish," she said. "That's what makes that mystical power work. And I can't risk falling apart. Not again. I've only just stitched myself back together, and my wounds aren't healed. Serena on the phone sounded like a sit-com laugh track compared to me at my lowest."

"When Ted Wilder died," he said softly. "Fourteen months ago."

She nodded. "It was on our wedding day." She squeezed her eyes shut and felt the hot tears splash onto her hands. She heard him open his door and get out; his door closed and a moment later, hers opened.

"Where's your key?"

"The side...of my...purse."

He released her seat belt. and supported her as she stepped out on her left foot.

"I should carry you," he said.

"Absolutely not, all I need is a strong arm to lean on." A dozen hops later she watched him insert the key in the lock.

"Do you have an alarm?"

She shook her head. "Just Laddie and Max, and they worship you."

He turned the key and opened the door. "I'm very popular with big dogs and small children. Those creds don't grow on trees."

"Neither does money, as Finn Wilder reminded me. I'll tell you the saga of Suncatcher after I talk to him." She padded barefoot into the house and shivered.

"Shall I lay a fire?" he asked. "And don't give me that look. Just because I don't ride horses doesn't mean I have no claim to manhood."

"Are we back on manhood again? Because you've

already convinced me." She grinned.

"Maybe later you'll reassure me. By the fire."

"Umm, the woodpile is out at the edge of the patio. I'll put a bandage on my foot and be in my office, down the hall."

"I have an idea. Let's eat in. Does anyone in Bitter Falls deliver food?"

"Meals on Wheels, but we're not old enough."

"Okay, second idea. I'll cook. Chef's Surprise." He paused. "You do have a phone number for poison control, don't you?"

She stopped, facing the hallway, and exhaled slowly. If she turned around, he'd see right through her, see that her defenses weren't just low, they were gone. Not only was the drawbridge down on her fortress, she was on the verge of running pell mell to throw herself into his arms. Running to shout the word she told him not to say.

She inhaled and kept on limping toward the bathroom and the first aid kit.

Reassure Rand Monahan of his manhood? By the fire? With flames reflected in his eyes and his hand on the side of my breast? Oh—my—goodness. Yes, yes. *Hell, yes.*

Chapter Seven

Rand watched the flames flare on the kindling and lick the three split logs he'd set at strategic angles to keep the air flow going. Laying fires was something he did very well.

That and lanyard weaving were the only two skills he'd learned at Camp Mohasset. Well, three skills. He'd mastered computer hacking under the sly tutelage of Jeff Adler, but that wasn't on the camp schedule.

Lanyard weaving was a dead end. Computers had quickly become his life's blood, the pathway to a fortune. Being handy with a fire eventually paid off, too, with some spectacular nights with sensational women at his ski cabin in Vermont. Nothing was more erotic than firelight, a soft quilt, and a lot of skin.

However...He sighed and looked down the hallway where Luanne had gone. *The times they are a-changing.*

A power surge of memory, Luanne in his arms by the light of the Hunter's Moon, erased all other women from his hard drive. What would she look like by firelight, her curly hair fanned out and her skin flushed with excitement?

The noise of increasing wind and pathetic whimpering drew him back to the patio door.

"Come on, boys, let's see if I can find some food for you."

He'd dated a woman with a dog about the size of Laddie and Max, so he guessed how much dry food and canned food to give them.

107

"If I give you too much, let's not tell the boss, okay?"

They danced daintily and licked their chops. He set the bowls out on the patio and called them to eat. Before he went inside he filled his arms with wood. If he got lucky enough to cuddle Luanne in front of the fireplace, he didn't want any interruptions.

Before he rummaged through her refrigerator and cabinets, he pulled out his phone and a small notepad. Messages were in the queue from Jeff, four calls; Serena had called twice before he'd received the brief call up on Apple Mountain Road; and Dinah called half an hour ago.

He called Jeff first—and got an earful.

Since his call to Rand that morning, bemoaning Serena's refusal to sign the pre-nup, Jeff had discovered that she'd taken a leave of absence from her job and disappeared. His rant caromed like a billiard ball from worry about Serena's safety, to anger that she'd be so selfish as to make him worry, to regret that he'd presented the pre-nuptial agreement at all.

"What the hell did your lawyers put in that broadsheet, anyway?" Rand inserted the question edgewise when Jeff took a breath.

"It's just—I don't—oh, hell. It was a lot of legalese, a little on the up-tight side, but I was willing to negotiate. She didn't give me a chance."

"Negotiate? Women who want a meal ticket negotiate. Women applying for Trophy Wife status negotiate. Women who marry for love are insulted by that notion. Especially a babe like Serena who could do a hell of a lot better."

"Oh, yeah?" Jeff snapped. "Who died and made you Prince Charming? You, who would have flunked *savoir faire* in front of that luscious banker from Zurich if I hadn't tipped the *sommelier* in the Rainbow Room in advance?"

"Exactly who are you mad at Jeff? If it's me, shove it. I have other calls to return, and a fire, and a beautiful redhead to share it with. Someone I didn't have to tip a *sommelier* to impress."

"A beautiful redhead? You bastard."

Rand said nothing. Waited. It wouldn't take long.

"Who is she? Anyone I know?"

"No, she's not one of my former girlfriends from New York. Her name is Luanne Holt and she was born and raised in Montana."

"Small town girl, huh?" His tone was dismissive. He couldn't muster interest in anything to do with Montana; he had New York problems.

"Maybe Serena went home to see her family," Rand suggested.

"No, I already thought of that. I called her sister in Texas. She said Yes, she'd heard from Serena, and No, she wasn't in Texas, and Furthermore, I'm a horse's ass."

"That's pretty much proof that Serena called her. Or maybe she figured that out on her own."

"I only met her once."

Rand chuckled. "Once is enough. Why don't you go over to Serena's old apartment? See if she told her girlfriends where she was going."

"If she told them about the pre-nup, they'll be waiting with tar and feathers."

"Hell of a risk, but what else have you got?"

"I'll call you later."

"Not later tonight, my friend. See for reference above, cozy fire and beautiful woman."

"Small town woman. Okay, I'll bite. How beautiful is she?"

"As beautiful as Serena."

"You're a bastard. Call me tomorrow."

Serena didn't answer her phone, and her voice mail was full. He redialed two more times and swore. He was worried. He hoped she was in Texas with her family; her sister's denial could be meant to keep Jeff away.

He called Dinah, chatted about his kayak trip and how he was doing a favor for Grandpa, looking at antique photos.

"Antique photos, my ass," she said. "Grandpa says Luanne Holt is hot. Tell me about her."

"You knew? He told me she was something like a spinster."

"Is this the first time he's fooled you?" She laughed like a performing seal. "Huh? Huh? I didn't think so."

He sighed. "Are the kids still awake?"

"Erik is. Sophie fell asleep at the restaurant and Kurt carried her to bed. They both miss you a lot. Erik! Come here, honey, it's Uncle Rand."

"Hi, Uncle Rand, guess what?" All Erik's sentences started with the same two words. *Guess what.* Rand's favorite was Erik's news bulletin by phone from England during an intense period of potty training. *Guess what? I went poopy in London!*

"What?" Rand asked his nephew.

"We're gonna go to Montana!"

"Someday, sure. That'll be fun."

"No, I mean really. We're gonna go to Montana on, umm," His reedy little voice drifted away as he spoke to his mom. "Mommy, what day are we going to Montana? Oh, yeah. On Thursday. It's gonna be a surprise!"

"Well, that's, uh, that's quite a surprise, all right. Let me talk to Mommy, please."

"I guess the feline's out of the bag, huh?" She laughed. "I'm taking the advice I give you so easily. *Carpe diem*, and all that jazz. Don't put off 'til tomorrow, et cetera."

"How many of you are coming? And where are you staying? My cabin is the size of your guest bathroom. No, it's smaller."

"I had a heck of a time getting a place. Some festival is a big honking deal this weekend. But a dude ranch that only operates in the summer, the Rocking Star, is opening up for five nights to handle the tourists. Erik is out of his mind with excitement. The first cowboy he sees will supplant Spiderman forever in his pantheon of heroes."

"So, who's coming?"

"Erik, Sophie, me. Kurt insists he has to work. I've already started a campaign to get him to come with us to the dude ranch next summer."

"Good luck with that." Rand's brother-in-law was, regrettably, a lot like him. Dinah usually let the kids stay up until ten o'clock. It was the only way they saw their dad since he left the house in Greenwich at five forty-five a.m. to catch the train into Manhattan. Of course, the Daddy they saw at ten p.m. was ready to fall asleep standing up. If Erik said he caught rabies, Kurt would say, "Good job."

"Maybe you could talk to him." She laughed ruefully. "Yeah, I know. The pot calling the kettle black."

"Maybe that's the only one the kettle will listen to. I'll try. In fact, I'll call him tomorrow and try to talk him into taking a long weekend. This place is heaven." He laughed. "And yes, she's hot. Kiss Erik and Sophie for me."

"Erik heard some malarkey in kindergarten about being too big for kisses," she said. "I'll shake his hand for you."

"What kind of commie-cell school are you sending him to?"

"Goodnight, Rand."

He poked the fire, added a log, and tried again to reach Serena. No luck. In the kitchen he did a survey of Luanne's food supplies and cross referenced what he found with what he knew how to make. Bacon and eggs, check. Mac 'n cheese? No boxes in evidence. Pancake mix. Aha. He looked for the extras he'd need. In a cabinet beside the sink, yes, yes. And in the door of the refrig, the last essential. He pumped his arm in triumph.

The dogs scratched at the door.

"You think I'm a soft touch, don't you? Well, you're right." He let them in and told them to lie down. The thought of Erik and Sophie meeting Laddie and Max made him laugh out loud.

And Luanne would meet the munchkins, too. As Sophie liked to say when she slapped her tiny hand against his in a very-low high-five, "Kew-el."

He hoped the calls Luanne was making weren't tearing her apart. Finn Wilder. Hmmm. Who is he? Related to the late Ted Wilder, most likely.

He located a mixing bowl and a skillet, set them on the counter. Beside the measuring spoons he found a corkscrew and used it on a bottle of zinfandel.

Down the hall he glanced into a bedroom with a soft light beside the bed. He would have guessed Luanne's room would be quilts, antiques, and Americana tchotskes. He wouldn't have been surprised by heart-shaped pillows and porcelain dolls. Hell, he wouldn't have looked twice at a spinning wheel.

But instead he saw a sleek room. Gleaming hardwood floor, a queen-sized bed with a parquet headboard, gray and white bedcover tucked in tight, two pillows in plain white shams. One white chair; bedside tables with small gray lamps. It was a spare, elegant, modern look.

Luanne Holt, he was learning, was full of contradictions.

He heard her voice and tapped lightly on the door across the hall.

"Come in," she called softly. Into the phone she

said, "Don't sugarcoat it, Finn. What are the chances?"

He handed her a glass of wine, kissed the top of her head, and left the room, closing the door behind him.

In the living room, he found her CD player. Without looking to see what was inside, he pressed Play. The room filled with a male crooner. The song was lush, intimate, offering love that lasts forever and—oddly apropos of this October night—a hand to hold when leaves begin to fall. Curious, he examined the open CD case. Michael Bublé.

His phone rang. Serena's number showed up. Thank goodness.

"Hi, I'm sorry I lost your call before," he began. "I was up in the hills above town. I'm amazed it worked even for a minute."

He wanted answers to two questions: *Where are you, dammit?* and *How are you, dammit?* but he didn't want to scare her off by barking like a probation officer.

"I shouldn't have called when I was in the middle of a meltdown," she said.

"That's precisely when you should call. When you need a friend, call a friend. Me. Anytime, from anywhere. Collect, if absolutely necessary."

She laughed—not much of a laugh, more of a mini-guffaw—but it was enough that he breathed a sigh of relief.

"And by the way, where is anywhere?"

"In an existential sense? No, you're more a GPS guy. Life is nothing but a set of numbers on a grid. You and your buddy what's-his-name."

"His name is Iman Idiot, and you could do better, but he loves you." He waited for a response, then went on. "Jeff knows he screwed up. He's extremely worried about you."

"I don't want to talk about him." Her voice went

Lynnette Baughman

up an octave, and he could tell she was fighting another round of tears.

"Okay, forget him. I—Rand Monahan—am extremely worried about you. Please tell me where you are."

"I'm at a truck stop. Did you know you can rent books on CD at one truck stop and turn them in at another one?"

"Uh, no, I didn't. What state are you in?" *Texas. She was going to say Texas.*

"If I tell you, you have to swear on your hope of heaven that you won't tell Jeff."

"Can I tell him you're all right? Assuming you are."

"I'm all right," she said. "I need some time to sort out the mess in my head. In fact, I'm headed for a small town in the middle of nowhere."

"Nowhere is fine, but at least tell me the state."

"Montana. You're surprised, *n'est pas*? I took a cab to LaGuardia and the next thing I knew, I was on a flight to Detroit and another one to Missoula. Hearing your grandfather rave to you about Bitter Falls must have gotten to me."

Luanne came into the living room and the dogs ran to her. Rand didn't know what problem she was wrestling with, but from the frown on her face, she definitely was not kicking ass. She sipped her wine and patted the dogs on their heads.

He smiled at Luanne and spoke to Serena. "You're coming to Bitter Falls?"

Luanne looked up, puzzled. She mouthed the word, *Who?*

"Oh, for a day or two," Serena continued, then yawned. "I don't feel like facing my family in Dallas yet. And I hate New York."

"New York, Dallas...or Bitter Falls. When you say it like that, the choice is obvious." He chuckled. "When will you get here?"

114

"Tomorrow sometime. I've checked into a motel west of Missoula for tonight. A clean well-lighted place, as Hemingway would say. Speaking of well-lighted, you should see this truck stop. I'll bet it's visible from the moon. Hey, do me a favor, please."

"Of course."

"Is there a motel in Bitter Falls? The information operator was no help."

"Motel?" He recalled what Dinah had said, that the town would be full on the weekend. "I'll find you a place. Call me tomorrow when you get closer, okay?"

He said goodnight and closed his phone. "That calls for another glass of wine."

"Not for me, thanks. Maybe later. Who's coming?"

"That was Serena. She's at a truck stop west of Missoula. She's coming here tomorrow to spend a few days sorting out her options." He went into the kitchen and poured himself another glass of wine.

When he returned, Luanne was curled into a corner of the couch, staring into the fire. He placed the wine bottle on the coffee table, then adjusted the log and added more wood.

"And that's not all. My sister, Dinah, and her two kids are coming on Thursday. I'm going to try to talk her husband, Kurt, into coming, as well."

"Finn Wilder, Ted's brother, will get here Friday."

"This is beginning to sound like a French farce with people running in and out of doors. Or it would if it weren't for my promise to Serena. She made me swear I won't tell Jeff she's here."

"I heard you say you'd find Serena a place to stay." She frowned. "Every place is full. Finn is staying with Ted's favorite teacher."

"Dinah and the kids are staying at a dude ranch, the Rocking Star."

Luanne snapped her fingers. "Tree Autrey's place! I forgot they're opening for business during the festival. Let's call right away and see if Tree can make room for Serena."

She unwound her legs and limped to the kitchen counter. From a corkboard she retrieved a postcard, turned it over and punched the number into a cordless phone. While it rang she unscrewed the top of a small bottle of hand lotion and rubbed some into her hands.

She left a message, then shuffled through scraps of paper on the counter. "I'm looking for Tree's home number. Ah, here it is." She keyed the number and limped back to the couch.

Rand turned off the kitchen light. Firelight was far superior. As she settled back on the couch, rubbing more lotion into her hands, he poured a little more wine in her glass, getting it up to half full. "Medicinal purposes, ma'am."

"Aren't you afraid I'll get tipsy and try to take advantage of you?"

He grinned and filled it near the brim.

Her riposte was cut off by a deep bass, "Hello?"

"Tree, hi, this is Luanne Holt." She took a gulp of wine to keep it from spilling.

Rand prodded the fire as he listened to her chat with her friend at the dude ranch. He gave her Serena's last name and offered to pay with his card. Luanne raised one eyebrow comically and whispered, "Not necessary."

To Tree she added, "Rand's sister and her kids will be there, too." She listened and asked Rand, "Angelo?"

"That's right." He watched her talk animatedly about the number of tour buses that would be in town for the Harvest Festival, and the latest additions to the auction. A Hollywood producer had offered a part as an extra in a train robbery movie to be filmed in New Mexico's Jemez Mountains; three best-selling romance authors, all living in Seattle, would each critique a partial manuscript.

She tucked a pillow at the small of her back and rested her feet out in front of her on the couch. The hem of the green dress crept up her thighs despite her fingers tugging it in the other direction.

As soon as she ended the call, her effervescence fizzled before his eyes. In the cut-throat world of international investing, where everyone lied and their duplicity had to be seamless, Luanne would be an unarmed non-combatant mowed down by the crossfire.

A red, silky-haired pup stumbling across a dog-eat-dog arena.

Rand wanted to scoop her up and race for safety. But he was in her world, not his, and he didn't know which door led to safety. What should he say? The old four word conversation starter, tell me about yourself?

The fire popped a pocket of sap like a firecracker, and the top log rolled over in surrender. He poked it back over the hottest coals, and sighed aloud. Men who claimed to have a sixth sense about women were three senses ahead of him.

Or—they were lying.

At least he recognized one fact. For the first time in memory, the wrong four words were *I am a millionaire.* Luanne was the real thing.

He settled into the far end of the couch and took her feet onto his lap. He outlined the bandage with his finger. "Does it hurt?"

"Only when I laugh. And I'm not laughing much tonight." She poured a dab of lotion into her hand, screwed the lid back on, and rubbed her hands together.

"I noticed." Gently, he pressed his thumb in circles on the bottom of her uninjured foot. As she

117

relaxed and bent one knee, the hem of her skirt inched further north, and his imagination popped like the sap in the log. He almost laughed aloud at how quickly he hardened. The sexiest thing about Luanne—and the list was growing by the hour—was that she didn't know she was sexy.

"Finn Wilder is Ted's older brother," she said at last. "He's an attorney in Virginia. Ted was a brilliant engineer. He invented an inexpensive and extremely efficient way to fabricate solar cells. Named the business Suncatcher. But thanks to lying, conniving venture capitalists, he lost his rights. Finn is trying to recover them."

"So, was the factory ever operational?"

"No. Getting the factory open is the goal of the Harvest Festival, and everyone's upbeat and excited. What they don't know is that we've run into a Gordian knot of legal problems."

"And that's why you're working overtime on an ulcer?"

"You could put it that way. But I don't want to read entrails right now." She smiled. "You'd be doing me a favor if you distracted me."

She wriggled her shoulders downward against the pillow and extended her feet beyond his lap. The skirmish raged between the modesty of the dress and the risqué lace rim of her pale blue panties. With more leg to admire and reach more easily, Rand upgraded his foot massage to her calves and thighs. At first her legs were pressed primly together at the knees, but gradually she relaxed.

He took the lotion from the coffee table, squeezed a little into his hand and massaged it into her calves, widening the circles and reaching higher as her legs parted.

She made a purr of pleasure and stretched. Her eyes closed and her lips turned up in a sultry smile. "Ummm. I don't know your name, Stranger, but I'm giving you thirty minutes to stop that," she murmured. "All right, forty, but not a minute more."

Her heel grazed his erection, and Rand clenched his teeth to keep from making a most unmanly sound.

"Is that a threat, ma'am? 'Cause I don't go down without a fight."

The literal meaning of his words hung in the air, and he quit breathing. *Dear Dr. Freud...*

Luanne opened one eye and laughed. "Stranger, I believe your face is red."

He laughed, too. "That is so not a guy thing. Now we're going to have to revisit the manhood issue."

She responded by rubbing the side of one foot against the mound in his lap. This time he couldn't stifle the groan. Had he ever wanted a woman more than he did now? He could pull her into his arms and work that dress up over her hips and all the way over her head.

Luanne admired the shape of his jaw and the part of his chest she could see, the part above the third button. She hardly knew this man, and yet she felt she'd known him for years. Was that a good thing or self-deception?

The weight of the top log shifted, and light flashed from the coals beneath. Pockets of sap in the log exploded. Luanne's inhibitions whooshed out of her and flew up the chimney in a column of sparks. A stranger named Desire flooded into her to fill the vacuum. Lost without her internal meter maid writing up a ticket for parking in a Lascivious Zone without a marriage license, she rubbed her arch against his straining erection.

Firelight played around the room, exploring the ceiling, tasting her arms and bare legs, teasing Rand's eyes and igniting two tiny fires in his dark pupils. Warmth came to her from every direction, and her dress clung too tightly against her breasts. Too much heat. Too little freedom.

Rand would leave in five days; that was a good thing. She was free to explore this sensation, to be overwhelmed by her own need. Free to tell him what she wanted. To lie here in a cave a thousand miles from the real world, with firelight tickling her skin, and say with her eyes, fingers, and even her toes: I want pleasure. *I want you to stroke me and lick me, to fill me and carry me away.*

Two strangers, surrounded by shadows. Two. *Rand Monahan, and the one inside me.*

His hands kneaded the muscles of her calves and explored above her knees. She closed her eyes, relishing the feel of his strong hands on her thighs. Circles within circles, each orbit moving closer to what used to be her erogenous zone. Panties and bra territory. But now the zone was her entire epidermis. No, even more. The fuzz of air around her carried impulses to her core. Impulses...

Impulsive. Not a word she'd use to describe herself. Not until tonight. No, she'd been *patient.* Willing to wait. Willing to accept life on someone else's terms instead of diving in.

His fingers crossed the line, crept under the lace, and she moved her hips, a silent Yes. A soundless More. Mute, an invitation.

Both hands now, tugging gently. Her hips floated for a moment; the panties came off without a whisper. Protest was the furthest thing from her mind. If she said anything, it would be a rush of want and need and hurry.

His fingers read her message and parted her curls. Her shoulders pressed into the pillow, and she thrust herself against the fingers of his right hand, rocking, seeking release.

"That's a girl," he murmured. He lifted her legs from his lap and moved to the floor beside her. On his knees, he slid his left arm beneath her shoulders. As he pressed his lips to hers, he circled the sensitive nub between her legs with one finger and inserted another finger into her wetness.

She broke the kiss long enough to let words escape and take a deep breath. "Oh, my—oh!"

"You're so beautiful." He touched his lips to hers and she opened her mouth. His tongue explored her mouth while his fingers made tantalizing circles between her thighs, pressing, retreating, returning.

She circled his shoulders with her arms and clutched herself tight against him. The tight sleeves of the dress constricted her.

Again she broke their kiss. "Help me take this off. The zipper's in the back."

She rolled to the side and heard the zipper slide down, down. With a quick movement, she bunched the dress around her waist; Rand pulled it up and free of her arms. Before she lost her nerve, she unsnapped the bra and tossed it toward the dress.

He stood and gazed down at her. A shove from his knee moved the coffee table out of the way. He took the big afghan from the back of the couch and spread it in front of the hearth. Slowly, at least to her it seemed slow, he unbuttoned his shirt and pulled it forward over his head. With a snap of the fabric, he hung it by the collar on the rocking chair.

His shoes and socks were gone. He draped his belt on the chair, stretched out on the afghan with his back to the fire, and patted the space beside him.

She swallowed hard and crossed her arms over her nipples. "I picked a hell of a time to get modest, huh?"

"Come here. I'm aching to taste you."

"That's an intriguing thing to say. It gives me goosebumps."

"Me, too." He patted the crocheted throw. "Manly goosebumps."

She rolled onto her knees and crossed the three feet to his side. "I hope the phone doesn't ring."

He chuckled and kissed her shoulder. "Phone, hell. I hope the Hunter's Moon doesn't crash into the earth and obliterate life as we know it. Short of that, nothing will take my attention from your body."

She felt four kinds of heat at once. Her flush of embarrassment at her nudity; the fire in the grate. The heat inside Rand that burned in his eyes—and then, suddenly, in his mouth, on one breast and then the other. The fourth source of heat was deep within herself. A burning need to be loved. For her, that meant the whole package. Sexual passion, yes. A man to share life, to grow old with, yes. But she wanted more. She wanted to have a family.

That fire had to be banked. Nurtured, but kept secret.

Rand offered passion. For tonight. She told herself it was enough.

He sucked gently on each swollen nipple, and she felt her pulse in the hot, wet space between her legs. His hand cupped her rear and strayed to the front. She moved to show him exactly what she needed.

Rand tasted her skin, here, there, unable to get enough. He left her breasts to test again the sweetness in her mouth, left her mouth to kiss the tender spots below her ears, all the while listening for cues. Sounds she probably didn't know she made. Happy moans. Fast breathing. A throaty giggle he was sure she'd deny. For that matter, what were those growls and deep-chest laughs? Were they coming from him?

He nuzzled and nipped at her neck and traced his tongue slowly down the valley between her breasts, lower, to her navel. Lower still.

He moved, his knees straddling her ankles, and kept his tongue traveling to that tiny spot where she wanted pressure. Blowing softly, as he would on a tinder box, coaxing a flame to catch, he parted her curls and kissed her the most intimate way a man can kiss a woman.

"Oh, yes, Rand. Oh my—yes."

He wanted to make it last, but she was wound up. She twirled her hands in his hair. He gave her what she wanted, as hard as she wanted it, and felt her shake as the powerful orgasm rocked her whole body. An explosion of pleasure.

He returned his mouth to her breasts and then to her shoulder. He lay beside her, entranced by the dance of firelight on her skin.

She turned to him and kissed him hard. This time her tongue took charge, and her fingers worked feverishly at his zipper. His heart rate, which had been high while he focused on Luanne's pleasure and release, now surged higher still.

The fear that accompanied him like a late-afternoon shadow since his near-death threw up a black shape on the ceiling. He braced for pain—but it didn't come. His body, already flooded with hormones, flooded again with relief.

He lifted his hips and shoved his slacks and briefs off. Before he tossed them aside, he took a foil packet from his wallet and sheathed himself.

Staring into her eyes, he lifted himself on his arms, probed gently between her legs, and penetrated her welcoming center. Four deep strokes, another, another, and she cried out his name. As she grabbed his neck and pulled his lips to hers, he joined her in oblivious, refreshing, unforgettable release.

Chapter Eight

Rand set the single plate of crisp bacon and scrambled eggs in the oven, set to keep them warm, and poured pancake batter in the pan to make one large pancake. What Sophie would call a hu-MON-gu-ous pancake. While the first side browned, he set the table for two, and placed a plate of apple wedges near the place settings, and a book of matches at the ready.

He looked into the living room and grinned to see Luanne was still asleep in front of the fire. Her hair draped over the pillow he'd taken from the couch and inserted beneath her head without waking her; the afghan wrapped her like a burrito.

With a sigh, he leaned against the door jamb. He knew two things now that he hadn't known an hour ago. One, his equipment was all in working order.

Apollo, you are good to go. We have liftoff.

And two, "B.T.S.," his old inside joke with Jeff making money being the best kind of rush, was unadulterated bullshit. Nothing—not one thing—was Better Than Sex.

Joking about his manhood to Luanne had covered his secret fear. What if his manhood really was impaired by all that had happened with clogged arteries and his heart attack, and angioplasty? Dr. Brogen had said, "Kiss a pretty girl." He hadn't said anything about falling like the Crash of 1929 for a sensational woman and having mind-blowing, awe-inspiring, never-forget-this-night sex.

For a minute—okay, a millisecond—while Luanne found his zipper and took his stiff member in her hand, he'd hesitated to complete their love-making. "What if's" blew through his mind like the sparks from a roman candle, but faster.

What if he had another heart attack? Hell, he'd heard the joke everybody told at the cardiac rehab center.

"Can I have sex, Doc?"

"Yes, but only with your wife. I don't want you getting excited."

But right on the heels of that hypothetical question pressed another. The flip side of the silver dollar; the dark side of the moon.

What if...what if I dropped dead tomorrow *without* making love to Luanne?

Another inane joke from rehab, this time about the rigid dietary restrictions they all faced: Think about the people on the Titanic who said, "Dessert? No thanks, my doctor says I've gotta watch my weight."

As he'd looked down at her face in the firelight, all the "what if's" had ricocheted through his oxygen-deprived brain and followed his blood supply to his ecstatically happy groin.

Luanne wants me. Luanne wants me.

With those words looping in his mind and thrumming in his blood, he packed Reason, Caution, and Alarm into a Saturn V rocket and fired them directly at the transforming, magical moon that silently stole into the sky.

Houston might have a problem, but I don't.

Deftly now, he loosened the edges of the pancake, worked the wide spatula to the center, and flipped it. As soon as that side browned, he put the pancake on a dinner plate, poured the remainder of the batter into the electric skillet to make four normal-sized pancakes. Next, he turned the first one into a work of art. Maraschino cherries, chocolate chips, yes. And the last essential, whipped cream from the nozzle of a spray can. Perfect.

Flip the other pancakes; get Luanne's bathrobe from her bathroom door; turn off the skillet. Press Play on the CD player; vow to buy every CD Michael Bublé ever made or will make.

"I promised you something to eat." He went down on one knee beside Luanne. He unfolded the afghan as he held out her robe.

She stretched, languid as a cat; stood, and slid her arms into the pale blue robe. "I'm not very hungry."

"Good, because I'm not much of a cook." He steered her to the dining room table and held out her chair.

"What do you usually make for dinner?" she asked.

"Reservations."

He lit the candles and went into the kitchen. As soon as he put his four pancakes on a plate, he carried that plate and her warm plate of bacon and eggs in.

"This looks delicious."

"But wait, there's more." He returned to the kitchen, looked at her pancake, and rolled his eyes. Thank goodness no one in his real life could see him now.

"The chef sends his compliments, madame." On her placemat he set the pancake. Red eyes, wavy white cream eyebrows, a broad chocolate chip smile, and a bad hair day in loops and swirls of cream two-thirds of the way around the circle. "I'd wager there's not another one like it in Montana."

He would also wager that all the *maitre d's* and *sommeliers* in Manhattan—as well as Calista Karan—would declare him *persona non grata* if they saw this monstrosity. Tough. They could all jump in the East River. Only one opinion mattered.

"A happy face pancake," she exclaimed in

transparent delight. "It's—beautiful." She took a bite and licked the cream off her upper lip. "Delicious, too."

Rand sat down, took a bite of his pancakes, and grinned. Luanne Holt was beautiful—and delicious, too. The overused epigram, "Today is the first day of the rest of your life," swelled in his mind like the crescendo of a great symphony.

Turn a corner...Open a door...See with new eyes...New day dawning...Happy as a king. No cliché was too trite for him tonight, no truth too obvious to state. For the first time in his life that didn't involve financial profit, or Erik, or Sophie, Rand floated atop unalloyed joy.

Was this feeling...love? And if it was, what should his next move be?

Michael Bublé made a musical suggestion about offering love that warms the winter night, concluding, "That's all, that's all."

Luanne savored the taste and texture of whipped cream melting in her mouth. Was it her imagination, or could she still taste Rand's kisses? She traced her lips with her tongue.

She was glad the only light on her flushed face was candlelight. The words of the song she—yes, she—had placed on the CD player, about love that lasts forever, made her feel more naked than she'd been in front of the fireplace. She couldn't be more obvious without putting up a marquee by her bedroom door: Lonely Woman Seeks Lover, Apply Within.

"Is this a New York delicacy?" She took another bite of the happy face pancake.

"New York, Paris, Istanbul. They don't call it the International House of Pancakes for nothing. It's very popular at Chez Monahan on the Upper West Side. Prepared without fail whenever Erik and Sophie come for brunch."

"I have a question." She took a forkful of eggs and bit off a piece of crisp bacon. "Personal."

"Fire when ready."

She stalled, changed the subject. "Should I eat the cherries? It seems, I don't know, ghoulish."

He stabbed one of the maraschinos with his fork and popped it in his mouth. "Um-umm. Eyeballs are a great delicacy in Istanbul." He stabbed the other one and held out the fork so she could take it with her lips. "In for a penny, in for a pound. Sophie will gladly arm tickle you for the cherry eyeballs."

"I'll let her win. I prefer my maraschinos in a Shirley Temple where they belong."

"She'll want those, too. That girl is mad for Shirley Temples." He cleared his throat. "You had a personal question?"

She took a deep breath and exhaled slowly. "Is there a reason you don't have children of your own?"

"You mean have I been unable to perform sexually with other women?"

"Good heavens, no!"

He burst out laughing, and she knew she'd stepped into a trap. "You answered a question with a question."

"That's true." He poured more orange juice in her glass and then in his own. "Okay. It's a fair question. I'd like to have children, but I've never found anyone to settle down with. Anyone to m—m—m—"

"I think the word you're looking for is 'marry.'"

He sat back, looking thoughtful. She continued eating her eggs, bacon and pancake, glancing at him from time to time. When he spoke, it was to ask her a personal question.

"What happened to Ted Wilder? You said he died on your wedding day. That must have been horrific for you."

She set her fork on her plate, took a drink of

juice, and wiped her lips with the linen napkin. "Let's talk in the living room. I still have about a quart of wine in my glass."

He stood as she did and they carried the dishes into the kitchen. Laddie and Max tumbled into the kitchen and sat, rigid as stone lions on library steps. Luanne broke her last slice of bacon in half and tossed a piece to each of them.

"That's all, folks. Out of the kitchen." She picked up the phone on the counter. "I'm amazed this hasn't rung."

"Blame me. Or, better yet, thank me. I turned the ringer off so you could get some rest." He picked up the base and changed the setting. "Looks like you got eight calls in the last forty-five minutes."

The phone rang immediately and startled her. "I knew it was too good to be true. Hello? Oh, Cory, how are you?"

She gathered up her clothes from the living room floor and drifted to her bedroom in search of her slippers. For more than half an hour she talked on the phone, first to Cory, then to Finn to answer one question, then Cog Cochran in Scottsdale about a new auction item. Four of the messages were from Dexter. He'd received the documents that Finn had faxed to him. He wanted to go over them with her tonight.

His tone changed with each message he'd left. Friendly, cool, annoyed. Then hostile. With as much enthusiasm as she felt for checking mousetraps for furry bodies, she called him back.

No answer. Leave a message at the beep.

"Dexter, I'm sorry I missed your calls. I'm so exhausted I fell asleep. I'll stop in to your office tomorrow morning at ten-thirty or eleven. By then Finn should have more news. More encouraging news. We can sort it out for your Thursday morning paper."

She tried to shrug off her alarm at his hostility. They had common interests, Suncatcher and what the factory meant to Bitter Falls, but he had no claim on her personal life. She had to make that clear. Diplomatically. She didn't want Dexter Stone for an enemy.

She dropped her head forward and rotated it, trying to loosen the tension in her neck and shoulders. It didn't help.

This day, long as it had been, wasn't over yet. She'd told Rand she'd tell him about Ted. She might as well get it over with.

In the living room, she watched Rand fold the afghan and drape it back over the couch. As he tended the fire, she tucked herself into a corner of the couch. Laddie and Max walked in circles until they plopped down, each with his nose to his tail.

This is hard, she thought. Hard to know how much to tell, and where to start. She'd known Ted for so long. Ever since she was eight years old; Ted had been nine.

"Ted and Finn moved here when Ted was in the third grade. I was in the second grade. Finn was an older man. Sixth grade. They lived with their father's brother, Malcolm, and his wife Anne."

She sipped her wine. "People didn't talk openly about why the boys came from Oregon, but everybody whispered it. Their father had been convicted of killing their mother. Lincoln Wilder always claimed he was innocent, and Ted and Finn beat up anybody who said he was guilty. They spent a lot of time nursing black eyes and split lips, but kids learned not to talk about their dad."

An image flared in her mind. Dexter Stone, the school bully. Blood pouring out of his nose and tears of rage pouring down his red cheeks. Finn Wilder getting dragged by the collar to the principal's office. Dexter was bigger, but Finn was angrier.

Another pause to sip wine. "Their dad's defense attorney, God bless him, never gave up. After twelve years in the state pen, Lincoln Wilder was cleared by DNA evidence. The so-called eyewitness who convinced the jury that Lincoln was guilty was the real killer. Their dad wasn't even in that town when his wife was murdered. I'm sure Finn's admiration for the attorney is what led him to become a lawyer."

"And Ted?" Rand added one small split log to the grate and they watched it spontaneously ignite in the superheated air. He sat at the far end of the couch, angled toward her.

"He was very close to his uncle. Malcolm was a mechanical jack-of-all-trades. He could fix any piece of farm equipment, drill a well, build furniture. Build a house. Once he built a Model T car from a giant pile of parts and won a big contest. Ted learned from him. After high school he won a scholarship to M.I.T. He became an engineer and an inventor, but he always gave ten percent of the credit to college and ninety percent to his uncle."

"And somewhere along the line, the two of you fell in love."

She nodded. "There was never anyone for me but Ted. Unfortunately, he was as bashful as I was. He didn't notice me until he came home after college. We dated, and gradually we planned to get married. He worked crazy hours on his inventions, especially his solar cells." She swallowed hard and sipped wine to ease the tightness in her throat.

The phrase "gradually we planned to get married" was ice barely thick enough to walk across. She didn't want to touch the cold black water beneath it. So much time had been lost while Ted lavished his love on his work—instead of her. It had been, in some ways, like loving a priest.

Her hand trembled as she sipped the wine and splashed a few drops on her robe. She set it down on the end table.

"He died of an aneurysm on our wedding day. I was already in my wedding dress, upstairs at Albion House. It was to be a small wedding in the parlor, followed by a reception in the solarium."

"I see now why you had a problem inside the house. You must remember that day every time you go in."

"It's worse than you know. Today was the first time in fourteen months that I walked in the door. The only reason I did was to show you the pictures, seal the deal, and get Amelia's donation into the Suncatcher Fund."

"And that's what we need to do first thing tomorrow? At the bank?"

She'd told him on their way back from Apple Mountain Road about the Daguerreotypes in the bank vault and how the payment should be wired into the Suncatcher Fund's account at the same bank.

She elaborated now on the tangled legal jungle Finn Wilder was hacking through, and how much it was costing.

"Ted made a deal with a venture capital firm, Percival. Then there was a boatload of trouble, wholly owned subsidiaries, and holding companies, and a receivership, and a stock buy back by some entity. I can't even recite the litany of things that went wrong. Somewhere in there was a hostile takeover; the falling dollar was part of the mess. There was even an embargo by the State Department that held up delivery of an essential mineral. The bottom line was that Percival's interest in Suncatcher was bought out by a company that plans to build the solar cells in China. Not only will that company not have to pay U.S. taxes, there won't be any jobs in Montana."

"A deal," she repeated, then paused. "Someone

made a deal with the devil."

The dogs lifted their heads, gave one bark each, and slumped back into instant sleep. Whatever threat they'd sensed wasn't worth a run to the door.

"So, it's Finn Wilder and you against the universe. Or, at least, against a man-made perfect storm."

She nodded. "I think my problem is I've seen too many movies where the underdog triumphs. I keep expecting the music to swell and the Death Star to explode. But in a movie, there's always an identifiable bad guy. In real life, evil is more like a wall that's higher and wider than the hero can see, or a toxic gas that hugs the ground."

Rand rose and pressed Play again on the CD player, and the track number for "That's All." Michael Bublé sang again of country walks in springtime and fall, and how love could warm the winter night. As tired as she was, her pulse quickened and her mind raced. Had she really made love with this man?

The taste of his skin clung to her lips, and her fingertips itched to stroke the muscles in his chest and arms. If he so much as breathed on her skin, she'd be on fire from her toenails to her hair. She lifted her hair off her neck and tried to cool down.

He's leaving in five days. That was her good angel reminding her that she was acting like a loose woman, making love with a man she barely knew. That wasn't like her at all. No, she'd waited years and years to make love for the first time—and that had been with the man she was going to marry.

Her bad angel was ready with a sharp rebuttal.

Waited for years? Oh yeah, you waited. And how'd that work out for you?

It was her bad angel who'd gotten her into this situation with Rand. It was she who'd whispered what a good idea it would be to have a harmless fling.

Rand Monahan and I have nothing in common.

Good angel; such a sensible girl.

We have p-l-e-n-t-y in common. A laugh, more like a cackle, inside her head.

"Luanne?"

She heard her name as if from across a frozen pond. Skates sliced the ice. She pulled her arms in close to her body and spun. Arms up, spin faster, a blur of motion...

"Luanne?"

She opened her eyes, disoriented.

"You need to get to bed." Rand took both of her hands in his and pulled.

She was upright, but only half awake. "That's true." She let him guide her down the hall and kissed him goodnight at the door of her room.

"I'll see you at the bank," he said.

In the living room, he broke up the chunks of wood still on the grate and scattered the coals beneath it. It would die out pretty quickly. With urging, Laddie and Max made a visit to the back yard, then trooped down the hall to Luanne's open door.

"Lucky dogs," Rand muttered. He poured the remainder of her wine and his own down the sink and washed the glasses by hand. Taking care to lock the front door behind him, he strode down the moonlit driveway and drove "home" to his cabin.

The air had turned substantially cooler since the two of them had been out at his grandfather's land. The moon that had looked so romantic the evening before, the color of cheddar as it rose, was high in the sky now. One day closer to full, but smaller, whiter, and colder without the benefit of atmospheric refraction. Now *there's* a romantic thought.

He stood in front of the cabin and listened to the

wind high in the pine trees. The only illumination was what was left of the moon's light after scudding clouds and swaying pine trees took their unfair share.

A howl began, increased, and died away. A wolf? Not a frightening sound. A lonely sound.

Another howl now; perhaps an answer? Rand laughed and leaned against the front of the SUV.

I'm all alone out here. New York might not exist any more. My bank accounts, all the powerful ones and zeros stored in a supercomputer, the proof that I'm a man to be reckoned with, that I'm worth millions, might be erased. Identity stripped.

An image appeared in his mind's eye. The top of the head and the torch of the Statue of Liberty showing above the sand. He hadn't seen the movie, *Planet of the Apes*, but that final image and Charlton Heston's cry of tragic loss was an icon. *Snap!* Instant recognition. Like the dour farmers in American Gothic, and Janet Leigh screaming in the shower, you couldn't live in America and not see it.

He clicked "lock" on his key ring and the Lincoln bleated and blinked once. *Aye, sir.* He climbed the three wooden steps and sat on the porch swing.

Without bank accounts, who am I? In a primitive world, how would I cope? Could I cope?

The wolf howled again and Rand chuckled. The wilderness version of internet dating. MyTerritory dot com.

Rand was sure of one thing. He didn't want to go it alone anymore. Not since he'd walked into Memories Mine and looked into the depths of Luanne Holt's green eyes. It was like walking through a hall of curved mirrors. His view of himself, of the whole world, had changed.

He wasn't sure yet which view was correct—and which was a distortion. But he knew with rock solid certainty that he was close to the answer.

Chapter Nine

The headline Wednesday morning made Luanne throw up.

Injunction Blocks Suncatcher.

She'd thought Dexter would hold the story, that he'd give Finn Wilder and the intellectual property attorneys—and her—another day to work a miracle. One more chance to—to what? Batter their way through the wall of the Bastille?

Did she believe in fairies and Santa Claus as well?

Her first call was from Cory. "Oh, Luanne, I'm so sorry. You must be sick!"

"You nailed that one," she muttered. "But the paper made it sound worse than it is. I still think we have a chance. I have to call Finn now, and I have to meet Rand at the bank."

"Call me later. I'm on my back, eager to talk on the phone."

"How are you feeling?"

"Good. The doctor was right. I'm following his orders to the letter. Couch, bed, couch, bed. No contractions."

"I wish I could be more help to you."

"You take care of business. Kent's sister will stay with me when Kent can't be here."

Luanne reached Finn and read him the article. His silence made her already queasy stomach roil. "Finn? Are you still there?"

"This can work to our advantage," he said thoughtfully. "I know that's hard to believe, but it can. I would like to break Dexter Stone's nose, but—

okay. Prepare to have your phone ring like it's never rung before."

"Why? What are you going to do?"

"Make Suncatcher the most famous all-American business since Colonel Sanders tucked fried chicken in a bucket. I'll call you in a couple hours. Oh, and wear something red, white and blue. It will look good on the internet."

He hung up before she could get any more out of him. He'd succeeded, in any event, in lifting her spirits. She wondered if he was speaking literally about what she should wear, decided he was, and went through her closet. A navy blue A-line skirt with matching jacket, a white blouse, and a flashy red-white-and-blue silk scarf. She looked ready to march down Disneyland's Main Street. Or, come to think of it, to storm the Bastille.

She was running short on time, but she managed to put on makeup and tame her curls. Her part-time employee, Nancy, had agreed to work alone at Memories Mine through Friday, and two high school girls would help her with the increased business all weekend. One less thing to worry about.

The look on Rand's face when he met her outside the bank told her he'd seen the Bitter Valley News. She repeated what Finn had told her.

"I don't pretend to understand why he's optimistic, but Finn knows all about being an underdog, and he has a lot of friends in the media thanks to work he does for some powerful politicians. I'll move on."

"I'll do anything I can to help you." He opened the door and followed her into the bank.

The bank president, Hugo Hall, welcomed them, asked after Amelia, and told Rand how much he enjoyed fly-fishing with his grandfather. The three of them did an inventory of the Daguerreotypes in the vault. While Rand arranged the wire transfer,

Luanne moved across the aisle. Sitting down across the desk from an old friend, she tried not to show the desperation that churned inside her.

"Betsy, I brought the loan papers with me." She set a manila folder on the desk. "They're all filled out."

The vice-president in charge of mortgage loans opened the folder and her shoulders slumped. "Are you sure, Luanne? This is a big bet, and the paper—"

"I know what the newspaper says. But there's a lot Dexter doesn't know." A flash of anger made her empty stomach contract.

She took a deep breath and forged ahead. "Or maybe I should say there's a lot that Dexter didn't put in the paper. Ted's brother Finn is giving this everything he's got, and how can I do less than that? We've got Yost and Collyer, the best intellectual property firm in New York, working on the case, and I have to pay them."

As Rand said when he'd coaxed her to taste the maraschino eyeball, *In for a penny, in for a pound.*

"What does Yost and Collyer get, ten dollars for a comma?"

Luanne shrugged. "Ten dollars to think about a comma. Twenty dollars more to actually put it in the brief."

"I should have gone to law school," Betsy muttered. "But no, I thought, 'Where's the money? In banks.' I didn't think to wonder who it belonged to."

Betsy focused on the documents in the folder. She signed her name at the bottom of one sheet, then another, and another.

The loan against Luanne's house was pre-approved, but neither the borrower nor the lender wanted to complete the transaction. She wondered what her parents would think. She hoped they'd understand her passion for Suncatcher.

Betsy tapped the top of the pen against the

paper as she looked again at the first page. At last she put the pen down.

"Let's wait a few hours. If I put this into the system before five p.m. it's the same as now."

"The wire instructions are in the folder. I'll call you before five."

Betsy reached over to pat her arm. "I hope you'll be calling to say it's not necessary."

Luanne hoped the same thing, but she kept it to herself.

Betsy rearranged the paperweights on her desk. "What about the money Rocky Monahan is wiring into the Suncatcher Fund?"

Luanne had hoped that the unexpected money from the photo collection could be set aside as seed money. It was enough to open the doors and turn on the power to the factory. Instead, she was sitting at a poker table with her last stack of chips. Betsy was correct when she'd said this was a big bet.

I'm all in.

"I'll work on the wire transfer with Hugo," Luanne replied. "The money from the antique photos is all going to Yost and Collyer."

"Luanne, I know you loved Ted—"

"But he's dead. Buried. Isn't that what you're thinking? I know he's dead, Betsy. But his invention isn't dead. It's very much alive and worth millions of dollars. I'm fighting for what rightly belongs to Bitter Falls. Not to China and some blood sucker on Wall Street."

Betsy sighed and rolled her chair back. "I hope you're right. If you get the rights back, all of us at the bank will do everything we can to get the factory running. We're a small-town bank, but we have friends in high places."

Luanne stood and held out her hand. Instead of shaking it, Betsy walked around the desk and wrapped her in her arms.

"Two things, Luanne. First, don't let the bastards drag you down to their level. Remember what they say about fighting in the mud with pigs. And second, who's the hunk in the tan jacket who can't tear his eyes off you? I believe the voltage in the air might be interfering with the alarm system."

Luanne looked over and, sure enough, Rand smiled back. "Would you believe me, Betsy, if I told you it's strictly business?"

Betsy chuckled. "Try another one."

"Rand Monahan is a New Yorker. He'll be leaving in four or five days. End of story."

"Is that what you want?"

Before she had to answer, Rand strolled over and introduced himself to Betsy. Luanne walked to the window and looked out on her hometown. She tried to imagine what it looked like to a New Yorker, but her imagination wouldn't stretch that far. A nice place to visit?

Would Rand remember her when he got back to his real world? Could she forget him?

She had to forget him! She had to break off this—this—*distraction* and get her focus back where it belonged. Too much depended on what happened in the next three and a half days to let herself get sucked into a fairy tale starring herself as the beautiful princess.

She did the math. Seventy-two, no—eighty-six hours. Midnight Saturday. The auction would be over.

Piano music meant to soothe customers filtered through to her and had the opposite effect. She sang along in her head. *A hand to hold when leaves begin to fall.*

No. She didn't have time for hand holding. She had a job to do. More than a job. A mission. She stared out at the street and watched golden leaves shake loose from trees in the park and fly away to the east. The wind was picking up.

Rand answered Betsy's questions about New York and what business he was in, but his attention was tuned like a radio frequency to Luanne. She stood still as a mannequin at the bank window. What was she thinking? What was she feeling?

Did she have any regrets about...last night? As soon as he saw her, in front of the bank, he'd detected a wall between them. He wanted to get her alone and reassure her of his motives. He wanted to trace her soft lips with his finger—no, with his tongue.

"Your grandfather is the nicest man." Betsy went on to tell how Rocky sent flowers when her mom died. "He was crazy about Mom's biscuits. She used to do all the baking for the Round-up Café, you know. Have you eaten there yet?"

"Not yet."

"You'll be there sooner or later. Be careful of their breakfasts, though. They'll give you a coronary for sure."

A coronary? "Thanks for the warning." He saw Hugo Hall walking toward them. "Excuse me, please."

"Mr. Monahan," Hall said, "the wired funds came through perfectly. Thanks for all your help. Would you like a cup of coffee while I work with Luanne?"

"Thanks, no. I have several calls to make. I'll sit over there by the window, out of the way."

Hall shook his head. "People wander in and out of the lobby all day and holler at their friends. Why don't you use my office? Luanne and I need to work with Betsy anyway."

"If you're sure..."

"Positive. Close the door, make yourself at home. There's cold water and soda in the refrigerator beside the desk."

"Thanks. I'll do that." Rand glanced at Luanne; she gave him a nod, but no smile. Was she paler than yesterday? That bonehead Dexter Stone deserved a kick in the ass for breaking the story before all the facts were in. Who did he think he was? Montana's answer to Carl Bernstein?

In Hall's office, Rand pulled out his cell phone to call Jeff on his direct line. In the middle of the trading day, as it was now, Jeff's phone would be answered by any of six people.

"Morning Select." Merry Lou Shore answered.

Before he could say anything, she added, "Hold on for a moment, please." An instrumental version of ABBA's "Money, Money, Money" played in his ear. Music he'd chosen.

Merry Lou had a voice that bespoke honeycombs and Georgia peaches, but the woman would step over your bleeding body to steal your business. A lot of people he knew would do no less, but Merry Lou did it so smoothly you'd look up from the floor and thank her.

Her accent and southern expressions were irresistible, like the lure of a Venus Flytrap. Merry Lou would say, "Bless your heart," while her leaves snapped closed on your still-warm carcass and began the digestive process. It was said on Wall Street that Merry Lou Shore not only knew where the bodies were buried, she'd tossed dirt on half of them. An exaggeration—he hoped. A click and she was back.

"Merry Lou, this is Rand. Is Jeff available?"

"Hold on just a tad bit, Rand. I see him coming this way. How are you? I understand they have *electricity* where you are! Or will soon."

"It's a good first step, Merry Lou. Everyone here is excited."

"Jeff," she called, "Rand's on the phone for you. Rand, you take care. The longer we work for Jeff, the more we miss you."

"Thanks, Merry Lou."

A shadow crossed his mind like a sudden eclipse of the sun by the Empire State Building: *The longer I'm away from New York, the less I miss it.*

"Hold on," Jeff said. "I'm taking this where I have some privacy."

Rand hoped that didn't mean Jeff would be peeing while they talked. The man was an inveterate multi-tasker.

"All right," Jeff muttered at last. "Have you heard from Serena?"

"Yes. She's all right, but I'm sworn to secrecy as to her location."

"Sworn to—? Hey, asshole, I'm your best friend!"

"Why, Jeff, you should write for Hallmark. So warm, so friendly. So persuasive."

"Stuff it! Where is she?"

"All right; you wore me down. She's in Istanbul."

"She's in—? Funny. I take back what I said about you being worth more alive than dead."

"I had one purpose in calling this number. To tell you the woman you love is all right. Bye, now."

"Okay, okay, hold on. I'll just climb out on this ledge. Whoa! It's windy out here, and—oh, my god— thirty-two stories to the street below. Now, Rand, please—*please*—tell me where Serena is."

"Key-man insurance is a wonderful fall back position, isn't it, Jeff?" He chuckled. "I promised her I wouldn't tell you where she is. I will, however, say that she was crying like her heart was broken."

"That's what her roommates said, too."

Rand heard the sound he hoped he wouldn't hear. "Jeff, is there a urinal out there on the ledge?"

Flush. "I decided not to jump. I'll go to Istanbul instead. To find the woman I *love.*"

"Best of luck to you."

"Rand—wait." Jeff sighed. "I have a hard time with mushy stuff, you know that. I also have a hard

143

time admitting that your health, pathetic as it is, might be better than mine."

"What the hell are you talking about?"

"My blood pressure is 200 over 90."

"Crap! Have you been to a doctor?"

"What do you think, I get my blood pressure measured by a cab driver? Of course I've been to a doctor."

"And what did he or she say?"

"That if I don't marry Serena I'll drop dead. *Now* will you tell me where she is?"

"Is this a trick? Swear on something you hold holy. Assuming such a thing exists." He waited. "Jeff?"

"I'm thinking, I'm thinking. Listen, this is the absolute truth. I tore the pre-nup into confetti. It was a huge mistake. Money has nothing to do with love."

"'Money has nothing—?' Who are you, and what have you done with Jeff Adler?"

"I'm telling the unvarnished truth. I love Serena."

Rand weighed his options. "All right. I'll try to get her to call you. One time. Tonight—at your apartment. You'd better not be at work. If you can't convince her you love her, I can't help you."

The door to the private office opened and Luanne came inside just enough to close it behind her. She looked like a stockbroker who'd sold everything for a dime on the dollar one hour before the market soared to new heights.

Without saying good-bye, he ended the call and snapped his phone closed. "Luanne, what's wrong?"

She wet her lips and cleared her throat. "Rand, last night was a mistake. If I hadn't been—you know—in front of the fire, I would have been on top of things." She blushed at the double *entendre*. "I mean, I would have taken Dexter's calls and studied the papers Finn faxed to both of us."

"And you could have—what? Controlled Dexter's thought process?"

"I don't know; maybe. What I'm trying to say is, I have a goal, and I have to finish what I've started. I don't think Dexter would have printed what he did if I'd been paying closer attention."

She swallowed hard and held out her hand, perhaps to hold back whatever he might say to sway her position.

"Closer attention," she said ruefully. "That's a good one. All the time I was with you I forgot Bitter Falls and Suncatcher existed. I forgot..." Another swallow; tears gathered in her eyes and threatened to go over the spillway. Her face reddened.

"While you were with me, you forgot Ted Wilder," he said. "Is that what you were going to say?"

She shivered, nodded vigorously, and wiped away the tears.

"Bitter Falls, Ted Wilder, Suncatcher Factory, economic salvation," he said. "Where is Luanne Holt in that equation?" He stood and moved halfway across the room. There were only inches between Luanne and the door, but somehow she moved backward.

"I'll have time. Time for...myself." She sucked in a lungful of air. "Later. This is a bad time for me to be acting like—like I have been ever since you walked into the store."

He closed the distance and his arm shot up, above the left side of her head, to hold the door closed. He winced inwardly to see her shrink back from him. Even though he knew that what she was afraid of was corporate voodoo, infinitely outside of her control, he hated to think she mistrusted him.

"Luanne," he said softly, "time isn't like that. Time is now; later may or may not exist. You said you loved Ted for years. Why didn't you marry him five or six years ago?"

She stood taller and her eyes flashed with anger. "You have no right to ask that! Who do you think you are to criticize my life?"

"From what I've seen and experienced with you—and don't pretend you didn't feel the earthquake, too—I'd say Ted Wilder was the luckiest man on this or any other planet. Did you refuse to marry him? Did you tell him, 'Later, when the time is right'?"

In a heartbeat he saw her go from anger to defeat. It was like watching time-lapse photography of a proud flower wilting. He turned the lock on the doorknob and wrapped her against him. Walking backwards, he guided her to a chair. Instead of seating her, he grabbed a fistful of tissues from a box on a side table, turned her sideways and sat himself. In the same movement, he pulled her onto his lap.

"I'm only guessing here," he said, "but I don't think you said, 'Let's wait five years for a wedding.' I'll bet Ted the inventor had his head in the clouds."

Or up his ass, he added to himself. *It takes a meathead to know one.*

He fed the tissues into the mask she'd formed with her hands. Each zipped inside like a reverse vending machine. As she snuffled and keened against his chest, he kissed her hair, rubbed her back, and murmured, "It's going to be all right."

Gradually her shoulders stopped quivering and her hyperventilation morphed to normal breathing. She sat up and used the soggy tissues to wipe away the quarter moons of mascara under her eyes.

"You're right about the wedding," she said on one long exhalation of breath. "He put it off. Suncatcher was a demanding mistress. But that was then; I'm dealing with now. Today. I have to complete this work before I can move forward."

146

"Even if today is all you have?" he asked.

She met his eyes. For a long moment, she said nothing out loud, but her eyes were like a memory stick. *Transferring data. Do not disconnect.*

"Even if today is all I have," she repeated. "I have to finish this."

"If that's your mission, I have one, too. To do everything in my power to help you. Starting with the auction."

"I don't understand."

"Charity auctions to me are like salt water to a fish. And my sister Dinah, famed impresario of worthy causes, knows everyone who is anyone."

She stood and glared at him, hands on her hips. "It's not charity."

"Money-for-a-good-cause by any other name still smells as sweet. I think that's Shakespeare."

She took a few deep breaths and thought it over. "Okay, I'll admit it. I need help. And Finn has fastidiously ruled out a hit man for whoever runs Allied Advent Tech. So, yes, thank you. I'll be grateful for anything you can do to, uh—"

"Drive sheep into the shearing shed?"

"For a good cause. Then we'll turn them out to run free and make more money. I mean, wool."

He stood. "May I take you to lunch?"

"No. I can't be ruthless when you're around. You distract me."

"What a sweet thing to say." He grinned. "You had me at 'ruthless.'"

"Don't expect an apology. Staying away from you is the only way I can focus on what has to be done. Today."

"And tomorrow? Never mind. That will be 'today,' too, won't it? How about Sunday? The auction will be over."

"Sunday?" she repeated. "What does your airline ticket say? When do you go back to New York?"

He said nothing, knowing he'd answered her question with his silence.

"Sunday will be fine," she said.

Her bright tone was as artificial as the insipidly cheerful voices on Sophie's favorite TV show. Little airplanes with faces. He shuddered at the thought of her little mind, wasted.

"Sunday it is, then," he said, "for a serious talk. And just so you know, airline reservations are just ones and zeros on a mainframe computer. They can be changed."

He heard the bank president outside the door and rushed to unlock it and open it wide.

"I'll get to work on that, Luanne," he said, a little louder than necessary. "Thanks for your ideas. I'll get in touch with Dinah immediately."

She dropped her handful of tissues in the wastebasket as she passed him. "Good. I'll talk to you this afternoon."

She thanked Hugo Hall for his help and asked him to give Rand the latest printout of items for the auction.

"Rand claims to be acquainted with the goose that lays the golden egg," she added. "Or did you say sheep?"

"Both. And cash cows, too." He nodded and smiled. "I'll call you as soon as my friend Serena gets into town. She'll probably have some good ideas, too. We won't go to dinner until you're free to join us."

Luanne's eyes flashed like she might protest, but he was counting on having her at a disadvantage with the bank president listening to every word. She gave him a curt half nod.

As he watched her cross the lobby and leave the bank, he stifled a laugh. *Luanne Holt couldn't find "ruthless" in the dictionary.*

Hugo invited him to have a seat and handed him a bottle of cold water. "Have you heard of Cog

Coughlin? He's handling the details of the auction. Let me pull up my email and see exactly where it stands."

Rand took a seat. He'd checked already; the bank had wi-fi. He could bring his laptop in from his car and work here.

"While you get your mail," Rand said, "I'll give my sister a call. Get her on board."

He was certain that getting Suncatcher open was a worthy cause, but he had his own reason to seal the deal. The sooner it was behind Luanne, the sooner she'd focus on her own needs. And when she did so, he'd be there to, uh, sharpen her focus.

Chapter Ten

Luanne was hit by a gust of wind outside the bank and closed her eyes against the stinging dust. For once, she welcomed bad weather, because the forecast for the weekend was good. Excellent, in fact. This weak cold front was coming through right on schedule, Wednesday morning, ratifying the meteorologist's declaration.

Humidity was low, as usual, with winds gusting to twenty-five miles per hour. Temperature would be fifty for a high, dropping to thirty tonight; tomorrow, forty for a high, twenty-eight for a low. A whiff of winter. Frost on the pumpkins.

But Friday, Saturday and Sunday would be sunny, warm, windless, gorgeous. Days and nights perfect for the Harvest Festival.

It was as if Mother Nature dropped in today with a reminder. *You've got to weather the bad so you'll treasure the good.*

Pulling her jacket closed and holding her hair back from her face with one hand, Luanne headed down Main Street toward the Bitter Valley News. When she opened the front door, the wind whipped in around her and riffled the pages of a stack of newspapers. Her hair probably looked like she'd brushed it with a whisk broom, but she couldn't care less how she looked. In fact, she wished she had snakes for hair and that Dexter Stone would take one look at her and turn to Solid Stone.

Receptionist and classified ads clerk Phyllis Bloom looked up. Before she saw who had blown in, she automatically recited, "May I help you?"

Her eyes widened. "Oh, Luanne, hello. Uh, Dexter is in the press room. He should be back in a minute."

"The reporter? What's his name?"

"Dustin. He's not due back for an hour."

"Good." She bit off the word like a crisp Saltine. If Phyllis was wise, she'd skedaddle.

The grandmother who'd known Luanne since she was in Brownie Scouts slapped the cover of the bank book closed, stuffed it in a leather bag and zipped it closed. As she lifted her windbreaker off the coat tree, she mumbled that she needed to get to the bank before noon.

"Can't believe how soon the Harvest Festival will be." Phyllis jammed her arms into her coat. "I hope the weather is good. Oh, I hear Dexter coming now." She hustled out the door as if pursued by a junkyard dog.

Luanne exhaled through pursed lips and reminded herself she'd been brought up to have manners. Or had she? Wasn't she a descendent, though indirect, of Goldie Jones, a woman who'd survived two years in the Klondike and come out with fabulous wealth? In the dead of winter, with starvation staring her in the face, Goldie had poured out her anger at a partner who'd tried—unsuccessfully—to cheat her. By sputtering candlelight and in tiny print to save precious paper, she'd written in her journal: *Gentility is a nice addition if you already have every damn thing you need.*

"Did you want to see me?" Dexter asked. "I'm pretty busy."

"Of course you are. But there are some details of today's story—starting with your outrageous headline—that need to be corrected."

He shrugged. "When I have confirmation that you and Ted's brother own the rights to the solar cells, I'll be only too happy to run the story. Until then, people have a right to know what's going on."

"The injunction wasn't signed. You knew that last night. AATech can damn well ask for the moon. It doesn't mean they'll get it."

"Hmmm." He cocked his head as if trying to recall some fragment of fact. "Knew it last night? Actually, I didn't. I read those little black letters on the documents, not whatever you think was between the lines. Perhaps if I could have reached you by phone, you could have convinced me."

"I did call you back." Her confidence slipped a little, eroding at its edges like a sandbar in swift water.

"Oh, by then the story was in layout. You know how deadlines are. I have to get the papers done and put the press to bed by eleven. When I said I'd hold the paper Saturday night to get the auction results, I was making a big exception to my rules."

There was something so abrasive about him that Luanne felt off kilter. Dexter was usually overly friendly, overly attentive. Proprietary. As if she were his; as if she were a prize filly he hadn't saddled yet. One night she'd overheard him tell the mayor he and Luanne weren't dating "seriously" yet.

"I'm content to wait 'til she gets her feet under her," he'd said. Wink, wink. Guy to guy.

Got to coddle the little lady. You know how women are.

That social event honoring the mayor and his wife had not been the right time to confront Dexter with what she'd overheard. She'd seethed inside, but postponed the confrontation.

That specific delay was understandable.

What was beyond comprehension was why she'd continued to put it off. There's reticence—and then there's cowardice.

"I understand the need to put the paper to bed,

Dexter. And I appreciate what you're doing Saturday night." She almost bit her tongue to keep from adding snide congratulations on having tripled his usual ad income thanks to the Harvest Festival.

Jerk!

"When I couldn't get you on the phone last night," he said, "I drove over to your house. I didn't ring the bell, though. I could see you had company."

So that was his game. Rand's car in the driveway, smoke curling out of the chimney, and probably no lights. She squeezed her hands into fists and kept them tight against her.

"Failure to communicate. I see. Well, as they say on the banks of the Bitter River, that's water under the bridge, isn't it? The important thing is to get the correct information into tomorrow's paper, with—I hope—an equally large headline."

"Correct information? I'm all right with that, sure. But don't expect me to print what you wish or hope is true. Just the facts, ma'am."

The door opened behind her.

"Good morning, Luanne, Dexter." A man's deep voice. "Hell of a wind out there today."

She turned, glad for the interruption. Mayor Aldo Rasmussen hung his tan hat on the elk rack on the wall.

She took a breath and tried to get any twinge of anger out of her voice. "Good morning, Aldo."

"I ran into Phyllis down by the bank," Rasmussen said to her. "That's how I knew where to find you."

"What's up?" Dexter asked.

"What's up?" The mayor brushed dust off his corduroy jacket. "CNN and NBC, that's what's up! Did you know they have reporters coming?"

"What?" Dexter asked, clearly surprised. "What for? Somebody have a two-headed baby?"

Rasmussen grinned at Luanne. "I'll bet you can

guess what's up, huh?"

The tight muscles in her face relaxed a little and a smile replaced the thin zipper that kept her anger at Dexter in check.

"I think Finn Wilder is drumming up some interest in the plight of Suncatcher," she said.

"David and Goliath, that's how one of the producers put it." Rasmussen rubbed his hands together.

The phone on Phyllis's desk rang and Dexter grabbed it before it went to the message. "Bitter Valley News."

The mayor was chortling with joy at the prospect of national news coverage. "What they do, these big networks, is they have producers who call and arrange everything. They've been on the phone to me, and the library. They don't know yet when they'll have someone here in person. Hell, they're scrambling around, trying to find a map."

"I hope it's in advance of the auction," she said. "Finn is trying to build it up."

Even more important than money earned from the auction, she knew, was the chance to aim the light of public opinion on the rats who ran Allied Advent Technology. The brighter the light, the better for Suncatcher.

Dexter hung up the phone and swore. Sitting down heavily in Phyllis's chair, he brought up the internet on her computer monitor and typed in some commands. A full-screen photo of Ted Wilder appeared.

Luanne caught her breath and put her fingers to her lips. She saw from the logo above that it was the official news page of NBC's business network. Dexter scrolled down and the article began. "Rest in Peace? Not if Tech Powerhouse has its Way."

She leaned in and quickly read the first two paragraphs and almost hooted in delight. After a straightforward statement of the facts, how Ted had invented a new kind of plastic solar cells and designed a factory to manufacture them, it said his rights were essentially stolen by a corporate shell game.

The reporter threw in a few sentences about how Suncatcher Solar Cells were a breakthrough advance on the method that won the Nobel Prize for a UC, Santa Barbara, physics professor.

"Since Ted Wilder's tragic death from a brain aneurysm fourteen months ago, his brother, his former fiancée, and the whole town of Bitter Falls, Montana, have been battling Goliath to get his rights back and open the factory."

She called Finn on her cell; she only had time to ask one question before the mayor asked to speak with him.

"Aldo Rasmussen here, Finn. Yes, yes, we're looking at it now. Yes, I see. Sure. Hold on a second. Dexter, give me a piece of paper, would you?"

Dexter looked as if the mayor had asked him to hand toilet paper under the stall, but he tore a sheet out of a notebook and Aldo grabbed it.

She listened as Aldo wrote and read back what Finn was telling him, the name and number of a producer at CBS Evening News.

Dexter watched with a glower that—if focused through a magnifying glass—could ignite the paper he'd given to Aldo.

"Okay, I've got it, Finn, thanks. Great job." He handed the phone back to Luanne. "He needs a new picture of you, ASAP. I've got a digital camera over at my office. Come on over."

As Aldo swept out into the wind, his hat clamped tight, Luanne asked Finn what the latest was on the injunction.

"It's still stuck in the same court. The judge wants more briefs filed by five p.m. tomorrow. He set a hearing for first thing Friday morning."

She was disappointed that Finn would have to postpone flying to Montana, but it was the only chance they had.

"Yost and Collyer got the money this morning," he continued, "and they're pouring coal into the boiler. The producer at CBS, by the way, is Yost's sister. Further proof that God loves us more than AATech."

"They're going down," she said. It felt good to even say the words. How sweet would actual victory be?

"Absolutely. Chins to the floor. Hey, your new boyfriend is making some phones ring, auction-wise."

"He's not—" She caught herself, remembered Dexter was listening to every word she said. "That's good news."

"Is Dexter there?"

"Yes, he's here."

"Tell him I'll call him in thirty minutes. You get that picture shot and email the j-peg so I can send it to some news guys."

"Finn—I'm just, I mean, thanks. It feels good to have a door open for a change. Virtually, literally." She laughed. "Even metaphorically."

She closed her phone and tossed Finn's message to Dexter the way a queen discards a used hanky.

As she walked up Main Street to the mayor's office, she wondered what Sunday would bring. The only way to get there was by forging straight ahead. No distractions; she'd see as little as possible of Rand Monahan.

As little as possible!

She owed that to Ted, to the town, and to the definition of herself she carried around in her head, that she was good old reliable Luanne. Someone you could count on.

And yet—Rand had made it clear he wasn't taking "No" for an answer. She'd said "No" to lunch, and somehow in the space of two minutes he'd finagled "Yes" to dinner with his terribly upset New York friend, Serena. And tomorrow or the next day, he would want her to meet his sister, and Erik and Sophie.

Seeing "as little as possible" of Rand Monahan was a hollow promise. And—secretly—she was glad of it.

****

Rand locked his laptop in his car and strode up Main Street toward the park on the west side of the county courthouse. Out beyond the park bench and maple tree where he'd rested yesterday, on his bike ride, was a playground. Not the plastic play areas that seemed to be everywhere, all in primary colors with tubular slides. This was wood and metal. The fort really looked like a frontier fort for a small garrison. The wagon looked like something that exceptionally short pioneers brought west on the Oregon Trail.

Erik and Sophie were going to love it here. He felt a goofy grin widen across his face. That was the best thing about kids; seeing the world all over again with them. In his case, since he'd fast-forwarded past so much in his all-fired hurry to grow up and make gigabucks, he was seeing a lot of the world for the first time.

He spotted Serena on a wrought iron and wood bench. She was facing the empty playground; the flat board seats of three swings moved randomly in the wind gusts. No pattern, no purpose.

A lot like Sophie and her cohorts at their dance recitals.

"Ma'am, you look like you've lost your last friend, but I'm here to prove you wrong." He stood in front of her, expecting her to rise and hug him.

157

Instead, she wrapped her arms tighter around herself and seemed to shrink.

Her long blond hair, high cheekbones, and blue eyes had stopped many a conversation, and her graceful walk had slowed construction at uncounted worksites. He'd heard someone describe her eyes as "Vermeer blue." Today she looked less like an oil painting and more like a watercolor with more water than color.

He sat beside her and put his left ankle on his right knee. He thought of one thing to say, then another, but tossed them away like two-week-old cartons of Szechwan chicken. Silence didn't feel golden to him, not now, but he made up his mind to wait.

"I'm thirty-two years old," she said at last.

Rand didn't know much about women, but he was pretty sure anything he said, including, "I'm thirty-six," would be wrong, so he waited again. Never mind politics and religion. Age and weight were the fuses he wouldn't touch.

"When I was twenty-two," she said, "I had an affair with a married man. Nothing unusual; he said they were separated and waiting for the divorce to be final. I don't have to tell you how long that takes in New York. Well, it takes even longer if the son of a bitch hasn't filed. You want to know how I found out I was played for a fool?"

Yes? No? Neither seemed like a good answer, so he raised his eyebrows.

"He called me into his office and stood there like a pillar of salt while his wife called me a slut." She closed her eyes. "I was pregnant. I was going to tell him that night."

He put both feet on the ground and wrapped his left arm around her. "Serena, I'm sorry."

"A week later, a week when I couldn't get out of bed, I had a miscarriage. I changed jobs and blocked it from my mind." She snapped her fingers. "Poof. Gone. Never happened."

"I won't insult you by saying I know how you feel. But I'm sorry it happened and I hope the man roasts in hell. The sooner the better."

"Jeff doesn't want kids." Her voice was as flat as the yield curve on bank savings accounts.

"Oh, I don't—"

"He wrote it into the pre-nuptial agreement. No children."

"Good news—he's torn the pre-nup into confetti. Bad news—he had to stuff the confetti into his head to fill the space where his brain is supposed to be. Serena, he's begging me to beg you to give him another chance."

"Never."

"Good, then you'll at least consider talking to him tonight."

"Are you listening to me?"

"Better than you think I am. You could do a lot better than Jeff, but he loves you very much. Please call him tonight. He'll be at his apartment."

She sat up, stiff-backed. "Did you tell him I was in Montana?"

"No! I promised you I wouldn't. I told him that we'd talked on the phone, and I said I'd try to get you to call him—just one phone call. His last chance."

"He's already had his last chance."

"Poor choice of words on my part. Getting past who's totally right—you—and who's infinitely wrong—Jeff—and all the semantics related thereto, I'm personally pleading with you to call him, just once." He waited, then dropped the explosive into the well. "His blood pressure is two hundred over ninety."

She bolted onto her feet. "What the hell? He's going to have a stroke! Is he seeing a doctor? What does the doctor say?"

"That you should call him tonight."

She stared at him, her hands on her hips and her lips tight. "Rand, I'm pregnant. And I don't want anything to do with Jeff. I'm never going back to New York."

"Pregnant? That's wonderful! You'll be a fantastic mother. And Jeff will be thrilled once he gets over the shock."

"No, he won't. I'm not telling him. Now or ever. I'm going to put 'father unknown' on the birth certificate." She burst into chest-heaving sobs and sat down on the bench.

He put his arm around her shoulders. "Hey, listen. It's going to be all right."

She leaned against him, inhaling enormous amounts of air and letting it all out in ragged sobs.

"You're worn out," he said. "Have you been to the dude ranch yet?"

"No. I called you when I got to town. I don't know where the ranch is."

"We'll go out there this afternoon. Right now let's get some lunch. I can see that you've lost weight. How far along are you?"

"Four months. The morning sickness is pretty much over. And I always take my vitamins."

"That's a relief." But vitamins weren't enough, especially if she was throwing up. She looked awfully pale. "Have you been seeing a doctor?"

"Yes, right from the first. I want this baby very much. I was right on the verge of telling Jeff about the pregnancy and saying we could get married at City Hall, instead of having the wedding I've always wanted, when he presented me with the Declaration of Dependence. Sign here in blood."

Her tears started afresh.

He'd been torn between Jeff and Serena when there were two sides to this dispute. Now there were three sides, and he knew where he stood. This baby sure as hell didn't deserve the burden of *father unknown.*

Concern for the innocent bystander made his promise to Serena untenable, and yet he couldn't violate her trust. A promise is a promise, even if it's wrong.

Somehow he had to get Jeff to make a U-turn. The two of them had to be face to face, and it was clear that Serena wasn't going back to New York. So, how could he get Jeff to come to Montana?

With a little more urging, Serena agreed to have lunch with him at the Round-Up Café. He'd drive out to the dude ranch later; she could follow him in her rental car. Maybe by then he'd think of an argument persuasive enough to get her to call Jeff. The first step would be the hardest.

Chapter Eleven

Luanne looked across the table at the Mineshaft Restaurant at Serena, then to Rand, who sat on her right, then back to the dinner menu.

Last time she'd seen the menu had been her first night with Rand. She'd met him in her shop, and time had gone over a cliff. The minutes that had crept up to five o'clock exploded into a new deminision. One minute they were in his car; the next minute they ordered the trout. The next minute they kissed.

How many hours until we made love?

She needed time to process whatever was going on between them. Instead, she was on a moving sidewalk that sped up and slowed with no warning.

While they'd waited for a table, Rand brought her up to date on some of the amazing items added to the auction. He gave all the credit to his sister and to Serena, who'd climbed on the bandwagon as soon as he'd asked her to help, but Luanne was sure he was simply modest about his own arm twisting.

Antique furniture, a Marc Chagall lithograph appraised and sold at Sotheby's two years ago, a motorcycle that had belonged to Steve McQueen. The list had something to appeal to even the most jaded bidder. The auction was certain to raise more money than she'd imagined possible, especially with the Suncatcher story going around the world on the internet.

With immense relief, she'd called Betsy at the bank at three o'clock and told her to tear up the second mortgage papers she'd given her at ten.

The three of them ordered salads, steaks, and grilled vegetables. She and Rand were having rosé wine. Serena wanted only club soda with lime. She was pale and withdrawn.

"I need a roster to keep track of who's arriving when," Luanne said to hold up her end of the flagging conversation. "Bitter Falls is exploding in temporary population before my wondering eyes."

"It's a cute town," Serena said. "If I squint, and ignore the cars, the center of Main Street looks like an old west town in a movie."

"I wonder what it will look like on TV," Luanne mused. "That reporter from NBC Nightly News must have followed me, with the camera on, for an hour. And they'll use, what, forty seconds?"

"I'm playing catch up, here," Serena said. "I understand why you're having the festival and the auction, to raise money for the Suncatcher factory. But why all the national media?"

Rand smiled at Luanne. "I didn't have time to tell her the whole saga."

"Excuse me, Ms. Holt?" A man in a sport coat and slacks, the only man dressed like Rand in the restaurant, stopped beside their table. "I'm Chevy Keyser with CBS. My producer spoke with you on the phone."

Rand stood and offered his hand and his name. "Would you care to join us?"

"Oh, I don't want to intrude," Keyser said, as he pulled out the fourth chair. He and Rand sat down and Keyser shook hands with Luanne and Serena.

The waitress approached with a menu but he said he was sitting with a friend across the room. He ordered a Moose Drool on tap and asked if the three of them would care for a drink.

"Thanks," Serena said. "I'm good."

Rand and Luanne said the same.

"Well," Keyser said as soon as the waitress

163

moved away, "you've stirred up quite a hornet's nest, Ms. Holt."

"Please, call me Luanne. I can't take credit for the publicity. Finn Wilder is the man behind the curtain."

"The inventor's brother? An attorney?"

"That's correct. He's doing everything he can to get the patent rights back from Allied Advent Technology."

"That's the new company, isn't it?" Keyser asked. "By new I mean the last in line after the patents bounced all over. What was the first company, the one Ted Wilder dealt with?"

"Percival Partnerships Limited."

The waitress brought his beer in a tall glass. He handed her a bill and waved off the change.

Luanne could tell from her smile that it was a good tip. No wonder the town was buzzing. She answered a few more questions, then shook Keyser's hand again.

He stood and said he'd see her at ten the next morning, Thursday, at her store.

"The camera crew is staying in Missoula tonight. Ten o'clock should give them plenty of time for the drive. Thanks again for letting me interrupt you. Enjoy your dinner."

Luanne leaned forward and spoke quietly. "Finn told me the producer at CBS, the woman who called me to say Keyser was on his way here from Seattle, is the sister of one of our intellectual property attorneys."

"It's about time you caught a break," Rand said. "What were you asking us, Serena?"

The waitress appeared at Luanne's elbow and placed their salads on the table. The bus person was behind her, filling their water glasses.

"Umm, nothing," Serena said. "I mean, listening to Chevy Keyser's questions cleared it up for me."

Rand's phone lit up and wiggled a couple inches away from his plate. He glanced at the caller ID. "Excuse me, please. It's my brother-in-law." He rose and walked out of the dining area.

Luanne passed the rolls to Serena and broke one in half. "Do you know Rand's sister's family?"

"Oh, yes. They're great. Actually, I work with his brother-in-law, Kurt, at Lehman. Or, I should say I did work with him. Technically, I'm still employed, but I won't go back to New York; so, when my leave runs out, I'll have to make some decisions. My plans are in flux."

"I was standing next to Rand yesterday afternoon when you called," Luanne said.

Serena shrugged and moved her lettuce around but didn't eat anything. "It was a long day. I've never run away from home before. I've always been a team player, the one who gets people to calm down and settle their differences. Maybe I bought into the family legend that I'm as serene as my name. Anyway, when I was suddenly the angry one, my brain dissolved or something. It's a very strange thing to wake up in Montana."

"You have family in Texas, is that right?"

"Yes, Dallas. They want me to come home, but I'm not ready." Her lower lip quivered and tears welled in her eyes. "Could we change the subject, please?"

"Of course." Luanne took a bite of her salad greens, then another. "Umm, don't you care for your salad?"

Serena looked at her plate. She'd moved the lettuce all over, but hadn't eaten any of it. "It's probably good, but I don't have any appetite."

Another change of subject indicated, Luanne deduced.

"How is your room at the Rocking Star?"

Serena put her fork down and closed her eyes.

"I'm sorry. I'm not good company."

Luanne's hand shot across to Serena's. "Do you feel ill? Maybe something you ate?"

Serena gave a rueful laugh. "I can rule that out. I haven't been able to eat for two days. Or maybe it's three now. Oh, I've tried, but nothing stays down for long. And, no, before you wonder, I don't have anything catching."

Luanne gave a slight wave to the waitress.

"Yes? Shall I bring your steaks?"

"Something has come up," Luanne said. "We'll have to take our dinners with us. Please box the entrees." She pointed to Rand's salad. "And one salad."

The waitress took the salad back to the kitchen just before Rand returned. He slipped into his seat.

"Good news. I persuaded Kurt to come with Dinah and the kids." He put his hand over Luanne's. "I can't wait for you to meet my family."

"Rand, Serena doesn't feel well. I asked the waitress to box our dinners; we can go to my place. I'll walk Serena out while you get the food."

The three of them rose, and Rand handed her the keys to the SUV. He watched the two beautiful women cross the wooden dance floor and weave between tables to the exit.

His phone vibrated in the vest pocket of his sport coat. He sat and answered without looking at it. "Hello?"

"Any luck?"

He sighed. "Jeff, I can't talk now."

"You can say one word. I'll say, 'Is Serena going to call me tonight?' and you can say, 'Yes.' Now, ready? Is she going to call me?"

"I've been in touch with her, and I should know soon. She's—she's not feeling well." He'd almost slipped and said she looked as pale as skim milk. "How are you? Staying off ledges? Doing what the doctor ordered?"

Jeff said nothing for a long moment. "The doctor has his head up his ass."

"Call Brogen for a referral."

Jeff swore. "Brogen would refer me to Dr. See-More Montana for a rest cure. No thanks. I've got an appointment with Dr. Jack Daniels tonight. House call."

The waitress returned with a stack of round containers tied in a plastic bag. She set it on the table and gave Rand the check in a black folder.

"I'll call you in an hour, Jeff. Postpone that appointment with J.D. I'm sure Serena will call." He closed the phone and added a tip to the dinner amount.

He'd just been through the Oracle of Death conversation with Kurt, and he dreaded doing a replay with Jeff. Wasn't it enough that *he'd* nearly died from over-stress, over-exertion, over-work? Kurt and Jeff had both seen his face turn the color of oysters. Kurt had been at their office, early for a business lunch with the two of them, and had ended up riding in the ambulance with Rand, calling Dinah and Grandpa.

Wasn't that enough? Hello? Why did they still think nobody dies before the age of forty?

He signed the receipt and picked up his credit card.

That's when he felt the pain.

Left chest, shooting upward. Sweat beads broke out on his forehead. He fumbled inside his jacket for the plastic container. Quickly, he shook one nitro tablet into his hand and set it under his tongue.

I'm okay, he murmured. To himself or out loud, he didn't know which. A twinge of angina, nothing to worry about. Kink in the hose, no big deal. Stable angina, stable. That's the most important word. Stable. Under control.

He sat still, climbing back to normal. The new normal. The one where he hadn't missed Christmas. The one where he could still buy the goose and save Tiny Tim.

At last he inserted his credit card into his wallet and stood. Carrying the food containers, he walked across the crowded restaurant. At the archway to the bar, a wild yell drew his attention. A TV screen above the bar pulsed with red and yellow around the words Home Run. Playoffs? World Series?

Rand had a long list of things he wanted to do with the time he'd pulled out of the trash compactor in the nick of time. Watching TV in a bar with cowboys—or with Wall Street computer jockeys—hadn't made the cut.

Someone started toward him. Dexter Stone. Rand walked faster, but it wasn't fast enough.

"Mr. Monahan, a question for you. Got a minute?"

Rand stopped. Luanne had told him Dexter was highly agitated about Rand's SUV being parked at her house the night before. Now all the media interest, which bypassed Dexter's newspaper as neatly as a diversionary channel around a cofferdam, was making him smolder.

"I've got a question about Allied Advent Technologies," Dexter said. "This big boogeyman that everybody's so excited about."

"Sorry, Dexter, I don't know anything about them. And I'm in a hurry." He held up the bag full of containers. "I can call you tomorrow, though."

"Yeah, uh-huh. You do that." Dexter held out his meaty hand, offering a handshake and blocking Rand's path to the door at the same time.

Rand showed that the bag of containers was looped over his right hand, and he made no effort to move it. The crowd howled and cursed, drawing Dexter's attention away enough that Rand could get past him.

Over his shoulder he called to Dexter, "Enjoy the game."

****

Luanne watched the play of emotions across Serena's face as Rand argued on Jeff's behalf. He'd started off with gentle persuasion and moved up the scale a little each time she refused to call Jeff.

At the same time, he coaxed her to take a bite of steak. One bite, good, now one more. The three of them were seated at Luanne's dining room table. When he set out the plates and two wine glasses, he'd poured a tall glass of milk for Serena.

Exasperated, he rubbed his hand over his face. "Serena," he said, his voice barely more than a whisper, "look at me."

She glanced at Luanne as if for support, then at Rand.

"When I promised you I wouldn't tell Jeff where you were, I didn't know you were pregnant."

"What?" Luanne looked from him to Serena.

She nodded.

Rand met Luanne's questioning gaze. "Four months. Hence the milk."

"If you tell Jeff I'm here," Serena said fiercely, "I'll be on the next plane out of Montana."

"Is that really what you want? Come on, Serena, Jeff loves you. He will love and cherish his baby, too. Give him a chance to man up."

Serena's shoulders began to shake, and she put her face in her slender hands. Luanne stepped into the kitchen and got a box of tissues, patted Serena's arm, and gave them to her.

At the same time, Rand got Serena's purse off the coffee table and set it in front of her. He said only one word. "Please."

As the uncomfortable silence stretched on, Luanne cleared the table. As she put the scraps of steak on one plate and divided them between the two dog bowls, Laddie and Max sat up ramrod straight, like Olympic sprinters on the blocks. They resisted the powerful urge to lunge toward the food, but they weren't saints. From deep in their throats a tiny forbidden noise—the sound of begging—escaped. Synchronized, their large pink tongues licked left, right, left again.

She carried the bowls out to the patio and gave the signal. They clearly wanted to fly toward the bowls, but instead they moved with grace.

"Good boys." She came back in and closed the sliding glass door against the cold wind.

Serena took her cell phone out of her purse and turned it on. Immediately it beeped that she had messages. She scrolled down. "He said he'd be at home?" she asked Rand.

"Yes."

"We'll leave you alone," Luanne said as she picked up her wine glass.

"No. Stay here, please," Serena said.

Luanne sat down, nodding yes when Rand held up the wine bottle, but holding her finger and thumb a half inch apart. Her kitchen phone rang but she ignored it.

Serena closed her eyes and pressed a button on her phone.

"Don't forget to breathe," Rand said.

She smiled, then the smile disappeared and her eyes went wide. It was pretty clear that Jeff had answered the phone.

"I, it's..." Serena took a sip of milk. "Yes, it's me. Rand talked me into calling. So, uh, what do you want to say?"

Luanne caught Rand's eye and smiled. She watched Serena's face. It was like watching a triple scoop ice cream cone in July. Whatever words Jeff was finding, he was melting Serena's icy core.

"No," she said. "I won't go back to New York."
She listened. "Yes, I'm willing to meet you and talk.
I don't promise any more than that. We need to—we
need to talk. I agree."

She sniffed and listened to whatever Jeff was
saying; her eyes filled with tears. "I've missed you,
too. Meet half way? Just a minute."

She covered the phone with her hand. With the
first hint of a smile Luanne had seen on her pale
face since they'd met at the restaurant, she asked,
"Where would half way be?"

"Somewhere in Minnesota," Luanne whispered.

"Half way is Minnesota," she repeated into the
phone. "I don't think you could find it. I don't think I
could find it either." She took a deep breath. "No, I'm
not in Seattle. Hold on."

She covered the phone again and closed her eyes
as if wrestling with a dilemma. Finally she looked at
Rand. "Okay, Mister Persuasive," she whispered,
"tell him how to get here." She held out her phone.

Clearly shocked by Serena's turnaround, Rand
took the phone. With a comical shrug to Luanne, he
spoke. "Hi, Jeff." He grinned. "Good guess, Sherlock.
The fastest way to get here on a commercial flight is
through Detroit. But Dinah and Kurt and the kids
are coming on a charter tomorrow, direct to Bitter
Falls. I'm sure there's room for you."

Chapter Twelve

"I slept ten hours last night," Serena said.

"That makes one of us," Rand muttered as he opened his laptop.

He'd listened to the coyotes—or wolves, or whatever howled in the woods—until two a.m. If he couldn't be with Luanne, he'd use the lonely hours to plan a campaign to win her heart.

As for Serena, he'd seen the change in her as soon as she arrived at the bank. Her shoulders were high and square to the world: her cheeks had a little color. And her blue eyes had some of their old Vermeer radiance back.

"Who else is going to use this room?" she asked. Hugo Hall, the bank president, had insisted they settle into the bank's modest conference room so they could use the bank's wi-fi network.

"Cog Coughlin, the auctioneer, has three assistants arriving today. They'll be in and out. Where's the outlet? Oh, I see it." He powered up.

Serena yawned. "I missed breakfast, but the cook took pity on me and fixed scrambled eggs and bacon."

His fingers froze over the keyboard. "You ate a decent breakfast?" He gave her a fist bump. "Ain't love grand?"

"Of course, I haven't dropped 'da bomb' on Jeff, yet."

"My advice? Start with, 'How would you feel about having a house plant?' Something needy, like an African violet. Then move up to timeshare ownership of a Pomeranian."

"No! No tiptoeing around; no games. I'm not getting any younger or any less pregnant. I can support myself and my baby with no help from him."

Rand sat back in the swivel chair and scratched his chin. "There's more to support than money."

"You're preaching to the choir, Rand. This is not all about me. Jeff is working himself to death, and I'm through watching it. I'm not—repeat, not—moving back to New York."

She ran her cord to the same outlet he'd used, plugged in her laptop and powered up. She tapped her nails on the wood and hummed a tune.

He could feel her staring at him. "What?"

"Luanne is just as hot as I heard she was."

He groaned. "And you heard this from whom?"

"Dinah, who heard it from Rocky. Pretty much everyone in the universe knew about it before you did."

A light tap sounded on the not-quite-closed door and Rand called, "Come in."

Hugo Hall stepped into the room. "Have you looked at 'Suncatcher-fights-back' yet?"

"I'm just pulling it up now," Rand said. "Holy motherboard! Nearly half a million hits? Is that right?"

Serena's fingers flew over her keyboard and she studied her screen. "That's right. All the eco-friendlies are on board. And it hasn't been on network news yet."

"Look on the right," Rand said. Hall came into the room and looked over his shoulder. "Links to electric cars, windmill farms, plus solar, solar, solar."

"Exciting, isn't it?" Hall asked. "Well, I'd better get back to work." He closed the door as he left.

"Click on Inventor," Serena said. "Up at the top right."

Rand clicked his portable mouse and sat back. A

snapshot popped up. A slender man with an enormous backpack stood on a boulder, with a rocky crag behind him. The second picture was of Ted with Luanne, not side by side, but Ted in the foreground. An interview in a Seattle newspaper, four years ago. The cutline beneath the photo didn't even mention her name.

The look in her eyes made Rand ache for her. He could almost hear her say, *What about me? What about our future?*

It's possible that even then a blood vessel in Ted's brilliant brain was thinning, or thickening, or whatever blood vessels do when they veer from normal.

And were blood vessels in my heart, even then, changing, narrowing? Was plaque stacking up along my artery walls??

Was Ted Wilder warned, as I was?

"The Seattle article says he was talking to a venture capital company," Serena said, "but he didn't say who. I wonder if it was Percival."

A cartoon drawing of an old western melodrama villain, the kind who tied the heroine to the railroad tracks, got Rand's attention. He clicked on a highlighted word. *Whodunnit?*

The screen morphed to a black screen with the handle of a knife protruding and red drops trailing from the knife off the bottom of the page. He scrolled down. The red drops rained on the words: *Who killed...?*

Below the question was a list of high-profile murder cases. He clicked on the first one he recognized, a young pregnant woman in California whose body was found, along with her unborn baby, on a cold, rocky beach. He went back to the black *Who killed?* page and clicked on *The Electric Car.* Instantly he was on a site that lionized the movie by that name.

Back again. *Who killed...? Suncatcher Solar Cells.*

He told Serena and she went to the same site. The room was quiet as they read.

"Wow," she said at last. "Who writes this stuff? I need to disinfect my keyboard."

"The thing is," he said, "nothing starts from zero anymore. Conspiracy theorists are everywhere, ready to pounce. All they need is a cell phone, a laptop, or an internet café. Finn Wilder got a lot of angels who want to join his parade. Stand up for Suncatcher, for the little town with the big dreams and the empty factory, and you'll be standing up for the American economy. Finn tapped into a reservoir of goodness. That's what will be on the network news."

"But?" Serena asked.

Rand nodded and leaned back in his chair. "But the blogosphere is on fire to find a villain. Someone to excoriate. For every Jean Valjean, a Javert."

He thought of the Enron scandal, of the tape recording of Ken Lay's minions, laughing as a forest fire shut down a major transmission line into California; saying, *Burn, baby, burn.*

"You sound like you don't buy that."

He shrugged. "The tendency in such cases is to assume the blackguard is the rich guy. Being rich, I take issue. Let's say I buy a company that's a day away from bankruptcy. I close their factory that employs one hundred people to make a product that sells for less than the cost of making it."

She nodded. "Hence the bankruptcy."

"Yes. Then I invest in a new factory that employs fifty people making a product that sells for ten times the cost of making it. Wages go up; jobs are stable."

"But you're a villain who put fifty people out of work."

"That's right. The fact that the next day one hundred people would be out of a job with nothing on the horizon is ignored in favor of Name That Villain." He took a long drink from his bottle of water.

"Jeff and I aren't involved in anything like my example," he said. "We don't count widgets or add up payrolls. We don't close factories. But we do invest money and we do look for profit."

"More like the oil can than the ax," she mused.

"Say, what?"

"The Tin Man, in the 'Wizard of Oz.'"

He said nothing and she sighed in exasperation.

"The Tin Man with the ax," she said, deliberately, as if speaking to someone who'd missed the twentieth century and for whom English was a fourth language. "He had a job to do. Cut down trees. Hence the ax."

Rand nodded slowly. "An ax. Pre-Industrial Revolution."

"Yes. And he rusted. No moving parts. Dorothy used the oil can. You, and Jeff, are Dorothy. Analogy complete."

Another knock on the door. This time Serena rose and opened it. "Luanne! Hi."

"You look like you feel a lot better," Luanne said.

"How 'bout me?" Rand asked.

She grinned. "You look like you need some sleep."

"Nailed it," Serena said. "I think he's got a w-o-m-a-n on his mind."

"You don't need to spell in front of me," he groused. "I'm not a d-o-g."

Luanne caught sight of his screen. "What's up?"

"Oh, lots of chatter about Suncatcher and other green energy companies. Don't you have an appointment with the CBS guy at ten?"

"His crew got pulled off to cover something else.

176

We'll either do it after three or tomorrow."

Rand tapped on some keys. "Look at this car. It was designed in a wind tunnel to reduce drag. It's a two-seater hybrid-electric that gets three hundred miles to a gallon."

"Have you heard anything new from Finn?" Serena asked.

"That's why I'm here. Hugo said to use their fax for anything I needed, and Finn faxed the brief filed by Percival on behalf of Suncatcher. I don't have time to read it." She held out the papers to Rand. "You want to see it first?"

"Sure." He set the pages beside his computer.

"Serena and I are going to see Cory. When will your family and Jeff get here?"

"Around four. You want to meet for lunch?"

"No, thanks. We're making an early lunch for Cory. She's got cabin fever. Oh, do you want to be in the pool? Everybody's betting on when the babies arrive." She pulled a folded sheet of paper out of her purse. "It's a buck to get in."

He pulled out a ten. "I want ten chances to be right. What do you have?"

"Most of the bets are for next week, starting Monday. I can put you down for Wednesday afternoon and Thursday night."

"What about sooner?"

"Sooner? Do you know something her doctor doesn't know? Her due date is fourteen days from now."

"Put me down for this Sunday. Ten bets, all on Sunday."

She wagged her finger back and forth. "No, no, no. You can't take Cory for a ride up Apple Mountain Road."

"Rats!" He glowered. "Put me down anyway."

He walked them out to Luanne's car and watched them pull away. Serena was a new woman today. Most of the change was thanks to Jeff saying the right thing. And doing the right thing, flying to Montana to tell her in person.

Rand hoped his buddy would say the right thing when he got the baby-on-board news, but somehow his level of worry didn't rise above his ankles. Jeff's sincerity and Serena's determination would carry them through. And there's usually more than one right answer.

Or maybe he was seeing everything through rose colored glasses. Love-tinted lenses.

Serena had confided the night before, when he drove her out to the Rocking Star Guest Ranch, that she was looking forward to meeting Cory and her family, especially since Cory knew so much about babies.

"I don't have girlfriends, Rand," she'd said. "I haven't had girlfriends since I got out of high school. No, before that. Around the time I applied to Harvard my friends closed their doors; I don't go to class reunions. I've been living in a man's world ever since. Competing. Trusting no one. Jealous of every wedding, every pregnancy."

She'd grown quiet, looking out at the moon.

"I can't go back to Dallas. I don't fit in that box any more."

"You don't have to sign any contracts tonight. Talk to Jeff tomorrow," he'd urged.

He went back inside the bank, spoke to Betsy and Hugo while he poured a cup of coffee, and returned to the conference room.

Before he read his email, he picked up the *amicus curiae* brief filed in Federal District Court by Percival Partnerships Limited. Who were these business bozos who'd "helped" Ted Wilder lose his shirt?

He skimmed through the first three pages, slowed down. Went back. Read the first three pages carefully, the fourth, turned to the fifth.

"Oh, shit!"

****

"Fifteen minutes of fame is a lot more than I want," Luanne said. She sat on a stool in the bar of The Mineshaft, the mayor on one side of her and the bank president on the other. All over town DVD recorders were saving copies of ABC, CBS, NBC and CNN news. The NBC affiliate in Boise, Idaho, was doing a substantial feature on companies in the Pacific Northwest that were changing history by changing the way people produce and use energy.

Advances in solar energy and improvements in windmill technology were the tent poles of the feature, the reporter had explained to her, but there were segments about geothermal energy, hybrid cars, and the enormously important oil shale business in Canada. Also, they emphasized conservation.

The feature had expanded so much, the reporter said, that it would be in two parts. He didn't know if Suncatcher would be featured tonight or tomorrow. All his footage was available to the NBC Nightly News producer, but since that producer was sending a business-energy expert from CNBC, the guy from Idaho would probably be ignored.

"The bartender will turn up the volume when the news comes on," Mayor Aldo Rasmussen said. "You want another beer, Luanne?"

"No, thanks." She didn't want the one she had, either. She swallowed four ibuprofen pills with bottled water she carried in her purse.

Dexter walked in and greeted the two men, tipped his hat to Luanne, and looked for a place to sit.

She was glad to be at the bar with all the seats filled. Dexter made the rounds of the tables, called out to someone he knew to save him a seat, and

179

came back to stand behind Luanne.

"What are you having, Luanne?"

"I'm set, Dexter." She put her hand over the top of her glass. "One is plenty."

He called out his order to the bartender and reached around her to get a handful of beer nuts. "You on TV tonight?"

"I don't know. It's gotten to be a blur." She'd started off the day in a light gray dress with her red, white and blue scarf. She'd gone home late in the afternoon to feed the dogs and change into jeans and a Levi jacket.

"I talked to Finn about half an hour ago," he said. His left hand snaked around her again and emptied the glass nut bowl. "He thinks it's a toss up tomorrow. I guess the judge is a jerk or something."

"We'll see." She doubted that Finn would make any such statement to Dexter, but she didn't want to prolong the conversation. She turned to the mayor and asked about the set up time for the vendor's booths. Her headache was getting incrementally worse.

"Excuse me, Aldo," she said before he finished answering her question. "I'll be back in a few minutes."

In the ladies' room she took her time. Brushed her hair, touched up her mascara and lipstick. A break from the noise in the bar took the edge off her headache.

The day had been long and intense. She'd gotten the first phone call ten minutes before six, eight o'clock on the east coast, and agreed to a radio interview at seven. It had been a mess at first; she kept stepping on the interviewer's questions. After doing that four or five times, she got the hang of it.

She hoped she sounded passionate about the subject, which she was, but not like a cock-eyed optimist, which she wasn't. In the light of what Finn told her about the judge and the hearing scheduled for nine o'clock Friday morning, optimism was hard to come by.

Finn had called at eight-thirty. He wanted her to see some papers and wondered where she'd like to pick up the fax. She could have said, "The mayor's office," but instead she'd said the bank. More convenient, since she was to pick up Serena there.

Yeah? Better chance to see Rand Monahan is more like it. She could barely keep her hands off him. And yesterday in Hugo Hall's office she'd been the prissy one—the *ruthless* one—who said she would avoid him and concentrate on business. "Until Sunday" had been her declaration.

She'd been proud of herself last night, at the Mineshaft and then at her house. Friendly, but at arm's length. Of course, they were both concentrating on Serena.

When the two of them left, she'd sagged against the door. About as ruthless, and toothless, as a jellyfish.

Then all night she'd dreamed of being in Rand's arms. Maybe she should admit defeat. Tonight? No, his family was here. He was with them now, at the dude ranch. He'd invited her to join them for dinner, but she'd said no. Why?

Some kind of self-flagellation campaign? I want to be with Rand, so I should say No and build character?

She returned to the bar and slid onto her stool.

"Just in time," Aldo said, pointing at the TV. "Here it comes."

The earnest young man from Boise, Kenny Thorn, was shown on a ranch near Bitter Falls. He showed the roof, covered with large solar panels, and went inside the garage to show the equipment that turned the solar heat into electricity.

"Here's something I've never seen before,"

181

Kenny said. "An electric meter that runs backward. When the system makes more electricity than the family needs, they sell it back to the grid."

Suddenly, there she was on the screen. All the people in the bar whooped and whistled. "Lookin' good, girl!" she heard someone call. She felt her face turn the color of a very bad sunburn. She listened to herself answer Kenny's questions, keeping the emphasis where she wanted it, on how this *American* invention, based on groundbreaking work that won the Nobel Prize in Chemistry for an *American* physicist, should be developed and manufactured in *America*.

A bellow of "Damn right!" and "Luanne, you rock!" filled the bar and turned the heads of all the diners in the restaurant. She laughed, grinned, and continued to blush.

But she noticed one person wasn't sharing in the party atmosphere. Dexter Stone. What a jerk.

On the TV screen, Kenny Thorn was standing by an old ranch windmill. He'd shot that scene before interviewing Luanne. He told her he'd even gotten the rancher to drive two cows over to the stock trough so he could make his point. The footage that followed, of enormous windmills, was file footage shot elsewhere. Some was on the island of Maui; some was Washington along the Columbia River.

She ordered a club soda and watched the ABC Evening News. They interviewed Finn in front of the federal courthouse in New York City where a three judge panel would meet at nine the next morning.

"Bitter Falls, Montana," said the anchorman, "is The Little Town That Could. They're chugging uphill against powerful forces, but they won't give up."

Pictures of Ted filled the screen. Ted working on the solar cells, Ted hiking. Back on camera, Finn made the same point she had: American invention, American manufacture. The bar erupted again in chauvinistic delight. Bitter Falls, of thee we sing.

"Thanks for the beer," she said to Aldo the mayor. "Time for me to go."

"Anything I can do to help, any hour, you call," Aldo said. "Good luck tomorrow."

"Thanks, Aldo." Both the CBS and NBC interviews would be in the morning. What she feared was that the court ruling would come down—against Suncatcher—and she'd be in front of a camera when it happened or shortly thereafter.

Her intention was to drive home, but she wasn't surprised when her car aimed itself toward Rocking Star Guest Ranch. She was eager to meet Dinah, Kurt and the kids. She knew Rand wanted Erik and Sophie to meet Laddie and Max. And he'd called from the Bitter Valley Airport to tell her his grandfather surprised him by coming, too.

Maybe the two of them could take Erik and Sophie to the carnival on Saturday, and then take the dogs for a long walk. Images of herself in the heart of Rand's family teased at her mind.

"Oh, face it," she muttered. "I'm in this up to my eyebrows."

She drove over a ridge and saw the glow on the horizon where the full moon was about to appear. If she hurried, she'd be with Rand when it rose over the beautiful valley ranch.

Moonlight, fresh-cut grass, horses nickering to each other. Mountains in the distance; constellations winking through the gathering darkness. Rand's lips on hers.

She didn't believe in magic, any more than she believed in ghosts, but there was something about this full moon in the month of harvests and hunting that pulled at her, as if the water in every cell of her body was surrendering to a tidal tug.

What had Rand said as he'd kissed her on his grandfather's land on Apple Mountain Road?

Resistance would be futile.

She drove faster, under the huge timber frame that marked the entrance to the ranch. Aloud she repeated what she'd told him out on the sunsplashed hillside.

"I'm not resisting."

Chapter Thirteen

Rand stood on the patio of the sprawling guest ranch and stared toward the rim of the ranch, at the area where the paved highway veered close to the Rocking Star, then angled away toward a scenic canyon. Was a car slowing? Was it turning? He blinked, trying to bring the details into focus.

Could it be Luanne?

Five days ago, when he'd driven past a sign that said, "Welcome to Bitter Falls," he didn't believe in magic.

And now?

He chuckled and leaned on one of the smooth pine logs that supported the patio roof. Now he had an open mind.

He was used to making huge bets. That was every-day life on Wall Street. A million here, a million there. No reward without risk. The market was no place for a wuss.

But when he passed that Welcome sign, and especially when he saw his cabin, he wouldn't have bet a buck-and-a-half he could last seven days in the back woods.

Now, as he recognized Luanne's car beginning the serpentine descent through rolling fields to the ranch headquarters, he was all in. His money was all on Hunter's Moon to win by a quarter mile.

He looked out on the magnificent lawn, at Erik and Sophie laughing and running like colts turned out of a corral. Grandpa, Dinah and Kurt reclined in comfortable Adirondack chairs, in a large semi-circle with a dozen more guests of the Rocking Star. At the center of the group but downwind of them, two ranch hands were adding wood to a blazing fire in a concrete pit.

The air temperature had stayed about forty-five degrees most of Thursday and the forecast was for a freeze before morning. The wind would calm and it should turn warm again. Just in time for the festival.

Judging from the swirling leaves on the ground, Rand guessed the massive shade trees on the ranch must have lost half their leaves today alone.

Inside the lodge, in a book-lined room with its own fireplace and reading lamps, Serena and Jeff were talking about their future. She'd whispered to Rand that she would tell Jeff about the baby tonight.

With regret, Rand had pulled Jeff away from Serena soon after their emotional reunion. He'd spent an hour closeted with his partner in Jeff's room. Serena understood the crisis; she'd read the *amicus curiae* brief prepared by Percival before Jeff arrived.

A chartered executive jet, a Cessna Citation 10, had delivered Rand's family, Jeff, and two of Rocky Monahan's extravagantly wealthy, auction-addict friends to Bitter Falls just before two p.m. The jet left immediately for Seattle, to pick up more of Rocky's friends, and returned.

The crew was now on required crew rest, twelve hours, sleeping in a cabin at the ranch. They'd be ready at four a.m. to fly Rand to New York. Six o'clock eastern time. He'd be cutting it close, but a helicopter would get him into the heart of Manhattan.

And he'd done a lot of the work already, by phone and computer.

In the process, he'd discovered that Dexter Stone was a more skilled newsman than he'd given him credit for. Dexter hadn't sniffed out the right tree yet, but he was getting close.

Rand had no time to waste—not with the Percival mess in New York, nor with Luanne in Montana.

Just as Caesar crossed the Rubicon, Rand had crossed the Bitter River. This was where he belonged.

He strode from the patio to the parking area and took Luanne in his arms the first instant she stepped out of her car.

"Right on time," he said as he kissed her cheek and pressed his own cheek to her soft, curly hair. "Here comes the moon."

****

Luanne was halfway home when her cell phone rang. She glanced at the number and pulled off the road.

"Hi, Finn. What's up?"

She hated to have harsh reality force its way in and crush her perfect evening, but Finn's evening was far from perfect. He would probably prefer a thousand things to staying up most of the night preparing to battle in federal district court.

"I'm just calling to say goodnight." He sounded tired. "I'm as ready as I can be. If it goes in our favor, I'll be in Montana by this time tomorrow night."

"And if not?"

He sighed. "I'll stay in New York and work on the appeal. Yost and Collyer both—the top guys—are in their office now, working. They gave me some temporary space down the hall."

"Don't tell me you're sleeping at their office," she said.

"Okay, I won't tell you. But don't worry, my best suit is hanging on the back of the door, clean and pressed."

She glanced at the clock on her dashboard. It

was a little past midnight on the east coast.

"I'm talking to NBC and CBS in the morning," she said. "Promise me you'll call me the minute you know something."

"Yeah, I promise." He said nothing for a long moment and she wondered if he'd dozed off. "Have you seen the Whodunnit site in the past hour and a half?"

She'd looked at the black screen with the handle of a knife protruding four or five, maybe six times, during the day. A click on the question *Who killed...Suncatcher Solar Cells?* went to a separate website and blog. Conspiracy theories and tirades competed for space. Finn had set the P.R. war in motion, but he didn't get to pick his soldiers.

"I haven't seen it since about five o'clock."

"It's gotten stranger. Some guy—or it could be a woman—who goes by the name 'Nobuddy' is trying to expose some company he says is behind AATech." He yawned. "Maybe he's just a pervert, and he wants to expose himself."

She laughed. "I'm not going to look at it tonight. I'd rather sleep peacefully."

"I'll talk to you tomorrow," he said. Another yawn.

"Good luck in court." She closed the phone and pulled back onto the road. Rand had followed her car for two or three miles, then turned to go to his cabin. He would be at her place in about thirty minutes.

She headed straight for her place and let the dogs in. She shivered and weighed whether or not to turn up the furnace. No, Rand had said he'd build another fire, said it made him feel manly. Not that he needed any help with that.

IMHO. She laughed. *LOL.*

Whoa. I spent too much time on the internet today.

She took off her jeans and western shirt and

took a quick shower. She'd just dried off when she heard the doorbell. She slipped into her long terrycloth robe, looped the belt end over end, and padded barefoot to the front door.

A peek through the eyepiece showed it was, in fact, Rand.

"Come in. Would you like a cup of Irish coffee while you build a fire?"

He said nothing, but as he closed the door behind him she could read *fire* in his eyes. With one quick tug from him, her cloth belt fell loose and her robe gapped. The cold air that had whistled in with him brushed across her naked body, but only for a moment.

Before she could think, he'd slipped his hands inside the robe and pressed her tight against him. He claimed not just her lips, but her mouth. Not just her mouth, but all of her.

His silence was more intimate than any words could be.

He picked her up and carried her down the hall, kicking her door closed with his foot. Gently, he set her on her feet. With one hand, he pulled the neat gray cover and sheets loose where she'd tucked them in that morning.

She dropped her arms and the robe fell to the floor. Shivering a little at the cold, she sandwiched herself between the white sheets. Or was the shivering from anticipation?

He turned on the small gray art-deco lamp on the bedside table and quickly removed his tailored shirt, slacks, and briefs.

She had a moment to admire his erection in the soft light, and then he was under the sheets with her. His hands, his lips seemed to be everywhere, and she floated in another world, another dimension. Ecstasy.

So this is what it's like to be cherished.

It was all physical—and all mental—at the same time. Nothing was spoken, and everything was said.

He kissed the valley between her breasts and sucked gently on one nipple and the other. His tongue was by her ear, his voice whispering the words she wanted him not to whisper but to shout: *I love you. Luanne. I love you.*

She wrapped her hand around his shaft and wondered which of them was getting more pleasure. Laughing and nipping his shoulder, she rolled on top of him and centered herself over him. Inching down, again, then up, she teased them both. She was right on the edge of a climax.

"I have to get—" he said.

She pressed her fingers to his lips. "No. I want all of you."

"Are you sure?"

In answer she pressed her hips down and took all of him inside herself, then stopped moving.

Rand felt the muscles inside her clench his shaft and release, driving him to the edge of a canyon, staring into a lake with no known bottom. He'd thought their first time to make love was perfect, but that didn't compare with this.

He moved, raising her rhythmically with his hips. Each thrust was better than the one before. Each thrust a promise of forever. And the last one was the best.

"Oh, Rand!" she called. "I am...yes!"

He felt her shudder of pleasure pass through both their bodies like a wave breaking on the beach.

He cried out, but what words he spoke he couldn't say for certain. Her name, and yes, and love. Spent, he panted and felt the wave recede, leaving him on warm, sparkling sand. He trembled like the gold leaves he'd studied by the river, leaves held to the branch by a molecule, begging the wind to gust once and fulfill their destiny.

Luanne made a noise that might be a giggle of delight. Her left hand stretched out to a flag of tissue in a dispenser beside the lamp. Gently, she rolled to her right and snuggled up against him.

"I hope..." she began, then kissed his shoulder.

"Tell me."

"I hope we made a baby. It's the right time for me."

"Oh, sweetheart, nothing would make me happier. You'll be a wonderful mother." He laughed and sat up. "I have a surprise for you. But first we have to have a fire."

He got up and put his pants and undershirt on. "You rest. I'll come get you when the fire is suitably romantic and the Irish coffee is hot."

By the light of the lamp he could see her smile of contentment. Her glow of love. He was the luckiest man alive.

Half an hour later he woke her with a kiss, helped her into her robe, and followed her to the couch. Only firelight and a floor lamp in a distant corner of the room gave off light.

He went down on one knee in front of her. Taking her left hand in his, he smiled. "Luanne, will you marry me?"

Her breath caught and she coughed. "Will I—?"

"Marry me. Have a family. Have a future together."

"I—I want to. But how could we? I mean, live in New York? I've never even been there."

"Where we live doesn't matter. Just as long as we're together."

She rubbed his hands nervously. "I want to say yes, but—"

"Then say yes. I promise you, we'll work out every wrinkle. I'm sick of New York."

As soon as he said it, he knew it was true on another level, too. His life in New York was killing him, just as Jeff's maniacal money fetish was killing him. It was time for a major change. A rejuvenation.

He reached in his pocket and pulled out a turquoise blue box. "I had some help getting this today." He opened the hinged box.

"Oh, Rand, it's—it's beautiful."

He lifted the one-carat solitaire in a simple platinum setting from the box and slid it onto her finger. He'd called her grandmother for her ring size—and for advice. Amelia Holt said if he bought Luanne a five- or six-carat diamond ring she would never wear it; she'd keep it in a safe deposit box.

"And while she wouldn't say it for fear of hurting your feelings," Amelia added, "I know she'd think it was an obscene misuse of money. Ever since she was a little girl, she's gotten more joy from buying toys for poor children and goats for African villages than receiving gifts herself."

With Amelia's advice, and Dinah's contacts at Tiffany's in Greenwich, Connecticut, plus email, he'd chosen the ring and had it delivered to Dinah in time for their flight.

Luanne turned her hand one way and the other, catching the firelight in the facets of the diamond. Again she marveled, "It's beautiful. Exactly what I'd want if I had a thousand rings to choose from."

He stood and she rose, throwing her arms around his neck. As he kissed her lips, he untied the belt of her robe and slid it to the edge of her shoulders. At that point, gravity was his friend.

"Show me again how much you love me," she said, with a wicked gleam in her eyes. Funny what tricks firelight can play.

She reached for the afghan on the back of the couch and helped him lay it in front of the fire.

After they made love, slowly, savoring every sensation, he listened to her breathing get slow and rhythmic. She had a smile on her beautiful face, and that put a smile on his.

He added logs to the fire and drank black coffee.

At three o'clock, with the fire nearly out, he carried her to bed and kissed her again.

Laddie and Max had taken over the bedroom in their absence. Supine on their dog beds, they opened their eyes a few millimeters to see who was traipsing through their dominion, identified the night visitor as Friend, not Foe, and dropped back into deep sleep.

Before Rand put on his jacket, he turned the ringer of Luanne's phone back on. The number eight blinked.

Outside there was only him, and the clear, cold air, and the white, full moon.

He drove to the small airport. Taking his briefcase and computer out of his car, he locked the SUV and walked with heavy steps toward the open tarmac gate. The pilot was walking around the sleek jet with a checklist.

Rand returned his wave and climbed the narrow steps into the luxurious interior. It was like walking the plank, backward. He strapped into his wide leather seat and tilted back until he was nearly horizontal.

If luck was with him, he'd sleep the three hours it would take to get to New York.

Chapter Fourteen

Luanne didn't feel right about wearing the ring. Yes, Rand's sister knew about it, and Grandma Amelia, but she'd still prefer to announce the engagement when she and Rand were together. Then she'd wear it everywhere and accept the gushing Ohhhhs and Ahhhhs of people around town, some of whom had known her since her front teeth came out on the same day and earned her a quick fifty cents.

When she awoke alone in her bed, she wondered if she'd dreamed the whole lovely scenario. But the diamond on her left hand said it was all real. Her Prince had come. She'd shivered once with sheer delight, and then again—when she tossed back her covers—with sheer frostbite.

Where is His Royal Highness now? He's not in my bed.

Her second and third clues that her Prince had come—and gone!—were, one, no heavenly fragrance of coffee, and two, no heat.

She swore softly as she put on her robe and scrounged in the bottom of her closet for slippers. In the living room, she went through a foggy-headed check list. Furnace off. No fire in the fireplace. Flue open. Oh, yeah.

She closed the chimney flue, turned on the furnace, put coffee on to brew, and got into a hot shower. Once all the essentials were taken care of, including getting her hair dry and finding an attractive wool pantsuit, coral scarf, and her best earrings, she was ready to face the day.

Or not. Thinking how the day included being interviewed on network television, *ready* was clearly an overstatement.

"Gotta do what I've gotta do!" she said.

Laddie and Max strolled in and waited politely at the sliding glass door to go outside. She opened the door and groaned to see their outdoor water bowls were crusted with ice. She brought them inside and set them in the sink to melt. The boys would be spending a lot more time inside now.

Rand was in for a shock when he met Old Man Winter. He said he was sick of New York and that they'd work out details of where to live, but in the cold—very cold—light of morning, Luanne had a lot to worry about.

Her home, her business, her dogs. Her whole life was in Montana. Sure, Grandma would only be here in the summer—a season loosely defined as July and half of August—but Cory lived here. And Rebecca and Rachel, and the new babies.

One word ricocheted through her brain. Baby, baby, oh baby.

Oh, my God.

She and Rand had made love with no protection. Right at her most fertile time of month. Was she—right this minute—pregnant? She returned to her bedroom and took a good look in the mirror. As if that was worth a soggy dog biscuit. Cell division at the molecular level wasn't likely to show up in her face. What did she think? She'd find a hickey?

In the kitchen she reached for the coffee carafe and noticed something she'd overlooked when she was suffering from hypothermia. A sheet of paper, folded over. With her name on it.

"Dearest love..."

She couldn't help herself. She cooed.

"...I have to be gone most of the day. Business. I can't take care of it from Bitter Falls, especially with

Jeff as hard to reach as I am. I'll explain when I see you—dinner time at the latest, at the Rocking Star. I miss you already. Good luck with the interviews. I know you'll be great."

He signed it, "All my love forever and ever, Rand."

She put the note in her purse and started to remove her ring, then decided to hurry over to Cory's. She had to share the news with her best friend.

Correction. Her second-best friend. From here on out until forever—and ever—Rand would be number one in her life. She'd be Luanne Monahan. Wife and, hopefully someday soon, a mother.

"Oh, my God," she said again. If someone stuck a microphone in her face and said, "Tell me all about the man!" she would run out of things to say in three minutes flat. What did she know about Rand Monahan? Not even his middle name, that's what.

Okay, she knew some urgently important things about his body, but she wouldn't tell anyone about that.

She removed the dry cleaner's plastic from her dressy winter coat and hurried out to her car. Thank goodness she had a garage and didn't have to scrape frost off the windshield.

On her way to Cory's, she listed the things she didn't know about her fiancé. He'd said his grandfather, and Dinah, and her kids, were his only family. What about his parents?

Has he—?

She almost drove into a ditch.

Has he ever been married before?

She turned on the radio, which was still set on CD. Like some perverse force in the universe, Michael Bublé offered her a hand to hold when leaves begin to fall. She pressed eject and listened to the farm report instead.

In her head she composed a personals ad. Small town redhead, thirty, seeks single white straight male, thirty-six, good with dogs and children.

Good in bed.

She laughed. Seriously, though, she needed to talk to him about his past, and where they would live. She'd been raised not to ask questions about anyone's bank balance, but she had to ask him. Maybe he was rich, but maybe he was horrifically over-extended and about to be poor.

"A million dollars is a lot of money," her father always said, "but not when you owe two million."

She'd just read in the paper yesterday about a movie director who was worth six million dollars, but he owed the government eight million in back taxes. Not only was he dead broke, but he was going to prison.

And the jeweler had repossessed his wife's five-carat diamond ring.

She looked at hers. Yes. Comfortable discussion or not, we have to talk.

If her parents were alive, her father would have the talk with Rand. The "no stone unturned" talk. If her dad and mom hadn't died so tragically, one year after she finished college, Hal Holt would have had the talk with Ted. Not just the "Can you support a family?" talk, but the "When's the wedding?" talk.

Her eyes filled with tears and she dabbed them gently with a tissue. She caught a glimpse of herself in the rear view mirror and swore. She'd have to touch up her mascara at Cory's before she faced the TV cameras.

It looked like it would be a long day. Right now, in New York, Finn Wilder was probably walking into the courtroom. *All rise.*

And the longest, bleakest, part of the day was that she wouldn't see Rand for hours. Where had he gone? Missoula? He'd said something when they drove back from Rocky's land about facilities for secure video conferencing at a large regional bank in Missoula. He could use it, he'd said, even if the other people were in Dubai, Shanghai, and New York.

She hoped that meant he wouldn't have to travel much when they were married. Missoula was far enough and big enough.

But here she was again—going off in her mind about living in Bitter Falls, when they hadn't discussed it, and it was probably impossible. Why would a man used to New York City consider moving to a place the size of a peach pit?

She sighed and muttered under her breath. "Time. For. The. Talk."

She turned down the road beside the irrigation canal.

That's when she saw the ambulance.

****

Rand waited for the helicopter's rotors to stop. Through the rain-streaked glass of the waiting area he saw Merry Lou Shore's assistant, Terrence Wong.

A woman in an international orange raincoat darted to the chopper and opened his door. Rand jumped down and sprinted to the executive elevator booth.

"How were your flights, sir?" Wong asked. "Your suit is in your office and the car service will be downstairs in seven minutes."

Merry Lou Shore greeted him as soon as he got off the elevator and began a rapid fire update on what she'd learned. Twenty blocks away, in his office, he peeled off his sleep-rumpled and rain-wet sport coat and shirt, dropping them where they fell.

In the closet-sized bathroom he shared with Jeff, he removed his slacks and dressed in the fresh clothes Merry Lou had placed so efficiently on the back of the door. In that space, he got a sense of what Superman accomplished in a phone booth.

He'd shaved as the plane taxied to the executive terminal.

As soon as he came out of the bathroom, Merry Lou swiveled his desk monitor toward him and pointed at the picture of a man, maybe forty, with deep-set, hooded eyes. There was something Mediterranean about him. Maybe Greek.

"What do you have?" He flipped the silk tie into a perfect Windsor knot without looking at a mirror.

"The real owner of Allied Advent Technology is a Russian national, Sergei Alexandrovich. This guy, Ollie Pappas, is his front. Sergei can't legally touch anything in this country. Of course, that works two ways. We can't touch him, unless he's on a plane that is forced by emergency to land on American soil. I think the FBI is hoping to stage such an emergency, but he might die of old age before that happens."

"What about Ollie Pappas? Is he in New York now?"

"Better than that. He's in New York—in federal custody."

He ran back into the bathroom and ran a brush through his damp hair. Merry Lou, so efficient that her nickname was Money Penny, stood by his open office door with his raincoat at the ready.

Wong stood just outside with his laptop, briefcase, and an umbrella.

"I uploaded the files to your computer, replaced your phone battery," Wong said, "and there's a printout to read on your way to the courthouse."

"And Finn Wilder is expecting me?"

He didn't hear the answer as the door of the express elevator closed behind him. He called Jeff in Montana. Without a hello, he asked, "Any news?"

"Yost's sister, the CBS producer, finally took my call. She's a brick wall. Nothing. But I buttered up the CBS reporter who's here, and he hinted that something big will break on the noon news in New York. He's pissed because it's going to cut into his air time from Montana tonight."

Rand strode across the lobby and out to the black Lincoln, staying dry thanks to the doorman's huge umbrella. He gave the address to the driver.

"Yes, sir. Be there in ten." The car shot out from the curb and Rand lurched to his left, right, left as the driver expertly wove through traffic.

"Have you seen Luanne?" he asked Jeff.

"Just from a distance. She's at the mercy of the reporters. NBC and CBS both. Oh, and her friend is in the hospital. The one who's having twins."

"Cory DeSoto. Sounds like I'll lose my ten bucks. I was betting on Sunday."

"I don't know the details—you know me and women. But there was some emergency."

"Oh, hell. See what you can find out. Luanne must be worried out of her mind. I've got to go. Showtime."

The car slid into a No Stopping zone, and the driver hopped out to open the back door.

Inside the federal courthouse, Rand closed and shook his umbrella, placed it on the conveyor belt, and began emptying his pockets and removing the computer from its case. The security guards moved like molasses in January, and he ground his molars in frustration. He knew that one word of complaint would be enough for them to slow down to glacier speed.

My tax dollars at work.

Finally he reached the correct courtroom. The guard studied his visitor's badge as if it were the first such badge he'd ever seen—and written in Sanskrit. He insisted on seeing Rand's phone to be sure it was off, and warned him of the dire consequences if he turned it on inside the courtroom. Finally, he hiked his gun belt up on his hips like

Wyatt Earp at the OK Corral and told Rand he could go inside.

Oh, please, Rand chirped in his head, *allow me the opportunity to kiss your fleshy buttocks, first!*

As soon as he entered the overheated room, with its tall ceilings, no windows, and air that had not totally re-circulated since New York was New Amsterdam, he spotted Finn Wilder.

This didn't seem like the right courtroom for what was, at its core, a patent case. Like a bacteria colony with unlimited food supply, the case had grown and swelled until it was more than the sum of its parts.

About half the seats were occupied; all the people looked bored. Although they were dressed for success, they were sweating like tobacco farmers. The bench was empty, but from the way people stared at the three massive chairs, it wouldn't be empty long.

Finn covered the length of the center aisle in four strides of his long legs. "Rand, good to see you." He held out his hand. "Finn Wilder."

"Is the court on a break?"

"Yes. They're working two cases simultaneously. Maybe more than two. They went to another courtroom fifteen minutes ago. Nobody dares step outside; they could be back in one minute, or an hour."

"I'd like to have the hand fan concession in here," Rand said.

"I think the judges have electric fans under their robes." He motioned to Rand to walk with him. In a corner, he asked if Rand's attorneys had made any progress with AATech.

"Yes, but their board won't deal until the court rules."

"They're pretty confident, huh?" Finn rubbed his jaw.

"If they win, and I'll admit they might, they think they'll be in a position to demand more on the buyout. But they'll be pissing up a rope. Did you hear that Ollie Pappas is in federal custody?"

"No shit? I haven't heard anything since I got here two hours ago."

"Trust me, a lot of people are working on it."

"What about Luanne?" Finn asked. "Does she know about your, uh, involvement?"

Rand snorted. "Involvement? That's a mighty delicate way to put it, Finn. I'm involved the way a pig is involved in frying bacon. And no, she doesn't know."

A door opened at the front of the courtroom and Finn slipped down the side aisle and back to his seat at the front of the room, facing the judges.

"All rise," the bailiff called.

Rand opened the massive carved door and left. He had appointments with bankers, lawyers, and the best fraud investigator money could buy. What he couldn't buy was a pass from the news media to keep his name out of this. If they discovered his "involvement," he didn't want to think how Luanne would react.

All he could do was—do the right thing. And pray for a break. He figured he had four hours, at the most.

In the limo he gave his next address to the driver.

"Sure thing, sir. Be there in fifteen."

The pain that felt like a bad crick in the neck since he woke up now moved down into his left shoulder. He got the vial of nitro pills out of his pocket and read the label. Instead of taking one, he pulled up a number he'd had on his speed dial for the past three months.

It could be a simple problem. Wasn't Brogen prone to exaggeration? Yes. The stents were a modern miracle.

He wracked his brain, trying to remember what he'd read about restenosis. Statistically...He couldn't think of the numbers.

But I've never needed a second nitro tablet. Brogen and everyone else had been very clear on that point. Needing one was nothing to be alarmed about. Even two wasn't that bad. If the pain stopped with a second nitro, a guy was probably okay. Three, well, that's another story. Take tablet number three, and call 9-1-1.

Through the sunroof, pelted with rain, he looked up at the blurred skyscrapers where the Masters of the Universe played chess with real kings and pawns. And they played for keeps.

He stared at Brogen's number. *No, not now.*

He took one tablet from the vial and put it under his tongue.

Chapter Fifteen

"Ma'am, excuse me," the nurse said. "You can't have a cell phone on in here."

Luanne looked at Finn's phone number on her caller ID, and turned it off. When it rang, she was already half-way down the hall to Intensive Care. She paused. Should she turn around? No, she'd check on Cory, and then call Finn back.

The waiting room was full of strangers; Kent must be in with Cory. She sat down and listened to the people, who all seemed to know each other, talking about a man with a heart attack. Kelly, or maybe they said Kiley.

The Bitter Valley Hospital was small enough that maternity and surgical ICU were together. Pediatrics and babies had their own ICU. And if it was a serious situation involving tiny babies, they were sometimes transported by air to Missoula.

Cory would go insane if she gave birth and the babies were whisked away on a helicopter.

When Luanne arrived at Cory's house, ready to blurt out her happy news, Cory was already in the ambulance. Kent was standing at the open door, waiting to get in beside her. In the two minutes she had to talk to him, she'd learned that Cory had fainted in the bathroom, and when she fell something had happened to her abdomen. She'd screamed in pain, Kent called 9-1-1, and that's all he knew.

Since then, Kent had updated her by phone between and after her brief interviews with the two reporters. The doctor on call and Cory's obstetrician had determined that she had a slight tear in the placenta. The babies were all right; heartbeats were strong, no signs of distress. Cory's blood pressure was fluctuating too much for them to do surgery now. She was being watched, with monitors all over her. The doctors said they were taking advantage of time to stabilize her.

The best obstetric surgery specialist in Montana was on vacation not far from Bitter Falls. If Dr. Jenna could be contacted by the ranger in the national park, the state police would rush her to the hospital. If not, and if Cory's obstetrician said he couldn't handle the surgery, they might have to medi-vac her to Missoula.

Kent came out and Luanne jumped to her feet. "How is she? Are they going to fly her to Missoula?"

"She's okay, really! They are keeping her still, and they say it will be all right. She's not in labor. They don't want to do anything yet." He wiped his fingers through his hair.

"Can I go in? I don't want to take your time, but—"

"Five minutes. And if that male nurse who looks like Shrek tells you time is up, believe him. She's in the second room on your left as you enter."

"I'll be back in five." She took a deep breath. *Phone off, check. Engagement ring on, check. Terrified look off my face, check.*

At the swinging doors plastered with Do Not warnings, she timidly pushed one enough to slip through. There were four glass rooms and a nursing station at the hub. Two of the rooms were dark and the curtains were half closed. The other two were lit up like stage productions with the curtains pulled wide so nurses could keep a wary eye. Machines beeped and bleeped and hummed. Phones rang at the desk.

Good luck getting any sleep in here.

She walked straight ahead, fearful that some overzealous nurse would throw her against the wall and say, "Who said you could come in here?" Instead two women looked up, smiled, and went back to what they were doing.

Second room on the left. *Made it.*

"Hey, girlfriend," Cory said. "Don't look so scared. I'm going to be fine. I'm just going over names for boys in my head."

Luanne put her left hand in front of her face as if covering a yawn and waggled her fingers. "I was on my way over to show you this when you turned into a drama queen."

"Oh, girl! That's gorgeous. I'd hug you, but that would set off more alarms than a ticking time bomb in the U.S. Mint."

"Do you really feel all right, or are you being all brave and dramatic?"

"Hey, when have I ever been brave? Honestly, I'm okay. Where's the groom-to-be? I want to congratulate him on his excellent taste in women." Her smile evaporated. "Oh, no. Does this mean you're moving away? I guess I didn't think about that part of getting you happily-ever-aftered."

"Nothing is decided. Rand said he's sick of New York. I'll tell you more after the two of us have time to talk."

The male nurse came in with a new bag of fluid for the IV and gave Luanne a pointed look.

"I'd better go."

"How did your interviews go? Any news from Finn?"

Luanne shook her head. "Any minute now." She blew a kiss to Cory and started to leave the glass-walled room.

Suddenly an alarm went off and the bald man said, "Stay here, please, ma'am. Don't get in the way."

206

He reached up and whipped the curtain three-quarters of the way closed. Luanne looked out through the opening.

The nurse moved fast, for a big man, into the room across the nursing station from Cory's room. Luanne watched, her eyes wide, as a team converged on the room. In a space around a bed that would be cramped for three people to stand, six squeezed in.

The alarm kept ringing.

On the loudspeaker she heard a woman paging Dr. Gupta; she knew he was a cardiologist. He burst in through the swinging doors, giving rapid orders for medication and asking for numbers.

"Clear!" someone called, and she saw them all shrink back from the bed, heard the bang of paddles to shock the poor man's heart. Silence. Then again, "Clear!" Bang, silence.

They did it a third time. The silence dragged on. She held her hand over her own heart, which was pounding, when she heard Doctor Gupta's accented voice. "I'm calling it. Eleven-nineteen."

She looked at Cory's face. Cory couldn't see anything but the curtain, but she could hear. Her face was so white the bleached linen could serve as camouflage. Luanne was sure hers looked the same.

She crept close enough to the bed to kiss Cory on the cheek. Tubes and wires seemed to be everywhere.

"I'll be back in a couple hours. I'm using up Kent's visiting time."

"Luanne," Cory said softly, "don't you want to know their names?"

"Of course." She laughed. "I never thought calling them Thing One and Thing Two like 'The Cat in the Hat' was a good idea."

"We're going to name one David for Kent's dad, and the other one Randall. Rand for short."

Luanne smiled broadly. "You amaze me. I'll let

you be the one to tell Rand about it."

She met Kent in the waiting room, painfully aware of the crying family that had just been told their loved one had died. Against her will, she remembered her own shock and grief at Ted's death. Unlike these people, who clung to each other and helped one another stand up, she'd shut everyone out. Sat in her wedding dress and rocked.

Alone, as if to share her grief made her love worth less.

For the first time, she saw her reaction as some kind of distorted mirror image of an only child who fears a new baby will take half—or more than half—of its mother's love away from her. But love is like a magical apple tree that grows a new and larger apple every time one is plucked from a stem.

Rocking upstairs at Albion House, hoarding her grief, had been selfish. The people who wanted to embrace her, to mourn Ted with her, deserved better than she could offer. By letting them comfort her, as this family was doing, she would have plucked more and more comfort from the tree.

Grief was just like love. There was always plenty to go around.

Kent walked her to the hall and gave her a squeeze around her shoulders. "I'll see you later. I'm going to hover near the ICU door like a persistent housefly until they let me in again."

She gave him one last wave and hurried down the hallways, eager to get outside so she could call Finn. Before she stepped on the rubber mat to open the automatic doors, she looked up.

The TV in the corner of the lobby was on CNN. The words SOLAR CELLS caught her eye and stopped her in mid-stride.

She moved closer and stared.

The reporter was standing in front of the Silver County Courthouse. Maybe a mile from the hospital where she stood. And the reporter was holding a microphone in front of Dexter Stone's face.

"...credit for unraveling much of this mystery. What did you think when you heard the Federal judges ruled in favor of Allied Advent Technology over the company founded by Ted Wilder?"

"There was something rotten about this from the start," Dexter said. He was lapping up the attention like an alley cat up to its knees in whipped cream. "Those Wall Street movers and shakers ripped him off and laughed all the way to the bank."

"When you dug through the tangled mess of who was behind the patent rip off, what did you find?"

"An outfit in New York, what they call a 'private investment firm,' goes by the name Morning Select Investments, stood to make a fortune off the Suncatcher Solar Cells. The owners are two New York millionaires, Rand Monahan and Jeff Adler."

"Are you all right, ma'am?" A cowboy put out his hand to keep Luanne from losing her balance.

"I'm, uh, yes. Thanks. I'll just sit down a while."

She felt with her hand until the plastic-covered chair was in line with her and sat. She looked away from the screen; her eyes fell on her hand. Her ring sparkled in the sunshine coming through the lobby windows.

She slid it off her finger and placed it delicately in the Tiffany's box, put it in her purse and closed the zipper.

CNN changed to a report of a fire in California. She rose, wobbled a little, then walked quickly to her car. Parking in the alley behind her shop, she called Finn. If she started crying, and that was a sucker bet, she didn't want to be a public spectacle.

"Hello, Finn. I'm sorry I couldn't take your call before. Tell me what happened."

****

Rand looked at the five men across the

209

conference table from him. They looked like they'd sucked lemons. In contrast, the two men on either side of him, all attorneys getting richer by the minute, looked confident.

Surreptitiously, the four of them checked their BlackBerrys beneath the table's overhang. Four racquetball reservations might have to be changed. Now things were getting serious.

"It's only money," Rand said with a magnanimous shrug. But he—and the board of directors of AATech who sat across from him—knew that a lot more than money was at stake. There was endless wrangling, and layers of lawyers, over indictments.

No, not endless wrangling. If that were the case, this would, in fact, be all about money. These red-faced, overfed men, whose trophy wives wore thousand dollar nightgowns to bed, faced the ultimate motivator on this rainy Manhattan day.

Prison time.

And the U.S. Justice Department had changed a lot since the Enron scandal. Wall Street criminals weren't incarcerated at country clubs anymore. Americans had lost enough jobs, seen enough pension funds stripped, and been kicked in the teeth by politicians enough times that the tide had turned.

Like in "Network," Americans were mad as hell, and they weren't going to take it anymore.

"Oh, wait," Rand said. "I forgot. It's not 'only money.' I have to leave in ten minutes to meet with the U.S. Attorney for the District of New York and the Deputy Director of the FBI. They'll want an answer. What do you gentlemen want me to say?"

They looked at each other, their eyes furtive and hooded, rather like plump raisins stabbed by Sophie into rising bread dough. Rand wondered if Seamus Brogen, M.D., would give them a group rate if they all showed up at Columbia-Presbyterian at the same time.

He looked at his watch, not to scare them more than they already felt, but to see if he could get in to see Brogen before he left for Montana. It took longer to fly west, against the jet stream. But it was two hours earlier in Montana.

"All right," said the man in the middle. "You win."

"No, I don't," Rand snapped. "Nobody wins in this crooked cock fight."

Especially me, he added to himself. *Especially me when Luanne hears the slanted, tainted, poisoned news.*

He'd seen the news on CNN, the interview with Intrepid Newsman, the Caped Crusader, Dexter "I'm So Smart I Scare Myself" Stone.

Luanne would believe the worst. And why shouldn't she? She barely knew the guy named Rand Monahan. Put that stranger on a see-saw with Ted Wilder, and what would happen? Ted's end, weighed down with years of love, expectation, and grief, would hit the ground like a boulder. Rand would fly off like a melon off a catapult.

Rand would never have guessed that something as weightless as a ghost could throw a shadow across everything he and Jeff had constructed and accrued.

But, setting aside that ridiculous seesaw image, he wasn't giving up. He could strategize. And as soon as he'd finished reading the *amicus curiae* brief prepared by Percival Partnerships, Limited, he'd known precisely where to aim his barrage.

"All right," the man directly across the table from Rand said again. "Our CEO will meet you at the U.S. Attorney's office. We'll give him authorization to make the best deal he can. But he doesn't know his ass from his elbow about the law you keep referring to. We want our top corporate attorney with him every minute."

Rand raised his eyebrows and consulted his four appendages, eye to eye to eye. They gave a shrug and looked at their watches.

He rose from his seat and reached his right hand across the table. One handshake. "I can delay the meeting thirty minutes. If your new CEO—what's his name again?"

"Luther Frist." The florid-faced man in the center, who'd risen to shake Rand's hand, glared at him. They all knew why Rand had emphasized how new the chief operating office of AATech was. Their old CEO, Ollie Pappas, was in federal custody, probably trying desperately to offload some of his guilt. The board's fear of Pappas making a deal before they could drove this whole drama.

"Oh, yes. Frist. You have the address of the meeting, I'm sure." He turned on his heel and walked out, four extremely well-dressed attorneys in his wake. He'd hoped to get the deal made and gift-wrapped in time for the evening news, but time was slipping through his fingers.

On the elevator, the pain was so sharp he had to hold onto the brass railing to stay upright. In the backseat of his limo, he called the number he dreaded calling.

When Brogen came on the line, less than a minute after the phone was answered, he had no time for chit chat about beautiful Montana.

"I'm in Manhattan," he said, "for another four—" He did the math in his head. Getting to the executive airport would be fast. The new crew would be there; the plane would take off immediately. Jeff had texted him that severe weather was moving north toward the Ohio Valley. He'd have to leave New York by four o'clock to avoid a time-eating storm detour well to the north of Toronto.

"I'll be in Manhattan for another three-and-a-half hours. I need to see you."

Chapter Sixteen

Luanne sat on the bench west of the courthouse. She'd parked behind the old stone building and circled wide to avoid any reporters who might be lurking. She half-expected to see Dexter Stone in klieg-lights, damning Ted Wilder with faint praise.

She'd gone home after talking to Finn. She couldn't sit in her car in the alley all day. As she'd pulled out, she saw the reporter from NBC's Seattle bureau going in the front door of Memories Mine. Thank goodness she hadn't sought refuge in there.

At home, she'd turned off the ringer on her home phone and turned off her cell. Laddie and Max, shameless as always, took advantage of her sadness. Huddled in front of the couch where she lay, knees to her chest, they took turns flopping their big heads against her, getting a week's worth of petting in an hour.

Staring at the cold, black fireplace, she could see only the blazing "manly" fire reflected in Rand's eyes. She pulled the afghan off the back of the couch and tucked it in around herself. Soon the edge was soggy with her tears.

The scent of Rand was embedded in the yarn.

About an hour of wallowing in self-pity was all she could stand, although Laddie and Max encouraged her to cry more. Their sympathy—and need for stroking—seemed endless.

Stay on the couch, they said with their soulful eyes, and the tips of their long tongues, and persistent head bumps. *Stay here. Don't get up until dawn.*

Another head bump. *Maybe not dawn. Maybe later.*

Oh, wait. What about suppertime?

She rose and they urged her toward the kitchen. *The can. Open the can.*

"You turkeys," she said. "If you could work a can opener, you wouldn't give me the time of day, would you?"

She fed them, early, and listened to her messages. Nothing from Rand. Nothing from anyone who mattered. Except two on her cell phone. Kent had called twenty minutes ago to say Cory was sleeping and everything looked good. And Serena had called an hour earlier.

Luanne made herself a cup of hot tea, drank it, then called Serena back and agreed to meet by the playground.

She looked around now, thinking Serena should be here by this time. The weather should reflect her dark mood: black clouds scudding across the sky and fierce dust devils churning the dry leaves upward, releasing them as particles that would blind and sting like angry wasps. But, no. The weatherman was right. The cold front had passed through, and the weather was spectacularly beautiful. Indian summer. The town was filling up with tourists, right on schedule, and the vendors in their booths must be happily hawking their wares and making change from their aprons.

From where she sat she could see the top of the Ferris wheel. Would Erik and Sophie enjoy the carnival? Or would they be jaded by having already been to Disney World? They were such cute kids.

"Here I am," Serena called.

Luanne waved and watched her stroll across the courthouse square. She wore jeans and a loose-fitting tunic in shades of lavender and purple, and wore high sling-backed sandals. Her long, straight

214

hair was tied back with a scarf.

"I'm sorry it took me so long to get here," Serena said. "Would you believe a traffic jam in Bitter Falls? A tour bus tried to take a tight corner and got wedged between a concrete island with a tree and an old fashioned light pole. The driver had to jockey forward and backward about six inches at a time until he could back onto Main Street and take a different route."

"I'm sorry I missed the excitement."

"When I told Dinah about this playground, she said she'd bring the kids in a little while. Jeff and Kurt are on a conference call. You can take the man out of New York, but—" She shrugged.

"What did Jeff say last night? Did you tell him about the baby?"

"He was great. He said he wished he hadn't torn up the pre-nup and thrown it away just so he could burn it in front of me. Greater love hath no man, I guess. At least no man on Wall Street."

"He's a lot funnier than I expected him to be. He and Rand are quite a pair."

Her mention of Rand seemed to hang in the air. Luanne wrapped her arms tight around herself.

"I don't know what to think, Serena. He hasn't called. I don't even know where he is. I feel like a—" She thought of Cory's word choice. "I feel like a ticking time bomb is inside me. That if he can't disarm it—and I don't even know if he wants to!— that I'll implode." She sniffed and wiped her nose. "Sorry. I'm having a pity party this afternoon. I need to face this head on."

"We all saw Dexter Stone's finest hour on CNN," Serena said. "Or finest ninety seconds. I hope you don't believe everything he says."

"My instinct says no, but my instinct is notoriously small town. Naïve. Chicken soup and a cheery smile facing down a pandemic of deadly disease."

"I'm sure Rand will be back soon and explain everything."

"You don't seem to be very upset that 'millionaire Jeff Adler' was named by Dexter. And that their company was named."

Serena shrugged. "There's more to this than meets the eye. Especially when the eye is in the head of Dexter Stone. Or in the heads of the breathless reporters who feed on character assassination." She looked toward Main Street. "Look, here comes Dinah."

Outpacing their mom, Erik and Sophie ran toward the playground.

"Hi, Luanne," Dinah said.

Luanne saw her eyes focus on her left hand. No ring.

The three of them talked about the weather, and how Cory was doing in the hospital, and the street dance that night. Dinah said she'd bought cowgirl boots for herself and Sophie.

"Kurt will take Erik shopping for western wear before the store closes." As Dinah spoke, her phone rang. She looked down at the number. "Hello?"

Luanne thought her voice, so relaxed and laughing a moment before, had turned brittle. Edgy.

To give her privacy, Luanne walked out to the swings to talk to Erik and Sophie. Soon she was roped into pushing Sophie on the swing. Erik insisted he didn't need pushing; he could pump.

Every few seconds, Luanne glanced over at the bench. Dinah was still on the phone, and Serena was staring at Dinah with an intense, worried expression.

Her phone rang. She glanced at the number and slowed Sophie down. "Sorry, Sophie, I have to answer the phone."

Erik, tired of declaring how well he could pump

while getting little hang time to show for it, called to Sophie and the two of them headed for the pioneer wagon and the fort.

Luanne sat on the swing he'd relinquished and closed her eyes. "Hello, Finn. Please skip the bullshit and tell me what's going on."

****

Rand took off his tie and unbuttoned the top two buttons of his dress shirt, but he still felt like the plane should do him a favor and drop the oxygen mask.

Finn Wilder looked like a man on his way to Mardi Gras. As the day wore on, after their first tense meeting in the courtroom, Finn's color improved. Tall and lanky from the get-go, he seemed to stand a few inches taller now.

Rand didn't need a mirror to know that his color had gone the other way. The wrong direction. Before-and-After was supposed to be a story of improvement. Like Rags-to-Riches. Like Sin-to-Redemption.

Finn got off the phone and grinned. "I gave Luanne the good news. The great news. Now can I send the story out to the reporters?"

Rand looked back at the laptop on his fold-down desk. He held up a finger to show he wasn't quite finished.

"You want something to drink?" Finn rose and opened the sleek refrigerator. "Or eat? This thing must have anything you could ask for."

Rand lowered his window shade half way so he could see his computer screen better. "What? Oh, just water. Lots of water."

"You're an easy man to please." Finn pulled the table of the aisle seat down and placed two chilled bottles and a tall glass of ice on it.

Rand rubbed his forehead and watched Finn shop through the refrigerator. He took a bowl of grapes, a carton of yogurt, and a root beer back with him to his seat.

Once again Rand concentrated on the story in front of him. During the long day, it had been constructed, and deconstructed, and reconstructed, by the lawyers. Paragraphs that purported to speak for the FBI and the United States Attorney's office had been read over the phone, texted, and revised by email until they were so antiseptic there was little there but nouns and verbs.

A word picture painted in the full range of color—from white to ivory.

Finn read it when they got on the plane and swore. "If these guys wrote 'War and Peace' it would be three pages. One page of story and two pages of footnotes, including threat of a lawsuit by Napoleon because it made him look like a loser—and too short."

He'd quickly rewritten it, told Rand he was the only one who could make a change.

Rand drank the first bottle of water, bypassing the glass and ice. "Okay. Good work. Fire when ready."

Finn took the laptop and began creating files and sending. TV stations would have to break in with the news or they'd be scooped badly by the internet.

Rand opened the second bottle of water and poured it slowly over the cubes. God, but he was tired. He was glad to "do the right thing," but why couldn't he do some of it today, some of it tomorrow, and some of it next week? *Do right* on the installment plan.

He reclined his seat part way and closed his eyes.

He'd hoped to keep his name, and Jeff's, and Morning Select's name, out of the mess, but that became impossible after Dexter Stone's premature ejaculation of all the news that's fit to print—or not.

The article, as it was going out now, was solid. Finn had done a great job of boiling it all down, getting the government's cover-your-ass-isms out of it while leaving in the human beings.

The one liberty Finn had taken with the whole truth was a small skip around how his brother had made the first deal with the first devil. Ted must have been selectively blind—or naïve—to think Percival could deliver on their grandiose promises. Somebody else up the line had the money, and Ted, out in Montana, was not in a position to ask any questions that mattered—even if, by some miracle, he'd known what to ask.

Part of what made it a great all-American story, the kind that would run on every network and the front page of hundreds of newspapers, was that it was a hero story. A hero-who-is-dead story. Why drag it down with news that the hero made some tragic mistakes?

Because whatever Ted Wilder had said and done—or left unsaid or undone—it was for the most noble of goals. If all went as he'd hoped, Suncatcher Factory would open. It turned out to be a mess, with more twists than a martini bar.

But now, with all that had happened in New York, it was turning out spectacularly well. The factory would open, people in Bitter Falls would prosper, the solar energy industry would get an injection of P.R. and investment that would lift all boats. And all around the planet people would have an efficient way to turn the rays of the sun into usable energy.

A scientist who'd filed his own *amicus curiae* brief with the court said there are at least a billion people on earth with no electricity. A small system using the kind of inexpensive cells manufactured by Suncatcher could produce modest amounts of electricity far from any grid and using no fossil fuels, enough to change the lives of a billion people.

The elegant arguments of Finn Wilder and the hotshot intellectual property firm of Yost and Collyer failed to win the case, but Rand would bet the judges cried a tear or two over the scientist's plea. It was about more than money, he'd said quite eloquently. It was about more than who would keep the profit. Suncatcher v. AATech.

The case was about the ordinary, common people—from Bitter Falls to Uganda—who would benefit if Suncatcher kept its patent.

AATech won in court, but at the end of the day, or, more precisely at two-thirty p.m. Eastern Standard Time, AATech's brand new CEO gave up all claims to the patent for Suncatcher Solar Cells. In return, they won the right to reorganize and stay out of prison. Of course, they had to do a lot more to mollify the U.S. Attorney. It would take a long time to dig deep through all the tentacles Sergei Alexandrovich and Ollie Pappas had dug into AATech, and Percival, and a dozen other American firms, but the CEO and the board of directors were "dedicated to helping the investigators."

The role played by Morning Select Investments was small. So small at its inception, in fact, that Rand and Jeff didn't know they'd invested— tangentially—in a criminal enterprise. Rand had discovered it, buried in Percival's Friend of the Court brief.

Percival Partnerships had defaulted on a package of municipal bonds. Four million dollars. They would have been bankrupt had Morning Select not stepped in and taken over their commercial bond paper. That bought Percival enough time to complete the sale of half their assets—mostly intellectual property contracts—to three buyers. In an ideal world, they could hold on to Suncatcher. But their backs were against the wall.

It's not an ideal world, Rand mused. It frequently sucks. But it's the only world we've got.

It happens all the time. Money doesn't know whose pocket it's in. Money has no brain, no conscience. The saga was a lot like the labyrinthine loans that propped up, and brought down, the subprime mortgage industry. Mr. and Mrs. Main Street take out a mortgage and move into their dream home. Then that loan—within minutes—takes on a chimerical life of its own. Sold, resold, packaged, repackaged. The question, Where did the money come from? becomes unanswerable.

"Here's a message for you," Finn said. "From Merry Lou Shore." He slid the laptop onto Rand's table.

Rand raised his seat back, read the message, and opened the attachment.

"Merry Lou amazes me," he said. "She must be holding the lawyers at gunpoint to get this done so fast." He laughed and handed the computer back to Finn. "She even got Yost and Collyer on board. I didn't know they ever did pro bono work."

"Until now, they didn't. They'd charge their own kids for advice on how to sell Girl Scout Cookies." Finn continued to type on the keyboard.

"What amazes me even more," Rand continued, "is how many of my traders want to shift our focus. Go green. Who knew I was standing every day in a pit of eco-vipers? They're probably out planting trees along Wall Street."

"It'll take a while to make a change like that," Finn observed, "and it'll cost you."

"It's only money." Rand looked out the window. "Where do you think we are?"

"I'll go ask. Here's your computer back. You've got a message from somebody named Brogen."

Rand folded the monitor part way down and

continued to look for landmarks. It was still daylight, but nothing looked familiar. Of course, the first time he'd flown to Montana he'd had such a bad attitude he didn't even look down.

"We're over western North Dakota," Finn said. "Almost over Montana. ETA is one hour give or take five minutes." He opened the refrigerator and removed a plastic plate. "Microwave for three minutes. Just like home. Are you sure you're not hungry?"

Not for food. "Yes, thanks anyway."

The only message he wanted was one from Luanne. Simple words. Love. Forever. Wedding. Family. Trust.

That was the hardest one. Trust. How could he win her trust after she'd learned about his and Jeff's involvement with Suncatcher's troubles? How could he explain, in the limited time he had, the complexity of Percival's money problems?

He'd pulled up her phone number a half dozen times, but this wasn't something he could phone in. Could he explain it, face to face?

He'd have to try. That's all he could do.

He opened Brogen's message. As he expected, the test results were bad. "How long will it take you to get to the hospital?" Brogen asked. "I can have a surgical team ready by six p.m. Don't eat anything or take any aspirin."

Rand gave a snort. *I'm getting that part right, anyway.*

"Dear Doctor," he typed, "Surgery tonight is impossible. I'm flying over eastern Montana right now, heading west to Bitter Falls. I have to take care of urgent business. I will call you when I can turn around and fly east. Maybe late tonight. Keep your knives sharp. Oh, and remember your advice about kissing a pretty girl? That was the best prescription you ever made. Her name is Luanne, which goes perfectly with Monahan."

He signed it and pressed Send.

This time he turned the power off and set the computer in its leather carrying case. He turned off the overhead light and opened his window shade.

He looked west, over the wing, and saw that the sun had gone down. The cloudless sky surrendered the light quickly. Beneath the plane, in Montana, it was already night. He looked as far behind the plane as he could, pressing his forehead against the window.

There it was. The full, orange face of the Hunter's Moon, trying to catch up with them.

Would he be here to see the next October moon? For that matter, would he be around to see next month's full moon, whatever it was called?

The pain increased. He shook out another tablet and again placed it under his tongue. It was time for Brogen and company to perform one of the miracles they were famous for.

Soon. Not tonight. Not until I see Luanne.

He closed his eyes and dozed.

Chapter Seventeen

Luanne had watched the news on every channel. Over and over she murmured, "Wow. Oh, wow. Oh. Wow." She couldn't string together more words. Emotion overran her vocabulary like a bottle of ink spilled across a letter.

Suncatcher, yes. Wow.

She didn't need to go on the Ferris wheel to feel her stomach fall like an ingot, then whoosh upward. She'd already been through a scarier ride than that.

When she got the news that Suncatcher lost the legal case, her stomach went lower than ground level. It fell into an open pit mine. Then, when she saw the words on the TV screen: "Breaking News, Reversal in Patent Fight," she'd shot up on top of the world.

As word spread that Suncatcher's lawyers had snatched victory from the jaws of defeat, the vendors' fair, and the carnival, and preparations for the street dance took on a holiday atmosphere. She'd heard that Dexter was wearing an egg face masque and wasn't taking any calls.

The only way it could be better was if Rand was beside her.

And yet—the jury was still out on Rand v. The Future. It would be so much better if he'd been honest with her. How could he care so little for her feelings that he let her hear from Dexter that he was in any way involved with Suncatcher?

The TV news was so brief that she couldn't understand it. She wanted details. A, then B, and so on. Instead the news was reduced to bites and non-sequitors. To her it was like listening to bugs flying into an electronic bug zapper. Buzz-zip. Snap, snap. Zip.

Serena had pulled up the stories online. Luanne had read and re-read them, looking for mention of Morning Select Investments. Apparently they'd had a tenuous connection with Percival. An attorney for Rand's company put out a statement that Dexter Stone had one day to print a retraction of his accusation against the principals of Morning Select Investments or face a lawsuit for slander and libel.

Where is Rand? And where has he been all day?

It was as if he'd proposed and then forgotten all about her. He must have been working in Missoula all day, in touch with his company's lawyers. More likely than not, she concluded, he had to handle every question since he'd been the one who'd gotten Jeff Adler to Montana.

And the two times she'd seen Jeff during the day, he didn't look worried. He looked happy. He'd even said to her, "Did you hear the news? I'm going to be a dad." The way he looked at Serena reminded Luanne of the sweet way Laddie and Max gazed at her when she came home from work. *Ahhhhh.* It was probably supper on their minds, but they *looked* like they adored her.

The second time she'd seen Jeff, while they watched TV in the lodge at the Rocking Star, he'd snapped his fingers.

"Luanne, I'm supposed to tell you. Rand is on his way." He looked at his watch. "Maybe get here in an hour."

He seemed not to hear her ask, "Where has he been all day?" Instead he left the room, muttering something about checking his email.

Instead of having dinner at the lodge, Dinah and Kurt wanted to take the kids to the carnival and let them eat junk.

225

"You want to come, too?" Dinah asked her.

"Little kids eating junk, then riding the Tilt-a-Whirl? I can't turn that down."

She was eager to see how the festival was going. She had five calls on her answering machine about the evening's three hayrides canceling because the wagon disintegrated, but someone towed a sturdier wagon into town. It would be fine.

She parked behind her shop and stopped in to see her part-time employee, Nancy, and one of her daughters. They'd done record business that day, and UPS had delivered the supplies they'd need for the busy weekend.

"It's past closing time," Luanne said.

"We've already locked the front door," Nancy replied. "As soon as we count the cash register, we'll be out of here. Congratulations on the wonderful news."

For a moment, Luanne thought word of her engagement had gotten out. "Oh, about AATech giving back the patent. The government must really have some leverage on them. I don't care how or why; I'm glad it's over."

She went out the front door and Nancy locked it behind her. The long walk to the fair and carnival lifted her spirits even more. If a town could sing, Bitter Falls would burst into rapturous vocal music any minute.

As she got closer she did hear music, but it was a cacophony of mismatched tunes from the Ferris wheel, a barbershop quartet in the ice cream tent, and Lainie McGee and the Night Riders in their first set at the street dance.

"This here's a tribute to Miss Patsy Cline," a male guitarist said. The microphone emitted some feedback and he stepped away from it.

Lainie took her mic off its stand and began singing "Crazy."

Lainie McGee looked fantastic on the band's poster, which had hung all over Bitter Falls for weeks now. Fringed vest and a beehive hairdo; pretty girl, maybe twenty-two, twenty-three. Seeing her live on stage, however, one's first thought might be: I'll bet that old gal knew Patsy Cline personally.

Luanne found Dinah and Kurt and held hands with Sophie while the others went on the Ferris wheel.

"Mine mommy says cotton candy is junk food," Sophie said.

"She's right, but junk is okay one time."

"Luanne?" A voice close behind her. Sophie turned first.

"Uncle Rand!" Sophie leaped into his arms and began listing all the junk she'd been eating. "...and a hotdog, and popcorn with butter, and cotton candy. And mine Daddy says I'm gonna upchuck. What does upchuck mean, Uncle Rand?"

"It means you need to get back on the ground and not upchuck on my suit." He set her on the ground as Dinah, Kurt and Erik arrived.

"Uncle Rand, guess what?" Erik was so excited he was almost levitating. "Guess what, I won this teddy bear at the balloon toss!" He held up a stuffed bear about six inches tall, displaying the enthusiasm of Indiana Jones securing the Ark of the Covenant.

"And it only cost me twenty-five dollars," Kurt murmured close to Rand's ear.

"Will you take me back to the balloon toss, Uncle Rand?" Erik pulled on his hand. "I want to win another bear for Sophie."

Rand dropped down to Erik's level. "I've got to tell you something, man to man. I need to talk to Luanne for a while. You try to talk your dad into feeding your gambling addiction."

Before either Sophie or Erik could launch another campaign for his attention, he stood and grabbed Luanne by the hand.

"Let's get out of here."

"There's Finn!" She called his name and waved her hands. "Finn, over here."

He looked up at the sound of his voice and ambled over. Luanne hugged him fiercely, standing on her toes to get her arms around his neck. "You did it. I don't know how, but you did. Oh, this is Rand Monahan." She smiled from one to the other, puzzled that they didn't shake hands.

Finn smiled broadly. "We've already met."

"Come on, Luanne, we need to talk," Rand urged again. Sweat dotted his forehead, and his lips were clamped tight.

"Is something wrong?" she asked.

"Rand?" Finn asked. "Stand by."

Finn took a few long strides to a food booth, apologized for taking cuts, and returned with a bottle of water.

"Let's go," Finn said. "I'll drive. I borrowed a car; it's right behind the ice cream tent."

In the back seat of the Jeep, Luanne took Rand's hands in hers.

"You're not wearing the ring," he said.

"I thought I'd wait until we told people together." She took the box out of her purse and slipped it on her finger.

He closed his eyes.

"Rand, where were you all day?"

He shook his head. "Wait."

"Finn," she said, "please drop us at my shop. My car is there."

"Sure."

"How is Cory?" Rand asked. "Jeff told me she had an emergency."

"She's in the hospital, yes. The doctor keeps telling Kent she's all right. They're monitoring her liver numbers, whatever that means. A specialist is on the way to do a Caesarean tomorrow morning."

He nodded and closed his eyes.

She studied his face, which was etched in fatigue. Had he slept at all in the past twenty-four hours? Where had he been, and why hadn't he told her?

She touched the ring, still foreign to her hand. Was she insane to utter vows, to publicly and legally braid her life with this man she didn't know?

And—her breath caught in her throat and her stomach did the Ferris wheel flop—had she already done so in a way more binding than any vow? Was she carrying within her...Rand's baby?

****

Rand looked out the passenger window, fascinated by the moon flying through the tree tops, still trying to catch him. Trying to tell him something.

As she drove, Luanne had chattered about Erik and Sophie, and the playground, and how Tree Autrey was bringing two Shetland ponies to the dude ranch on Sunday for Erik and Sophie to ride.

Crowding him in the front seat were invisible passengers: her nervousness and his fatigue.

At least, that's what he wanted to call it. *I'm tired. Pooped. Weary.*

Inside her house he said nothing about building a fire. The dogs ran to him but he sat on the couch and gave them each a perfunctory ear rub.

"Would you like some coffee?" she asked. "Or wine, or tea? I'd like some tea."

"Tea sounds good, thanks."

He rested the back of his neck against the couch and listened to Luanne moving about in her kitchen. The tea kettle whistled; the cups rattled; she returned.

He had so much to say. About the case, yes, and all the dramatic turns it had taken in the last

229

twenty-four hours. But there was so much more on his mind. He felt like the cliché "guru" in comic strips, the bearded guy on a mountain top who's supposed to know the meaning of life.

Now that he knew it, he needed words—and time—to tell it to Luanne. And Jeff, and Kurt. And any other fools who let precious time leak out of their lives while holding on to their blue chip stocks.

He waited until she sat beside him, her mug of tea in her hands. That Luanne wasn't having wine reminded him: she might be pregnant. She's doing everything in her power to protect our baby. *That's the kind of woman she is.*

He sipped his, then set the mug on the end table.

"I spent the whole day in New York," he said. "Made possible by the miracle of a chartered executive jet, the same one that brought my family and Jeff here. We took off at four this morning."

"Is that—? I mean, did you meet Finn in New York?"

"Yes. We'd talked a dozen times yesterday, and he was in close touch with my company's attorneys. He did a great job as the hub for all that was whirling around."

"And...some of what was whirling around, that was your doing?"

"Don't give me too much credit. When the FBI picked up Ollie Pappas, that gave us the keys to the castle."

"I read about that online," she said. "He was working for a Russian syndicate? Some sort of front man?"

Rand nodded. "My company's defense, and Suncatcher's interests, and the U.S. Attorney's agenda, all came together like a perfect storm."

"I wish I'd known," she said.

"I could have told you, but an hour later it might

have blown up. There was no way to forecast a good outcome. You've had enough shock and disappointment. Today, thankfully, was your day to celebrate."

"Are you...do you want to be in New York?"

He shook his head. "No. Everything I want is right here." He laughed. "And furthermore, to my amazement, all the traders in my company—whom I would have bet were as hard-assed as I was—are a pack of tree huggers. They're working now, probably all night, figuring out how we can become an earth-friendly investment firm."

He took a swallow of tea and grinned. "Even going so far as to franchise goats for African villages."

She chuckled. "Amelia's been talking to you."

"I reminded them what it costs to live in New York, specifically how much more it costs than being earth-friendly will pay, and you want to know what they said?"

"Ummm, that they're sick of New York?"

He nodded. "They're all insanely jealous of my forced vacation in Montana. They would kill to kayak."

"Forced? I don't understand."

"Yeah, right. That thud you just heard was the other shoe falling. I'm here on doctor's orders. Relax or die."

Her face went white. "That's what—"

"What?"

"That's what Ted's doctor told him. He knew he had an aneurysm. The doctor knew; Ted knew. Finn knew. Nobody told me."

He put out his hand but she wouldn't take it.

"I can't do this again." She reached to put her mug on the coffee table, missed. It hit the floor and broke.

She jumped up. "I'll get a towel."

Rand leaned forward and caught her wrist. "Luanne, it doesn't matter."

"Of course it matters," she said, her voice shrill with alarm. "I can't just let things lie around, broken."

She jerked her hand free of his and put it to her mouth. "I can't do this again, Rand. I'm not that strong."

She went into the kitchen and came back with a wastebasket and a wad of paper towels. He watched her sop up the tea and put the shards into the trash. When she'd finished, she took the wastebasket to the kitchen and returned. Instead of sitting, she looked out the window. Or, at least, that's where she directed her gaze. Rand doubted she could focus her eyes on anything.

Sometimes you don't know which way is up.

Where did that come from? he wondered. *Sometimes you don't know...*

Oh, yeah. Chalk it up to memory. Memory, mine.

He'd taken a wrong turn while skiing. It hadn't been his fault; a blinding blizzard had moved in and the ski resort abruptly shut down the lifts. He was already on top. In the whiteout, he'd been blown sideways off the ridge and tumbled helplessly into at least fifteen feet of drift. It was like being in an avalanche, only instead of snow coming downhill and burying him, he'd gone head first into it and cart wheeled.

Which way is up?

He'd clawed in panic, desperate to get air, desperate to feel wind again. Who would guess that sleet slamming into his face would be the best news he could have?

His legs, scissored apart at an angle that would make a modern dancer proud, wouldn't move. Statistics—his best friend for so much of his life—

now hammered in his brain. How fast would Vermont snow turn into solid ice?

How long do I have?

Which way is up?

One hand, ungloved, of course, was close to his face. He waved it like a windshield wiper, one inch, two inches, until he could see it. A jagged cut, probably from the edge of his ski, was smeared with blood. He licked it off. It welled again, and he focused his eyes on the fresh red liquid, warm enough to melt a path as it dripped. As it dripped up...up.

He was upside down. Just knowing that gave him a burst of strength to fight. His legs, his arms, his head—every muscle he had in his body—banged and battered the snow until he'd completed the cartwheel he'd performed to its halfway point.

He'd climbed free, dug out one ski, and crawled on his belly until he could stand and put it on.

When he was encased in snow, he thought, I'd give a million dollars to be out of this. When he was on his one ski, no poles, no gloves, absolutely blind and trying to remember which direction was the lift—and which way was the cliff with a five hundred foot drop—he thought, I'd give five million dollars to see a lift tower.

A shape appeared out of nowhere; a red jacket with a white cross. He'd called out, afraid the wind would swallow the sound. But the man, or woman, motioned to him, and he'd followed, all the way to safety.

The day he'd lain on the gurney, gasping for air, that mountain-misadventure had come back to his oxygen-deprived brain. In the middle of Manhattan, with unspeakable pressure on his chest, he'd watched the IV bottle swing wildly above him as the ambulance took a corner and a corner and a corner. It was like a clown car at the circus. Would it ever get there? Was everyone on the street laughing at the zany ambulance act, siren blaring as the clown driver steered it in a circle, then zigged, then zagged?

"Air," he'd shouted. *Tried* to shout. But you can't shout without air.

He'd thought about the deal he'd offered God in Vermont and never paid. Five million for sight of a tower. As the scene above him changed from the ambulance interior to the ER doctor, he upped the ante. He'd give six million for air!

He stood now, biting his lip against the pain, and walked to Luanne. He put his arms around her and felt her tears wet the front of his shirt.

She tried to stiffen her backbone, tried to back up, but her body declared a mutiny against her mind. Her arms went around his neck, and she surrendered.

However long they had together, it was better than another minute apart. It was time to close the door on the past and race headlong, hand in hand, into whatever the future holds. She kissed his lips, his cheeks, his neck, and held him so tight she wasn't sure where she ended and he began.

She knew that memories "mine" would always be with her, but it was time for "memories ours."

"Ted should have told you," Rand said. He pulled away enough that she could see his face.

"It's all—" she began, but he put his finger to her lips.

"He should have told you," he repeated. "And I should have told you, before I asked you to marry me. My excuse, that I love you, isn't good enough."

He kissed her forehead and her temples and her wet cheeks.

"Hey, no more crying." He chuckled. "I'm on a very low sodium diet."

She wiped her eyes on his sleeve and took a deep

breath.

"All right. I'm through caterwauling," she said.

"Good, whatever that is. It doesn't sound good."

"What does your doctor want you to do? Because I'm his new best friend. You will toe this line."

"He wants me on an operating table in New York City three hours ago. The plane I came on is waiting at the Bitter Falls airport."

"And he's a...what kind of doctor?"

"Cardiologist. I've had one heart attack. Mild. I have three stents in, and it's not working. I need a quadruple bypass."

"You are a bonehead. I suppose he already told you that."

"Bonehead, yes. He mentioned that. I said I wanted a second opinion and he said, 'Okay, you're an idiot.'"

She tapped her toe on the floor. "Get in the car. Don't argue."

"I'm not arguing."

"Laddie, Max, out. Now." She locked the door behind them, grabbed her purse and her cell phone. "I'll drive. You call your sister. Tell her to meet us at the hospital. You're not getting on a plane unless the cardiologist here says you can fly. And you're not flying all the way back across the country without medical assistance on board."

She locked the front door and strode toward the car as she added her final word on the subject.

"And you're not going anywhere without me!"

Chapter Eighteen

"Three across. Six letters. Putting placement problem." Luanne sat in the armchair with her bare feet crossed at the ankles on Rand's bed. The view out the window of the Hudson River and the George Washington Bridge kept pulling her attention away from the crossword.

"Putting?" he said, "like to put something down?"

"I don't know; I guess so. I've never been good at this."

Kurt rapped his knuckle on the open door and came in, followed by Dinah, Erik and Sophie. The kids were subdued, probably under strict orders not to hug Uncle Rand, who had a canopy over his bed and was surrounded by beeping equipment.

Luanne accepted a cheek kiss from Kurt and a breath-busting hug from Dinah. She lowered herself to the kids' level and assured them that Rand was going to be fine. They hadn't seen him since the Harvest Festival, ten days ago.

Kurt picked up the puzzle. "Putting placement problem." He pronounced it like a putting green. "Six letters. Stymie."

"How did you know that?" Luanne filled it in with a soft-lead pencil.

"First, the theme of the whole puzzle is sports. A stymie is an opponent's ball on the green, directly in the way of my ball's path to the hole. I play golf."

"How many times have you played this year?" Rand asked, scoffing.

"Yeah, yeah. Not enough. Now I have to save up

my vacation for Montana. Dude, where's my horse?"

Rand laughed, then winced. "No jokes. Doctor's orders."

"When have you ever followed the doctor's orders?" Dinah asked.

"Since I took over," Luanne said. "He responds to positive reinforcement, just like Laddie and Max." She grinned at Rand. "You're such-a-good-boy, such-a-good-boy!"

"I'm glad something works," Dinah deadpanned. "Oh, you have a fan club waiting down the hall. We have to take turns."

"Who else is here?" Luanne asked.

"Serena and Jeff, Grandpa, your grandmother Amelia, who is here to see Rocky, if you get my drift, and Merry Lou Shore. She followed Jeff so she could get signatures from both of you."

"That's not too many people," Luanne said. "I'll go get them. As long as nobody starts dancing like Zorba the Greek, the nurses won't care. Of course, with my grandmother, that's not out of the realm of possibilities."

"We have to go anyway," Kurt said. "We'll send them in on our way out." He lifted up Sophie to kiss Rand, then lifted Erik up, too.

"Are you really, really feeling better?" Dinah asked.

"Ummm, better than what?" Rand said with a wince.

She winked at Luanne. "Better than the alternative."

"Jury's still out. Okay, okay. Yes, I'm feeling better."

"Have you two decided when to get married?"

Luanne sighed. "We have to work out the pre-nup first. He won't sign it. And I can't get married until the matron of honor can walk down the aisle. Oh, and not until the groom can stand unassisted for fifteen minutes. Maybe Thanksgiving weekend."

"How's Cory doing?"

"She's supposed get out of the hospital tomorrow, which is way too soon in my opinion. The babies are fine, just a little jaundiced."

"We saw them through the nursery window about five minutes before we left for the airport. So cute!"

Dinah and family left and the others trooped in. Merry Lou Shore was ready to make the most of her time, slapping paper after paper, on a clipboard, in front of Rand. As soon as he'd signed, she handed each one to Jeff.

"And this one needs your signature, too." She handed one to Luanne.

"Why me?" She scanned it, said, "What is it?"

She sat down and read it slowly. "Are you sure about this?" She looked from Rand to Jeff and then to Merry Lou.

Jeff nodded, and gave Serena's shoulders a gentle squeeze.

Luanne took a deep breath and let it out slowly. The auction had been an incredible success, better than her wildest dreams, but the cost of opening the factory was beyond her wildest nightmares.

Morning Select Investments had already stepped in with the capital needed. As soon as the contracts were prepared, MSI would own forty percent of the company; Finn and Luanne would each own five percent; and the rest would be sold in a public stock offering. The first shares would be offered to investors in Bitter Falls, then to investors in the rest of Montana, and finally on the open market.

The agreement Merry Lou handed to Luanne today was a memorandum of understanding between Morning Select Investments and the Suncatcher Trust. Luanne was named chairman of the board of the new trust. Purpose was to use profits from the forty percent in trust to get Suncatcher Solar Cells into the hands of poor people all over the world. To change their lives.

Luanne wiped the tears away on the tissue her grandmother passed to her. "Okay, here goes," she said, and signed the document by the yellow flag.

Merry Lou gathered up the clipboards, secured them in her briefcase, and blew a kiss to Rand.

Jeff and Serena hugged Luanne, and Serena said to call with a progress report on Rand.

"We want to know when he can walk," Serena said.

"Oh, yes," Jeff exclaimed. "And when he goes poopy, we want to be the first to know."

"I'm thinking about writing a book about surgical recovery," Luanne said, "about what patients have to do before they get released. I'm thinking maybe a panda on the cover. Title is 'Eats Walks and Pees.'"

"On that note," said her grandmother, "I'm going to lunch with this gentleman." She kissed Luanne and gave Rand a finger handshake. "I'll hug you when you're less encumbered, Rand. I'm eager to get better acquainted. Maybe the four of us will go dancing."

Rocky kissed Luanne, too. "Welcome to the family. At last, a touch of class." He nodded to Rand. "I've got a call in to my lawyer. He should have something drawn up in three or four days. Or whenever he can bill enough hours to make the last payment on his three-masted schooner."

Luanne closed the door behind them. "What's Rocky getting drawn up by his lawyer? Or is it my business?"

"Everything about me is your business. Rocky is selling me—us—his land on Apple Mountain Road. When you get a chance, start looking for an architect, okay?"

She moved the equipment this way and that, tucking IV lines around metal clothespins to keep them out of the way. Slowly, trying not to jar him, she crawled onto the bed and lay beside him.

"You're full of surprises today, aren't you, Mr. Monahan?"

"I am, after all, a Master of the Universe. Not that I look too scary right now, but I can be ruthless."

"I don't think you're toothless."

"I said ruthless."

"Whatever. Listen up. I have a surprise for you."

"I'm listening."

"I told you I was going to take a pregnancy test tomorrow."

"Yes. And?"

"I couldn't wait. So, get well soon. You're going to be a dad."

He said nothing, so she lifted her head. Tears trickled out the corners of his eyes. His voice, when he spoke, was choked with emotion.

"I'm the luckiest man alive."

"And I'm the happiest woman. So that makes us perfect for each other."

About the author...

I live in Sequim, Washington, on the beautiful Olympic Peninsula (northwest of Seattle), with my husband, Bill, and our old, sweet-natured mutt, Laddie.

The name of my website, RainshadowRomance, refers to the climate of Sequim, which is located on the Strait of Juan de Fuca in the rain shadow of the Olympic Mountains. My favorite activity (after writing and reading) is downhill skiing, which we usually do in Utah.

My writing background includes time as a newspaper editor in New Mexico and four mystery novels. You can read about them on my website. "Love with a Welcome Stranger" was my first romance novel.

Visit Lynnette at www.rainshadowromance.com

Thank you for purchasing
this Wild Rose Press publication.
For other wonderful stories of romance,
please visit our on-line bookstore at
www.thewildrosepress.com.

For questions or more information,
contact us at info@thewildrosepress.com.

The Wild Rose Press
www.TheWildRosePress.com

Other Champagne titles to enjoy:

HOW MUCH YOU WANT TO BET? by Melissa Blue. Neil never thought a game of pool could change the course of her life, but against Gib she may lose both the game and her heart.

CATASTROPHE by Sharon Buchbinder. Cats! Twenty-three! Being evicted! Their handsome neighbor doesn't want to lose their curly-haired, curvaceous owner. So what's the rescue plan?

HIBISCUS BAY by Debby Allen. Picture love on a sun-drenched white sand beach surrounded by hibiscus-covered cliffs, with your yacht anchored in a blue Mediterranean Sea.

TASMANIAN RAINBOW by Pinkie Paranya. A concert violinist grapples with remote ranch life, intrigue and the mystery of a missing diary, the peril of a flood in which all could be lost, and the undeniable attraction of the man who would do anything to protect his son.

THREE'S THE CHARM by Ellen Dye. Rachel vowed never to speak to her ex-husband again. When her beloved horse needs a vet and Heath is the only one within three counties of West Virginia mountains, some vows need to be broken.

SEE MEGAN RUN by Melissa Blue. City-successful Megan goes home to the boonies to save her childhood home but finds she must not only agree to stay for her mother's wedding but also deal with the man she left when she hitchhiked out 12 years ago.

A MOTHER'S HEART by Misty Simon. Carrie wants a simple life. Helping Gran with the animal shelter: complication. When the new neighbor with two kids comes in for a dog, life goes out of control.

DAMN THE MAN by Michelle L. Witvliet. Maggie believes she was right to give Nick his freedom. He is patiently waiting for her to realize divorce was the only mistake they made. What's a woman to do?

Printed in the United States
152848LV00001B/2/P

9 781601 545282